SIMON & SCHUSTER CHILDREN'S PUBLISHING
ADVANCE READER'S COPY

TITLE: Children of the Black Glass

AUTHOR: Anthony Peckham

IMPRINT: Atheneum/Caitlyn Dlouhy Books

ON-SALE DATE: 3/7/23

ISBN: 978-1-6659-1313-3

FORMAT: hardcover

PRICE: $17.99

AGES: 10–14

PAGES: 368

Please send any review or mention of this book to
ChildrensPublicity@simonandschuster.com.

Aladdin · Atheneum Books for Young Readers
Beach Lane Books · Beyond Words · Boynton Bookworks
Caitlyn Dlouhy Books · Denene Millner Books
Libros para niños · Little Simon · Margaret K. McElderry Books
MTV Books · Paula Wiseman Books · Salaam Reads
Simon & Schuster Books for Young Readers
Simon Pulse · Simon Spotlight

CHILDREN OF THE BLACK GLASS

CHILDREN OF THE BLACK GLASS

ANTHONY PECKHAM

A CAITLYN DLOUHY BOOK

Atheneum Books for Young Readers
NEW YORK LONDON TORONTO SYDNEY NEW DELHI

ATHENEUM BOOKS FOR YOUNG READERS

An imprint of Simon & Schuster Children's Publishing Division

1230 Avenue of the Americas, New York, New York 10020

Text © 2023 by Anthony Peckham

Jacket illustration © 2023 by Galen Dara

Jacket design © 2023 by Simon & Schuster, Inc.

For information about special discounts for bulk purchases, please contact Simon & Schuster Special Sales at 1-866-506-1949 or business@simonandschuster.com.

The Simon & Schuster Speakers Bureau can bring authors to your live event. For more information or to book an event, contact the Simon & Schuster Speakers Bureau at 1-866-248-3049 or visit our website at www.simonspeakers.com.

The text for this book was set in Palatino LT.

Manufactured in the United States of America

0123 FFG

First Edition

2 4 6 8 10 9 7 5 3 1

CIP data for this book is available from the Library of Congress.

ISBN 9781665913133

ISBN 9781665913157 (ebook)

FOR J

PROLOGUE

Seka already had more than enough black glass to take down the mountain and trade for the coming winter's needs. He knew he should have been wrapping and packing it. But a few days earlier he'd spotted a particular crevice high on the shining vein. He'd looked away from it instantly, never letting his one remaining eye find it again, in case the other men saw it too.

To him, the shape and angle of the crevice hinted at a chance to cut the rarest of all pieces: a perfect, gleaming slab so thin it was almost see-through. These were called "sorcerer's glass" because sorcerers craved them and would bid high for them. The men of their village dreamed constantly of such a piece and the wealth it would bring.

But Seka also knew firsthand that sorcerer's glass was dangerous to cut, needing lots of force to cleave it perfectly from the mine face. As a young man, he'd lost his left eye to a flying shard while trying for one. With only one working eye, he knew exactly what he was risking . . . and he also knew that he had no choice. Sorcerer's glass would change any family's life forever, and theirs was a life that badly needed changing.

1

Tell and Wren, Seka's two children, had no idea of the risk he was about to take for them. They were far away on the mountainside, hunting for dinner. And dinner had just served itself up, if they could catch it.

In a jumble of boulders above them, the very tip of a narrow ear flashed pink for a moment, backlit by the low sun. There! That was all Tell needed to see. He already had an arrow nocked to the string because he always did when they were out hunting.

Just below him on the path, Wren knew by the way her brother stopped and curled his scarred fingers to the bow that he'd seen something worth taking. She had a good idea what it was. When he turned to her, she wiggled two fingers above her head, making rabbit ears. He shrugged yes. Wren pulled a face. Ugh! Mountain jackrabbits were lean and tough, like every living thing up there, including themselves.

Wren tapped her chest, pointed upward. Tell nodded and took off up the path, as silent as smoke. Even at fourteen, he was one of the best hunters in the village and brought in most of the meat they ate. He could've taken the jackrabbit by himself, but this way was quicker. Also, they liked working together.

Instead of circling back along the trail, Wren climbed straight up the low cliff separating them from the terrace above. The way she scaled the rock wall made it look as easy as walking, and for her it was. She was born to it. As a baby, she'd climbed the stone walls inside their hut as soon as she was old enough to pull herself upright. She had long, strong fingers, plus a jagged scar on her leg from a fall when she was just three. But then, everyone in their village had scars of some kind.

Wren was barely breathing hard when she slid up over the cliff edge onto the rocky terrace. She stayed on her belly until she heard the grinding sound of the jackrabbit chewing on a mouthful of spiny grass.

She stood up slowly and calmly, looking everywhere but at the jackrabbit, because all animals can feel eyes on them, especially animals that are hunted regularly. Then, not bothering to muffle her footsteps, she walked across the terrace—not toward the jackrabbit, just away from the cliff edge.

The jackrabbit stood up on its back legs, instantly alert. Wren sighed. This one was particularly skinny. A gamey old male. She could tell by the shape of his underslung jaw, even with just one fleeting sideways glance.

Because she wasn't looking directly at it, and because she wasn't getting any closer, the jackrabbit didn't flee instantly; it stayed upright, alert and ready to bolt if necessary.

Not alert enough, not ready enough.

The *hiss-thud* of an arrow let her know that her brother's shot had found its target. She finally looked directly at the jackrabbit as it succumbed with hardly a twitch.

"Not a bad shot," Wren teased.

"I like it when they don't know what happened to them." Tell nodded. He knew a good hunter made sure his prey didn't suffer. Plus, the meat tasted better that way.

There was no question they were brother and sister. They shared the same generous mouths and prominent, fine-bridged noses, a very visible part of their family inheritance. They'd been teased endlessly when they were younger. *Is that a mountain peak or your nose? Be careful of that blade on your face; it might cut somebody!* But as they grew older and bigger, their noses became less of a landmark and more just . . . interesting.

"Are you coming back down?" Wren asked as she slung the still-warm animal around her neck and tied its feet together with a twist of grass.

A familiar scowl settled across Tell's angular face, one that had been there for almost two years. He pointed up the mountain, away from the village. "I'll try for more," he said, then set off without looking back. Wren sadly watched him go. She knew that hunting was just his excuse to stay away, especially that day. But she had no such excuse.

She headed back fast, leaping from rock to rock until she reached the edge of the canyon. She paused to look down at the village directly below, her entire world, her entire life so far, all twelve years of it.

This was her favorite view, and in truth she scarcely had to look, she knew it so well and it changed so little. About thirty or so familiar stone huts were arranged along both walls of the canyon, at a place where it widened slightly and an ice-cold spring gurgled from a crack in the rock. The huts faced each other at various angles, depending on the vagaries of the rock, and they'd been built in all sorts of shapes. Her village had many rules, but none about the shape of your house. The rock determined that.

The huts all leaned against the canyon wall for the strength to withstand winter's heavy snow. With the canyon behind them, thick rock walls all around, and slate roofs above their heads, theirs was a life lived in stone, most of it cold. No trees worth the name grew this high. The timbers that supported their roofs had been carried up the mountain one by one long ago and were by far the most valuable part of any home.

Wren and Tell's was a sturdy rectangle on the high side of the village. Seeing it always gave her a solid feeling.

It got more sunlight than any other, especially late in the day, and Wren was proud that it was considered one of the most comfortable and well built in the village. The small summer garden she'd started years ago with her mother had gone to seed and, looking down on it, Wren made a mental note to gather the seeds before the first snow arrived. It would be soon, she knew, and once it arrived, their world of rock would become a world buried in snow and ice.

Voices bounced up the rock from below, clear as bells in the thin air, and Wren recognized every single one, no matter their age. Little kids were yelling or crying as they played one of their endless games, which usually ended when someone threw a stone and someone else didn't duck fast enough. Women were shouting at the children and across the canyon at their friends. Or enemies. There was an extra edge to their voices today. They should've rung with excitement and urgency because the mules were being readied for the long journey down to Halfway, but instead, Wren heard frustration, anger, and envy in the women's voices, and she knew exactly why. Because, for the second year in a row, they weren't going.

As for the men, she didn't hear any of them; it was too early. But their mules were tethered outside every door, ready for loading. Small, strong, sure-footed, and mostly mean mountain mules.

Except for Rumble. Wren smiled when she saw him

waiting outside her own door—the oldest mule in the village and, by far, the smartest. He wasn't tethered. He didn't have to be. He knew what was about to happen. He knew where he was supposed to be, and why.

Her eyes traveled automatically up the canyon to where it bent away from her. She couldn't see around the bend, but she didn't have to. She knew what was there: the reason for their existence, the origin of their name—the vein of black glass that some forgotten ancestor had found long ago. So much of it had been carved away over the years that the glass now lived at the end of a gleaming tunnel inside the mountain.

Movement! Small as an ant, the first of the men came around the canyon bend and headed quickly down the path back to the village, carrying the last of his season's haul, in a hurry to wrap it for the journey.

Without warning or hesitation, Wren stepped forward into thin air and dropped from sight, leaving no sign that she'd ever been there.

But she hadn't jumped to her death. Arms wide, her strong, slender body under control, her knees bent, she hit the steep scree beneath the canyon edge and rode a wave of small stones down to the floor with dinner bouncing on her shoulders: her own personal little landslide. It was dangerous, it was fast, and it was thrilling. It also got her back to the cooking fire well before her father arrived.

But Wren needn't have hurried. Seka stayed later at the

mine face than almost all the others, waiting for the quiet needed to try for the sorcerer's glass. To the People of the Black Glass, the vein was like earth's dark blood frozen forever. It belonged to them and them only, guarded by their remote, harsh location and their reputation for savagery.

A few men lingered at the mouth of the tunnel, but Seka finally had the mine face to himself. He removed his pika fur coat, folded it, and put it on the ground below the vein to cushion the piece when it fell. He took a few breaths to focus himself, then raised his hands and snugged his antler chisel into the promising crevice, angling it just so. He drew his hardwood mallet back all the way. But instead of turning his face away before striking, as he had been taught and taught to others and always did himself, he looked full on to the chisel and held his one-eyed gaze there, so that he could use all his strength for the blow.

"Guide my hand," Seka prayed to the gods of the mountain. He struck hard, and the last thing he saw was a perfect slab peeling from the vein, just before a stray sliver the size of a wasp's sting shot into his good eye. He dropped to the floor next to his fur coat, screaming in pain, instantly blind, knowing he was as dead as if the sliver had taken him in the heart.

2

Not that Tell would have cared much right then. He wandered a game trail miles away from the village. Alone, Tell had let the familiar sting of angry and poisonous feelings rise in him; they were particularly strong that day. The men would be heading down the mountain to trade, and Tell knew that he wouldn't be going with them, which was what put him in an especially dark mood.

He was sick of staying back up the mountain, sick of hiding the fear they all shared, that for some unknown reason the men wouldn't return, and they would all starve, trapped by the snow and the cold.

Tell was even sick of the stories about the trading trips, told endlessly around the fire once the men returned in triumph. The two-week journey down and back was the highlight of every year, and it provided great stories of daring, danger, good luck and bad, treachery, thievery, bravery, stupidity, and triumph. But more and more, the stories just aggravated Tell. He wanted to be part of the action, not part of the waiting. He didn't want to hear them; he wanted to *live* them.

He wanted to see the hot, filthy, brilliant streets of Halfway for himself. He wanted to breathe the perfumed lowland air he'd heard so much about, not hear about it all winter from those who had just returned.

But Seka had refused. Not this time. Next year. At the age of fourteen, Tell wasn't ready. He'd be a burden, not a help. He had to stay up the mountain with Wren. That was that. Among the People, a father's word was law—their first and most sacred law, broken only on pain of expulsion from the village, which meant certain death or worse.

And so that day Tell hated his father even more than usual. He blundered along the game trail, seething and muttering. He even hated his boots, which were a pinch too small but not small enough, according to his father, to justify a new pair. Tell was wound up in so much misery, he could hardly see straight.

It wasn't always so. Until two years ago Tell had been a shining light in the village, a boy known for his laughter, his level head, his clever hands, and his skill with a bow. The other children in the village liked him, followed him, copied his ways. Seka was next in line to be chief, and everyone said Tell would be chief one day too.

Tell had been welcome in every house in the village,

had been friends with one and all, even the chief's wolf-dog (which didn't like anybody and bit people randomly until a group of women got together and poisoned it; it was never a good idea to make the women too angry with you). Until two years ago. That was when his father and mother went down the mountain to trade their black glass as they always did . . . but only his father returned.

When their father had come up the trail to the village, head bowed, last in line and alone, Tell and Wren thought it was a joke, or that their mother had stopped to harvest medicinal herbs—women sometimes did that on the return trip. Their father said nothing, not a word about anything. His silence was heavy and impenetrable, confusing to Tell and Wren. By dark, their mother still hadn't come through the door. No one stayed out alone after dark. The terrain was too treacherous, the air was too cold, and the wolves and big cats hunted at night; it was too easy to die after dark. Tell and Wren realized slowly, sickeningly, that something had gone wrong with their lives. Greatly wrong.

"Where's Mo?" Wren finally asked their father, unable to contain herself any longer.

"She's gone. Forget her. Never say her name again," replied Seka, his voice terse, his face grim.

Tell pressed. "But is she—"

Before he could say another word, his father's hard hand silenced him with a smack. "What did I just say?

Never mention her again. She's dead to us, and that's that."

And that was indeed that. No mention of their mother ever again. Not in their house, nor in the village. Was she dead or alive? Did she run away? Or fall off the trail? Had she been captured and sold in Halfway? No explanation, no discussion, no sympathy. It was as if she'd never existed at all. The entire village turned its back on even the memory of her.

But she *had* existed, and Tell and Wren missed her hugely, even though, it was true, she'd often been difficult in their home and disruptive in their village. Beautiful but too clever for her own good, was what everyone had said about her. She'd challenged every idea, every decision, and every rule inside their house and out; she'd mocked the chief and others in a way that danced dangerously between funny and insulting; she'd started feuds with other women, then changed direction suddenly and made up with them. And then, some days, she never got up from her bed. She lay there silently, staring at the stacked stone wall, not even hearing their voices. Tell and Wren had learned to fend for themselves from an early age on those days. For them, all this was normal: the life, the home, the family they had known since birth.

And then, just like that, their mother was gone.

It was as sudden as if an avalanche had taken her; only, if it had, they would still be talking about her, remembering her, living with her, somehow. Not this unexplained nothing. Not this silence. Not this hole where Tell's heart used to be.

Tell blamed his father for this, as he blamed him for everything. He had said so to his face a year ago and had been beaten for it. He had hardly spoken to his father since. If he had known his father was freshly blind and thirty days from an eternal sleep on the glacier, he might even have said, "Good! Serves him right!"

But he didn't know. Wren was the one who found out first. She was cleaning the jackrabbit next to the cooking fire, trying to think of something to make it less gamey. They'd run out of aromatic herbs because she hadn't had time to gather any. Since their mother had gone, she did everything her mother used to do but not nearly as well. "Scut work," her mother had called it. Wren had every reason to be as miserable as Tell, but she simply wasn't.

Wren never stayed sad for long, no matter what. That's because she knew how to cheer herself up. This was one of her greatest strengths, a powerful skill, and highly unusual in their village. The People had learned the hard way to expect the worst, and they protected themselves with a bleak outlook on life. Not Wren. She could find a reason to lift her own spirits in the soft color on a bird's breast or the feel of Rumble's muzzle as he tickled her, looking for the treat he knew she'd hidden for him. By knowing how to cheer herself up, Wren was able to be happy, and the little light remaining in their broken family was thanks to her, because happiness rubs off in a home just as much as sadness or anger do.

Tell knew it, his father knew it, and if they agreed on anything at all, it was that without her their lives would be intolerable.

Wren abandoned the jackrabbit and went to the door; she heard a commotion in the village. It was the kind of excited, slightly out-of-control shouting that always spelled bad news for somebody, and it brought the women out of their houses and the children down from their playground in the scree to see where the finger of fate pointed.

Some of the men were escorting her father down the path into the village. When Wren saw him with an ice water-soaked rag wrapped around his eyes, his coat bundled neatly and clutched to his chest, she simply turned and went inside.

She pulled her father's rabbit fur quilt back so that he could lie down. She stoked the fire and filled the kettle. By the time her father arrived at the front door, Wren knew that their lives had changed as completely as if the mountain they lived on had blown itself to pieces, as mountains sometimes did.

3

"If Seka doesn't get his sight back in thirty days . . ." The chief didn't have to complete the sentence. Tell and Wren knew the rest.

Like all of them, they had been raised in the knowledge that the People of the Black Glass wouldn't—couldn't—care for anyone who was too hurt to look after themselves. The hurt couldn't work and ate food that belonged to those who could. They had thirty days to heal. If they didn't heal, they'd be taken up to the glacier with a gourd of apricot brandy. On the glacier, they would drink and laugh with friends and family until the ice felt as warm as a feather bed, and they lay down and drifted off to sleep, never to wake.

That's the way it is, was, and will always be. Wren and Tell both knew that. As far as the village was concerned, it was necessary—the harsh arithmetic of their existence. No one questioned it. For the People, the flow of their glacier was measured not in strides, nor in years, but in frozen bodies known to all, moving away from them at the mountain's slow pace.

Tell and Wren had already been to a few such goodbyes. They didn't understand why everyone laughed so much. Then Wren had stolen a sip of the apricot brandy to see how strong it was; it was very strong! Like a sip of apricot-flavored fire! It had burned her throat and muddled her head. And she thought to herself, maybe that's how you can laugh while someone you've known all your life goes to sleep on a river of ice.

"You should prepare." Those were the chief's parting words to the family as he went back to his own duties: making sure the mule train was ready for a dawn departure down the mountain. As he left, he turned and gave Wren a comforting smile and nod. Unusual for him and unnoticed in the face of much larger problems.

And so, while everywhere else in the village, mules were brushed, food and clothing packed, weapons sharpened, and grass-wrapped slabs of black glass loaded into baskets made of twisted tree roots, Tell, Wren, and their father faced up to a very different future than the one they'd woken to that morning.

"Prepare?" asked Wren. "What else is there to do but wait for your eye to get better?"

"I wouldn't count on that," said their father as he sat up and let the wet cloth fall from his face. When they saw his eye, any hope evaporated. It was angry and swollen and blood red from corner to corner. They had seen enough eyes like that to know. Thirty days, thirty months, thirty years. He was blind forever.

Tell could contain himself no longer. "How could you do that? How could you let this happen? You know you're all we've—" Tell almost said, *you're all we've got.* He stopped himself just in time. But their father nodded grimly. He knew.

That's something I've been asking myself is all he said. As close to an apology as the People ever got. They never said sorry for anything. "You can prepare by getting used to the idea that you'll be living with other families in thirty days."

Wren, as usual, focused on what was most important. "Which other families?" she asked. "Who do we go to? If— if we have to."

Their father smiled. They'd inherited their generous mouths—mouths made for smiling—from him. But he smiled so seldom these days that when he did, he looked like a different person, someone from happier times. A time they were already beginning to forget.

"Wren, you'll go to the chief's house. It's a great honor."

Tell grinned too when he heard that. He turned to his sister. "You deserve it."

"Deserve?" exclaimed their father. "He's lucky to have her, and he knows it!"

Both Tell and his father were surprised when, instead of sharing their satisfaction, Wren whipped around and ran out of the hut, slamming the door behind her. Tell took a step to go after her, but his father said, "Let her be. She just needs to get used to the idea. When she does, she'll be back."

Tell nodded, forgetting for a moment that a nod no longer worked in their home; then he remembered. He cleared his throat instead. "What about me? Who will I live with?"

His father paused, the way people do when they're about to deliver bad news. "Hammerhead agreed to take you."

"Oh!" Tell gasped, as if punched in the gut. Hammerhead? Hammerhead was the most feared man in the village. He wore a lion claw and wolf tooth necklace, made from animals he'd killed with his bare hands. Every time a new chief was chosen, the unspoken agreement was that it could be anyone but Hammerhead, which only served to make him even more brutal. People joked, when they were sure Hammerhead was far away, that even the fleas and bedbugs were afraid to bite him.

"But . . . why not Curas? Did you ask him?" Curas was the village's finest hunter, a very quiet man whom Tell admired greatly. "And what about the Mort brothers? Either one of them." The Mort brothers weren't especially good at anything the People considered important but were often asked to settle disputes before, or even after, blood had flowed. They were known to be fair.

Tell's father nodded. He'd asked them. He'd asked everyone.

"Do what Hammerhead says, do it well, keep your mouth shut, and you'll be fine." And then he added, more gently, "You'll have a roof over your head and food in your belly. It's the best I could do." He didn't need to add that Tell's own poisonous nature over the last two years was to blame for the lack of choice. Tell was routinely sullen, rude, contemptuous, hostile. Nobody wanted that. Nobody wanted him. Except Hammerhead.

"Why would *he* want me?" Tell asked.

"Because you're everything he isn't," Seka said quietly. "And everything he never was."

Tell had heard the stories from the adults, how they'd all picked on Hammerhead when they were young because it took him so long to learn anything. Then Hammerhead grew and discovered his own strength and became what he was now. Feared.

And then there was an awkward silence when Tell saw his father turn to where he thought Tell was standing, but he got it wrong and shrugged at the washbasin instead. Something about that helpless little mistake cracked the hard shell around Tell's heart. He bit his lip, fighting back tears—and not even newborn babies cried much in their village—then pretended he had to cough so that his father could face him properly.

"Boy, I know things haven't been easy. Not since . . ."

His father sighed, finally forced to say words he should've said two years ago. "Not since your mother left us. And I know I haven't helped. I've been too angry. And I don't really have any way to make it up to you. Except for this."

Tell's father reached into his coat, which was folded up behind him, and carefully slid out the absolutely smooth, window-thin slab of black glass that was the last he would ever cut.

"This is a perfect sorcerer's slab; I saw it just before I . . . lost my sight. You see only one of these in a lifetime, in the entire village, and then only if you're lucky." He paused, smiling bleakly at his notion of luck. "It cost me my eye and likely my life. And I'll be damned if the chief or Hammerhead's going to get their hands on it." Which was what happened by rule; in return for taking in Tell and Wren, the chief and Hammerhead would divide their father's black glass between them. The chief would decide what to do with their hut.

"It's yours. Take it."

When Tell reached out to take the sorcerer's glass, his father's hand touched his, as if by accident, and then held on and pulled Tell down so that he sat right next to him. Both their hands bore a litany of scars, recent and old— testaments of a life lived cutting, carrying, and shaping black glass. Tell sat close enough to feel the strength of his father's muscles and the heat of his blood. Closer than he had been in a long, long time. All the anger Tell felt for his father melted away instantly, to be replaced by the familiar feeling of loss, only now doubled. Tell said not a word. He just leaned into his father the way he used to when he was younger. It felt so good and so sad at the same time.

"Look after it until you're old enough to take it down the mountain yourself. Next year, maybe. Find a sorcerer—the most feared one you can because they're also the wealthiest. Sell it to her." His father kept their closeness. He wanted it too.

Tell was confused. "But . . . we don't go anywhere near sorcerers! It's too dangerous."

"Unless you have something they want. And this is something they want."

"Why?" The thought of dealing with a sorcerer made Tell's mouth dry.

"Nobody knows and nobody asks." Then his father smiled. Tell could feel his pride. "But they'll pay no less than a hundred sous for it, so it's important to them."

"A hundred?!" Tell blurted. The take for the entire season for the whole village would not add up to a hundred sous.

"It's worth that and more." His father squeezed his hand and put his face close, as if telling him a secret.

"Hide it well. Tell no one where it is. Someone will steal it from you the moment I'm gone."

Tell fought to control the feelings erupting hotly inside him.

"And protect Wren no matter what. There's power in her. When she finds it, there's going to be all sorts of trouble. She's your mother reborn from tip to toes."

Tell was shocked. He thought his father hated his mother, but the words and tone in his voice made it sound like something else. Questions formed on his lips—ones that still had not been asked or answered after two long years. And there was precious little time to ask them. They came tumbling out.

"What happened to her? Where did she go? Is she still alive? Why did her not coming back mean that none of the women could ever go down the mountain again? What did she do?" These were the questions that had burned themselves into Tell's soul.

His father nodded. "You have the right to know. I should've told you both . . . but it was too painful. Now it's time you learned the truth." He paused again. Tell held his breath. "Your mother, she—"

But before he could say any more, there was a fierce pounding on the door, which flew open and smashed against the wall.

"Where's my damn glass?!" It was Hammerhead, and he was angry. Hammerhead still had both eyes, but they were bloodshot and small. Tell's father stood up fast. Tell slid the sorcerer's slab under the quilt. He thought for a second that Hammerhead had seen it, then decided he hadn't.

Tell's father took two shuffling steps toward Hammerhead and stood as tall as he could. "I'll thank you not to curse under my roof." It was a strange thing. The People of the Black Glass stole and lied and even killed without a second thought, but, one and all, they considered cursing indoors to be unacceptably rude.

"My mule's waiting. I need to load." Hammerhead pointed a big, dirty finger at Tell. "You have an hour to wrap and pack your father's glass, boy, and do it right, or by the mountain's broken teeth, I'll be talking to you in thirty days." Hammerhead turned on his heel and strode out, slamming the door behind him.

Wide-eyed with fear, Tell turned to face his father. "You better get to it," his father said quietly. "It's going to take a while to wrap. I had a good year."

4

I had a good year. . . . I had a good year. . . . Those words went around and around in Tell's head as he padded and wrapped the slabs of black glass in rough, woven grass mats. How could you measure whether life was good or bad by how much black glass you had? According to that, Tell's father—and therefore Tell and Wren—had had a great year. But by Tell's reckoning, it was the worst year of his life. Worse, even, than the year his mother disappeared because she was still gone and his father would soon be gone and he and Wren would be living under separate roofs, little better than servants.

But as these thoughts boiled in Tell's brain and he prepared his father's glass for Hammerhead, an idea slipped into his head like a fresh wind from a strange direction. It wasn't gradual; it was sudden. It was an idea that would change Tell's world forever, and he knew it instantly. An idea so big and crazy, it made Tell sweat as if he had a fever. An idea so wild that every time he tried to shove it away or bury it, it would spring back stronger than ever. The idea burned inside him like a forest fire that could not be quenched, so that, when the hour was up and only half the glass was wrapped and Hammerhead's boots could be heard crunching toward the hut, Tell stood up straight and faced the door with eyes that almost looked insane. He had to force himself to breathe through his nose, not pant through his mouth like a dog.

Hammerhead slammed open the door as if their home already belonged to him. "Are you done with my glass, boy? You'd better be!"

"No," said Tell, struggling to keep a tremble out of his voice. "I'm not done."

Tell's father sat upright, alarmed. "What have you been doing?!"

Hammerhead grinned, clearly looking forward to the beating he would give Tell in thirty days. "Don't worry, Seka. I'll straighten him out. You never could. And I'll take care of the glass myself."

"No, you won't," Tell replied. "It isn't your glass. It's mine."

"What?!" screamed Hammerhead, the lion's claw and wolf tooth necklace rattling on his chest.

"Tell! Enough!" His father was trying to stop him from digging himself an even deeper hole, but it was too late for that. There was no going back. Words cannot be unsaid.

Ideas cannot be unthought. As Tell spoke to Hammerhead, every muscle in his body was taut, as if he were trying to lift a weight too heavy for him.

"The deal is for me to live with you. I'll never do that. I'd rather die. The deal is off."

Hammerhead raised his stone-scarred hand to smash Tell down, but somehow Seka sensed it and pointed his finger right at Hammerhead's tiny eyes.

"Not under my roof."

Tell had never heard his father's voice like that; nor had Hammerhead. It stopped him cold.

"Tell him!" Hammerhead roared. "Tell him once and for all! *A father's word is law!*"

Tell's father turned, trying to locate Tell. Before he could, Tell spoke again, and his voice was no longer trembling. It was clear with purpose. Once Tell made a decision, he acted on it without hesitation. He'd been that way since the day he was born.

"Da, I'm going to take the glass down the mountain myself and sell it. I'm old enough and I'm strong enough. I'm ready. You know I am. I'm going to bring back enough supplies to feed you and Wren through the winter. I'm going to get lowland medicine for your eye—the good kind. I don't care if it breaks some rules. All I need from you is permission to go. That's all that matters."

Hammerhead swooped in close to Seka. "First your wife—curse her heart—and now this? You can't allow it.

Everyone will be running up and down the mountain whenever they feel like it. Squash it and squash it now, or I'll make sure all three of you are cast out. Some of us thought it should've happened two years ago. You'll die on the mountain like vermin." This was no idle threat. People had been cast out for less.

"A father's word is the first law," repeated Tell. "Everything else comes after it, and you know it. You said so yourself." Tell drew himself up tall and turned to his father. "Da, I'll do whatever you say."

Tell's father bowed his head, thinking deeply. The rag fell away from his eyes. The newly injured one looked as though it was throbbing painfully. For a long time there was no sound but their breathing and the wind moaning through the village outside.

Finally, Tell's father fumbled behind him, reaching up the rough stone wall above his bed to where he kept his beautiful and deadly foot-long, razor-sharp knife of black glass in its beaded sheath of mountain lion belly hide. He pulled it down. Then he leaned forward and held it out to his son.

"It's a dangerous journey down and even more so when you get there. You're going to need this."

Tell swelled with pride as he took the knife, and he looked up at Hammerhead defiantly. Then he saw the naked hatred in Hammerhead's eyes. He knew instantly that he'd made an enemy for life—and there was no worse enemy than one of their own.

5

Tell urged Rumble down the steep trail. He was half a day behind the men, because he'd started packing so late and because of the trouble with Wren. When she'd finally come home and found out what Tell had done, she was overjoyed. She began packing. She assumed that all deals were off and that she was going down the mountain with him. But all deals were not off.

"You're going to the chief's house, and that's that." Their father wouldn't budge. Not only was the journey itself too hard and dangerous for Wren, but the city of Halfway was even worse. Women and children had been known to disappear in Halfway. Wren would be in constant danger.

Also, since their mother had failed to return two years ago, women no longer went down the mountain. Only men. That was a new rule, fresh and fierce in everyone's minds. It was the cause of the anger Wren had heard in the women's voices earlier, from her perch high above the village. It was the reason the women refused to acknowledge their mother's existence and ignored their whole family. The finger of blame pointed squarely at them, and in many ways they were already outcasts. The women had loved the trip down as much as the men did—maybe even more—and it had been taken away from them.

It made no sense to Wren that the women weren't angry with the men for *making* the new rule, just with their mother for causing it. In everyday life, the women were as powerful as the men—as skilled, as tough, as ruthless, as feared . . . and yet they let the men make the rules because *that's the way it is, was, and will always be.*

That was the favorite saying of the People, used every day by everybody. *But was it a favorite?* Wren asked herself, *or were they just words suited to the people who made the rules?* Meaning, the men. These and more were questions Wren had often heard from her mother but hadn't dared ask out loud herself. And anyway, none of them would have helped her own cause one little bit that day.

On every count, Wren was forbidden from going with Tell. That didn't stop her from using every trick she knew to change her father's mind, and when she couldn't, she disappeared again. No door slammed this time. She left quietly. Tell and his father knew that a quiet Wren spelled trouble.

In his restless sleep that night, Tell heard Wren return, move around stealthily, then leave again. He couldn't escape the tendrils of sleep in time to ask her what she was doing.

When the village mule train left at dawn and those who remained behind had gone back indoors to wait in smoldering disappointment and anxiety for the men's eventual return, Tell wasn't safely with them. He was still making spare strings for his bow. He made them as slowly as he could, because he was waiting for Wren to return. But she never did.

When he finally left, with Rumble fully loaded and a big pack on his own back, it was as if the village were deserted, as if he were doing something so wrong and scandalous that the rest of the village refused to watch him do it.

Only his father watched him go. Or, rather, listened. Seka stood hunched in the narrow doorway of their house, cloth across his eyes, as Tell made the final adjustments to the load.

"I'll be back in time," Tell said with more certainty than he felt. "With lowland medicine for your eyes. I promise—"

"No promises," his father interrupted. "Don't think about me. My fate is what it is. You have to think about yourself and Wren from now on, and that's all."

Unable to reply, Tell suddenly hugged his father hard, something that hadn't happened in a long time. Tell realized that they were almost the same height now! Seka was surprised for a second, then pulled Tell in tight and held him fiercely. As he did, he spoke softly in his ear.

"It's going to be hard—harder than anything you've

ever known. But you can do it. I've told you everything you need to know about the journey, many times. You have the hand, you have the head, you have the heart. You were going to be chief one day; that day won't happen now. But there've been many chiefs. No one your age has ever done what you're doing. This will be a great thing. This will change us. Show them, Tell. Show them who you are. Show them the son I know." Overwhelmed, Tell's unseen nod was the only reply he could muster. He lingered, casting one last futile look around for Wren.

"Go. You're late enough already."

Tell left while he still had the courage to do so. Seka kept his head tilted toward the fading clip-clop of Rumble's hooves until he could hear them no more. Still and silent, he stayed in that cramped doorway, unwilling to go inside and start the last, brief part of his life alone.

As heavy as Tell's heart felt about saying goodbye to his father, he felt almost as bad about leaving without even a wave from his sister. This journey would be dangerous and uncertain, and he had wanted to say goodbye.

But no more than a mile down the trail, Wren popped up from behind a big rock with her pack on her back, her short knife at her belt, and Tell's hand-me-down yew bow slung across her shoulder.

"Took you long enough to get moving," Wren said. She'd pulled back her shock of hair and wore her least-patched tunic. She even had the one piece of jewelry she owned around her neck: a fine-knapped disc of black glass on a woven mule tail string. She was ready for a journey.

Tell gaped at her. "What do you think you're doing?"

"I don't think. I know," she said firmly. "I'm coming with you."

"You can't. If you do, neither of us will be allowed back."

"I don't care. I really don't." Wren's face showed that she meant it.

"I *have* to be able to come back up!" Tell exclaimed. "I'm not going to sit back and let us become orphans. I'm going to get medicine to save Da's eye, and I can't bring it back if we're outcasts. That means you have to stay!" Quickly, before Wren could protest, he added, "Anyway, you've got it easy. You'll be in the chief's house. You'll be spoiled silly."

Wren moved closer so that she could talk very quietly, even though they were completely alone.

"The chief's wife hated our mother and hates me just for being her daughter. She definitely doesn't want me, even if the chief does. I'll be beaten every day, and then someone will try to push me off a cliff when I'm not looking, which means I'll be looking over my shoulder all the time. I'm not living like that." Tell didn't know what to say.

"You need me," Wren pressed on. "This is too hard to do on your own." With her brother still searching for a response, Wren took the opportunity to finish her argument on a practical note. "Anyway, Rumble listens to me, not you. And you *definitely* need Rumble."

Tell cast about as if looking for an avenue of escape, but there was none. "I wonder what else will go wrong on this trip" was all he said, finally. Then he started down the trail, leaving Wren to pat Rumble and continue right behind him, her feet light with anticipation.

But even though she was smiling then, Wren had spent a long night looking for the double-sided courage to leave. She knew full well the dangers she was walking into. Or she thought she did, from her mother's stories. But that was only one part of the courage she needed. The other part was the courage to leave her father to fend for himself. And she realized that she couldn't.

So before dawn, she'd gone to visit the old lady who lived in a tumbled-down hut at the low edge of the village. She was once the best boot maker in the village and had taught many of them how to make good boots, but everyone knew she wouldn't survive the coming winter, and so they'd begun to ignore her. When Wren asked her to move into their house and look after her father until they returned, the old lady had laughed.

"You aren't coming back, my sweet. Even I can see that. But your house is much warmer than mine." The old lady began packing her few belongings, humming to herself. "Let's just agree that I'll look after your da until one of us dies."

Wren was grateful. She knew it was the best she could do for her father, and it allowed her to leave.

6

Tell and Wren both hesitated when they reached the Narrows half a day down the trail, even though they were sure-footed and unafraid of heights and cliffs and plummeting drops.

In part, it was because this was as far as they'd ever been allowed to go. Children were absolutely forbidden from entering the Narrows. It was clearly the deadliest section of a highly dangerous journey. A thread of a trail was carved across a sheer cliff, with barely enough room for a mule. And sometimes not enough room. More than one family had lost a season's black glass plus their mule in an instant. Tell and Wren knew full well that bones were piled upon bones thousands of feet below them, and not all of them belonged to mules.

Just as bad, a gigantic mushroom-shaped rock loomed above the Narrows, hanging at an angle away from the cliff. Everyone in the village said that the rock stayed in place only because of an ancient spell, and all spells eventually wear off. All they could hope for was that the spell wouldn't wear off that day.

"We need to breathe evenly," Tell counseled.

"We need to look at our feet and nowhere else," Wren added. Lessons taught by the village elders.

And yet neither of them could quite take that first step into the Narrows. From where they stood, it seemed as though they'd be stepping into thin air.

So, Rumble took over. With an impatient snort, the old mule squeezed them aside and clip-clopped into the Narrows, looking as calm and relaxed as if he were walking a wide path on a flat meadow. There was no choice after that. Wren followed Rumble, and Tell followed Wren.

No one was supposed to look up at the hanging rock in case the force of their gaze dislodged it, but Tell and Wren couldn't help it. The sight of that huge, misshapen rock looming over them made them shiver.

"It's horrible," Wren whispered.

Tell nodded, not even wanting to speak while they were under it, and they continued on, following the slow, steady pace set by their mule, their eyes cast down at their feet.

And then, suddenly, they were through. The path widened, almost generously. Relief became excitement, which gave them renewed energy. Wren darted around Rumble and made him stop, which he didn't like.

"What are you doing? Why have we stopped?" asked Tell.

"Because . . . guess what?" Wren replied with a flare of her arms.

"What?" he barked, impatient to be moving.

"From now on . . . ," Wren said, ignoring his tone, "everything we see is *completely new*!" Her eyes were alight with the idea of it. Thinking this way was her talent. Her gift. It was contagious.

"By the mountain's cold breath, you're right!" Tell exclaimed, grinning fully for the first time in a long while. "We have to remember it all." He smacked his chest, pointed at his sister. "This is finally *our* story, not somebody else's!"

"Yes!" Wren laughed. "And we'll bore everyone silly with it when we get the chance!" Wren stepped aside for Rumble, who shot off down the trail. Even the old mule seemed frisky, maybe from surviving the Narrows for one more season. Surviving the downhill half, anyway. The return trip could be worried about later.

Wren's elation lasted all afternoon, until the wolves started howling at dark. She and Tell hadn't caught up to the others, hadn't even seen them. The only sign that they were even on the same trail was the incredible amount of fresh mule droppings they had to wade through. An entire mule train's worth. After a while they didn't even bother to scrape it off their boots. They just let it dry and fall off.

"Ugh!" Wren complained. "And these are my good boots."

"At least we'll never get lost," Tell observed.

That night they huddled around their tiny fire, kept Rumble close, chewed strips of dried mountain goat meat, sucked on brandied apricots for dessert, and washed them down with ice-cold mountain spring water. The wolves howled on and off all night, but they never saw any. They also remembered stories their father had told them about this journey, back when he still told them stories.

"It's not what you see or hear that gets you; it's what you don't see or hear," he'd say, which had never seemed particularly helpful.

Neither Tell nor Wren slept much that night, with the only solace being the fire and the sound of Rumble's belly burbling right beside them. It seemed to Tell that Rumble didn't sleep much either. At any rate, every time he opened his eyes, he saw that Rumble's were open too. It was immensely comforting, and Tell vowed to himself never to beat Rumble again, which he'd done many times. It's what everyone else did with their mules and told him to do. But he wouldn't ever again. As sleep crept up on him at last, Tell had a final thought: every rule you break makes breaking the next one easier.

They set off the next morning as soon as they could see well enough to put one foot in front of the other. Down,

down, down they walked. Down and across the sheer flanks of huge, sprawling mountains, one after another.

Neither Tell nor Wren remembered much about that second day's journey. All they did was walk as fast as they could without stopping. It felt like a horrible dream at the time—the kind you try to wake up from but can't—and it disappeared quickly into the mists of memory, as dreams do. At least nothing dangerous threatened them, or they never noticed if it did. They finally arrived at a flat, grassy campsite next to a stream, after dark. Rumble snorted softly and pawed the ground as if to say, *Now you can stop.*

They barely had the strength to take the baskets of black glass off Rumble's back. They wouldn't have made a fire at all except there was a freshly gathered pile of wood next to a fire ring that had been used for generations. Only when Tell scooped ashes aside to make room for kindling and burned his hand on a living coal did he realize that the others had camped there the night before.

This shook Tell deeply. It had taken him and Wren a day and a half to cover what had taken the men only a day. Not only were they not catching up, but they were losing ground. The men were walking as fast as grown men could, and Tell and Wren simply couldn't keep up the same pace.

Tell realized a humiliating truth. "He was right," he confessed, crushed.

"Who was? And about what?" Wren's feet were too sore for her to care about much else.

"Da. He said I wasn't ready. He said I would slow them down. I didn't believe him. But . . . he was right."

"Too late to worry about that now," said Wren as she lay back. "Anyway, what's the hurry? It's just us."

Tell shook his head and wished he could take things lightly, the way his sister did. But he couldn't. He lay back as well, looking up at the night sky as she fell asleep next to him, too exhausted even to eat.

It's never easy to realize that you're not as wonderful as you think you are. Especially at a time when you need to be. Tell rolled over to go to sleep, blanketed in humiliation and feeling a tickle of fear. He had never doubted he could do this. It was why he'd taken on Hammerhead in the first place. But maybe . . . maybe he *wasn't* up to it. The old people in the village taught that doubt is like the insect that lays tiny eggs under your skin. One day the eggs will hatch and the doubt-insects will begin chewing away at you from the inside, until you are hollow. A gruesome thought.

Tell looked up at the stars and constellations he knew well. They wheeled in the night sky, indifferent to him and his fears, until physical exhaustion overwhelmed him and he was taken by sleep as if by an avalanche.

Wolves howled. Big things and small things moved all around them through the night, but Tell and Wren didn't hear any of them. If an animal had chosen to make a meal of them, they would only have woken up inside its belly— that's how tired they were.

7

Sometimes fortune smiles on the young instead of sweeping them away, and Tell and Wren woke to a full sun, empty bellies, and warmth such as they had never felt up in their village. As they rubbed the sleep out of their eyes, they noticed small trees and big bushes scattered about, none of which they had ever seen before. The grass they had slept on was green and almost soft, not brown and dry. They were well and truly out of the high mountains for the first time in their lives. Anticipation spiced their breakfast, which they ate on the run, like wolves.

"Let's go!" Tell shouted with a grin.

"There's going to be a lot to see today!" Wren replied, heading for Rumble to load him up after a kiss and a scratch behind his ears.

They walked hard the third day. The night's sleep had

done them good. They felt strong. Wren sang, and Tell forged ahead looking for signs of game.

"The rabbits will be fat and sweet down here," he predicted.

Suddenly, Wren yelled from behind him, "STOP!"

Tell whirled, raising his bow, ready for anything. But there was no obvious sign of danger. In fact, Wren was on her knees on the path, staring intently at something in the grass on the high side of the path.

"What is it?" Tell asked, rushing back.

"You walked right past it!" Wren scolded.

Tell bent down, looked where she was looking.

"It's more beautiful than I ever thought it could be," she breathed reverently. And then he saw it: a tiny purple flower hanging like a bell from a slender stem. There was wonder in his sister's eyes. "Look at that color!" There was very little color up the mountain—gray, black, white, and brown mostly. Tell leaned closer, saw bold black and yellow stripes inside the rich purple throat of the flower. "Ohhh!" was all he could manage.

Every story they'd ever heard about the journey included the moment when the person telling it saw this flower and how seeing it washed away all aches and pains and made their feet faster on the trail. It was called the Halfway Flower.

Because, of course, seeing it meant that they were halfway to Halfway. This was as high as the flowers could grow. Tell stood up, poised to utter something.

"Don't!" Wren urged. "There's no need."

"I have to," Tell pleaded.

"All right. Go ahead."

Tell drew himself up, pointed at the tiny, delicate, lustrous flower. "We're halfway there," he declared. Wren rolled her eyes, but she knew that one of them had to say it.

Before they continued, they turned to look back toward their home. They couldn't see any sign of it. Their mountain was hidden behind the many other mountains they'd traversed. All they could see were glimpses of the path they had walked, getting smaller and higher until it disappeared for good around a distant rock face.

"We've come a long way," Wren said.

"Not long enough," Tell grunted.

Rumble agreed, evidently, and took off down the trail, leaving Tell and Wren to catch up, whooping as they hurtled downward on their mountain-strong legs.

And then, just like that, they were no longer in the mountains at all, but in the range of hills beneath the mountains, and their noses told them so. Rich new smells perfumed the air. Butterflies with colors they'd never imagined floated around them; in truth, they'd never even seen butterflies before, just the occasional small gray moth. Birds like flying jewels darted in the trees. There was even a bird as shiny and black as their glass, mocking them from above with its harsh cackle.

"I want to stop," Wren protested. "Just for the colors!"

She felt certain that knowing and remembering all these new colors would get her through the next winter.

"On the way back," Tell promised. "We'll take more time." Much to his surprise, Tell was struck by the smells. There weren't a lot of smells up the mountain either; the air was too thin and cold. Rich and clean, sweet, tart, pungent smells. He wanted to savor them all. But they couldn't stop, and they knew it.

They virtually skipped down the trail the rest of the day. Eventually, Rumble was the one who grumbled and groaned and had trouble keeping up. The air grew warmer by the hour. They shed their furs and started looking forward to the many wonders of Halfway, which they'd heard about from their mother. From the tiniest detail about buttons, which were a new thing, to the fact that the entire city was built of mud brick, plastered smooth with more mud, because mud was easy to make down on Halfway's low plain, she'd been an expert. They'd loved the new stories when she returned . . . until she didn't.

"They say you can buy oils to make you smell sweet!" Wren said.

"And people throw things away that are still useful," Tell added, scandalized. Even though their feet were only a little more than half the distance to Halfway, their minds were already all the way there.

Which was why they were such easy prey for a cutthroat ambush.

Cutthroats were lawless lowlanders or mountain men who'd been expelled from their villages. They had no homes, no families, no pride, no mercy, and no jobs unless you call robbery, ambush, and treachery a job.

The end-of-summer mule trains were a tempting prize, but generally the People of the Black Glass were left alone, on account of their deadly weapons and cruel reputation.

Not two children, though.

Tell only realized they'd walked into the ambush once he was hanging upside down above the trail, one ankle snared in a noose tied to a tree that had been bent double only moments before.

"Run!" he screamed at his sister. She turned to flee and ran straight into the hard hands of a cutthroat creeping up behind her—who soon found out that he was trying to hold the human equivalent of a wildcat. Spitting, snarling, writhing, kicking, biting, Wren fought with every ounce of her wiry strength. Her bow spun away as she twisted and turned. Her short knife was slapped out of her hand as soon as she reached for it.

"Dammit, little girl, hold still!" The cutthroat tried to hit her, missed.

Rumble let out a low, unhappy sound much like a growl and came back toward them.

A second cutthroat carrying a fire-hardened spear ran up to Tell, who was swinging in the air. "There's only supposed to be one of them! This one!"

"Look in the baskets! There's a hundred-sous piece in there. The gods preserve us if it's broken." Wren's cutthroat tripped her, fell on top of her, using his weight to try to subdue her—and still she fought.

Even upside down, with all the blood rushing to his head and making him dizzy, Tell realized this ambush was no accident. These two had been expecting him.

Hammerhead! The treacherous brute *had* seen Tell slip the perfect slab under his father's quilt after all! Tell's blood-heavy mind raced. He'd bet almost anything Hammerhead had made a deal to give the cutthroats everything but the hundred-sous piece of black glass, which he would take for himself. A fierce rage swept through Tell, but he forced the emotion away and made himself think.

The cutthroat with the spear was rummaging through the baskets of black glass, making a mess of Tell's careful wrapping . . . not noticing that Rumble was slowly turning his hindquarters toward him.

Even with the cutthroat squashing her, Wren's eyes were open and bright and looking right at him. She was thinking too. She mouthed, *Go!*

Tell drew his father's knife and swung himself upward so that he could slash at the rope above his ankle. The whisper-sharp blade parted the rough rope as if it were nothing more than a weed stalk, and he dropped to the ground.

"Oi!" Wren's cutthroat called out a warning, half rising.

The other cutthroat stepped back from the mule, hefted his spear, ready to skewer Tell. But you never step back from a smart old mule called Rumble.

Rumble lashed out with both hooves, smashing the cutthroat in the ribs. The spear fell harmlessly to the ground, followed by the stunned cutthroat.

Wren felt the weight leave her as her cutthroat rose to deal with Tell. She kicked upward with all her might, catching him where she knew it would hurt the most. An unusually high-pitched scream told her she'd found her mark.

Howling with agony, Wren's cutthroat stumbled down the path toward Tell, who drew his bow, ready to loose an arrow at point-blank range.

The cutthroat saw the lethal black glass arrowhead pointed right at his heart. He dropped to his knees, raised his hands in submission, and blubbered for mercy.

Tell hesitated. The cutthroat was no longer a danger to them.

"You have to," said Wren sharply. "You know it."

Tell's eyes told her that yes, he knew it, and yet . . .

"You *have* to!" his sister yelled.

So Tell gulped in a breath, aimed, and loosed the arrow . . .

. . . . deep into the cutthroat's right shoulder. With a shout of pain, the cutthroat toppled backward, clutching his shoulder.

"You missed!" Wren gasped in shock.

"I didn't! He'll never use that arm again," Tell countered.

"We're supposed to *kill* anyone who—"

"Then you kill them! Here!" Tell tossed the cutthroat's spear to Wren. "Put it through his heart! Go ahead!"

"I will!" yelled Wren.

But when she stood over the semi-stunned, broken-ribbed, totally helpless cutthroat Rumble had kicked . . . she found that she couldn't do it. Her mind said one thing, but the rest of her said another.

"You see? Not so easy."

Wren raised the spear high, screamed in anger, and broke it over the cutthroat's head, transforming him from semi-stunned to fully stunned.

Tell suddenly saw someone new when he looked at his sister, standing there holding half a spear . . . new and a little frightening. It seemed to him that she had just crossed a one-way bridge into another part of herself. She reminded him of their mother; a cold look of hers flashed in his memory. His father had talked about this just a few days ago. He decided not to think about it. Not now. They had to get down the mountain.

"Let's go," Tell grunted.

Leaving the injured cutthroats behind, they walked . . . then jogged . . . then ran full-tilt down the path, two children and an old mule trying to leave the ugliness of the ambush behind them as fast as possible. But you can't outrun memories. At least, they couldn't.

Eventually, Rumble slowed to a walk, and so did they. They no longer saw the beautiful things all around them, no longer heard the birdsong or smelled the stands of wildflowers they passed through.

"We should've killed them," Wren said once she stopped panting.

"I know." Tell shook his head at his own failure. "But I couldn't."

For the People of the Black Glass, mercy equaled weakness, and revenge was to be taken no matter what. Every child learned that before they learned to walk. Mercy was the first step toward their own extinction. Any attack on any of them was repaid with a life, instantly. That's the way it is, was, and always will be.

"What if they come after us?" Wren asked.

"I don't think they can," said Tell. "They're badly hurt."

Wren nodded, satisfied.

But what if they warn Hammerhead? Tell asked himself silently. *What if they tell him we're still alive?*

Fear clutched his gut as, suddenly, he realized what lay ahead for him: he would have to find a way to get rid of Hammerhead. There was no choice. Because once Hammerhead found out they'd survived, he would do his best to kill them and would never stop trying until he succeeded.

8

It was hours after dark when Rumble finally slowed and turned off the trail onto a tiny, overgrown path that seemed to lead straight into the heart of the mountainside. The lesser part of a moon was all the light they had to see by, but they were grateful for it. They turned a tight corner, crossed a gully, pushed through a narrow gap between huge, jagged boulders, and entered an amphitheater full of . . . ghosts, writhing in front of them?

Utterly exhausted, it took them a moment to realize that they weren't actually in a haunted place. They were looking at steam rising from a big pool of water.

"It's the Night Before hot springs!" Wren exclaimed, her exhaustion lifting instantly. The hot springs were steeped in lore. They were secret. They were the final stopping place before Halfway. They were the place where the People hid their heavy mountain furs for the return journey.

They were the place where the People had a much-needed bath (rare for mountain people because their water was so cold). Best of all, the water itself had healing properties that soothed the aches and pains of the journey—in fact, of the entire mining season.

Many of the People believed that the afterlife had hot springs aplenty. Those who believed in an afterlife, anyway. Some did and some didn't.

Though eager to try the water, Tell and Wren first took the load from Rumble's sweating back, so that he could wander off and forage in the dark. Only then did they shed their clothes and slide into the steaming water. It was a moment they'd never forget. It was the first time they'd been truly, deeply warm since they'd been born.

"Oh!" gasped Wren. "I could stay here forever."

Tell nodded, grinning almost drunkenly. "Don't drink it, though. It tastes really bad."

"That's because Hammerhead's been in it!" Wren decided.

Usually, Hammerhead jokes were a sure source of laughter. But not for Tell, not ever again. The very name put a knot in his stomach.

"I wonder which of our people found this place?" Wren mused. "Why don't we know their names? We should."

"What difference does it make?" Tell shrugged.

Wren thought before answering him. "Everyone we know . . . and everyone they know . . . and everyone who came before them, going back and back and back—maybe even to whoever found the black glass in the first place and started our village—they've been right here in this pool, warm and happy, and . . ." Wren saw her brother's confused look. "I don't know *why* it makes a difference; it just does!"

Tell said nothing but was obviously deep in thought.

"You're thinking about them, aren't you?" Wren said quietly. "Two winters ago, they were both in here, together."

"On the way down, anyway." Tell nodded.

"I wonder what happened. I wish we knew," Wren murmured, head down as if she were asking the water.

Tell paused, then said, "Da was about to tell me."

"He was? So, what happened to her?"

"Hammerhead came in, and then I was too . . . too busy to ask again." Tell tossed a double handful of hot water over his head, as if he were trying to wash away thoughts and memories. "All I know is, you never see the big changes coming," Tell said, dolefully echoing his father's words. "If it's really big and really horrible, it's sure to smack you right in the back of the head."

Wren let herself slide all the way underwater, held her breath, then came up and said simply, "Then there's no point in worrying about it until it happens, is there?" She got out, dried off, and went to her bedroll. It felt so good to be warm and clean that, despite all that had happened, she slept like a baby, the day's events already put behind her. Wren's ability to move on from horrible events and her ability to be happy went hand in hand, and Tell was envious.

He did not sleep like a baby. He had nightmares about the cutthroats, who had merged into one cutthroat, shuffling closer, begging for mercy and groaning at the same time. Tell had killed many things in his fourteen years—they had to eat, after all—but never another human being. There's a difference, and the difference was measured in nightmares.

Wren was first up. She let Tell sleep. She'd heard him murmuring restlessly in the night and knew he needed it. She folded their furs and leggings and looked around for the secret cave to stash them safely. It was easy to find, just from the stories. What was not easy was seeing all the other bundles of fur. It was like seeing the outer skins of the men—and only the men, now—she'd known since the day she was born. Good, bad, and in Hammerhead's case, treacherous, these were her people. Barely thirty men from barely thirty families.

"That's all of us," she said to Tell later, when she showed him the cave. "We're as rare as our black glass."

"And just like it," Tell realized. He found the sight of the bundled furs as haunting as Wren did.

"What do you mean?" asked Wren.

"Well, we're hard and sharp, but also . . ." Tell searched

for a word he'd heard once, around a winter fire when they were making arrowheads. "Brittle."

Wren agreed. "That's why we have to kill our enemies. Otherwise we'd be gone."

Many years ago, a band of outsiders had journeyed up the mountain, planning to plunder the vein of glass by force. This was a story told often in the village, and Tell and Wren knew it by heart. The broken bones of the outsiders lay in bleached piles all over the mountainside. A lone survivor had been allowed to take the story of the People's cruelty back down the mountain. No outsider had tried to steal their black glass since.

Tell stared at his sister. The very same sister who had slammed the door on her way out of their home and yet not. Older. Tougher. Changed in just a few days. He hoped that he was too. He needed to be.

"That goes for you and me too," he added. "Especially down here. We're going to have to be as hard as black glass."

"Is that your way of telling me there's no hot water today?"

"On the way back." Tell nodded. "When we've done what we set out to do."

"It'll be our reward," Wren concurred.

The rest of the journey was easy and lush, the path wide, the footing solid, and the nightmares disappeared in the wake of their growing excitement.

Just before noon, they turned a sharp corner of granite, and Tell suddenly put his arm out to grab Wren.

"Look! There it is!"

They stopped in their tracks. Even Rumble stopped and whinnied softly. Below them was the vast city of Halfway, far away across a hot, dry plain. All their lives they'd heard about the glory of this first glimpse. But nothing they'd been told could prepare them for what they saw with their own eyes.

"By the mountain's white crown, it's . . . it's . . . ," Tell stammered.

"It's *huge*!" Wren breathed.

They'd known Halfway was bigger than their village, but they'd never imagined it was a thousand times bigger and more, contained within the curve of high, thick walls. Their mother had told them that it took a full day to walk from one side to the other, inside the walls; she'd done it. They knew it was loud and full of people from every corner of the land; they never imagined they'd be able to hear the faint hum of their voices from here. They'd been told it was full of strange smells; they never realized that Halfway would actually spice the very air around them, this high up and far away. Tell felt a surge of triumph. They'd made it! Or they would if they got moving.

"Let's go!" Tell barked, and strode forward.

"Wait," Wren implored. "I love this view—from up here we're like hawks hovering." She sat on a flat rock, feasting with her eyes. This was her favorite viewpoint, her favorite way of seeing their village, too.

Tell returned, sitting impatiently next to his sister. But he knew that he also needed a moment to take it in.

The people below seethed like ants from a freshly disturbed nest, only they never settled. Every now and then, the wind would carry up fragments of music in voices, languages, and instruments they'd never heard before.

"Look." Wren pointed. "That's our gate!" Halfway had four gates, one for each quarter. Theirs was big enough to be seen all the way up here.

"That's the Mountain gate." His father had told him, more than once, that he would never forget the first time he entered it.

"Then . . . that must be the marketplace, on the other side of the wall." Wren leaned forward as if she actually were a hawk about to open her wings and glide all the way into the marketplace.

A sudden thought sobered Tell. "I wonder if that's where we buy medicine for Da's eye."

"Maybe there's a marketplace just for medicine. There probably is, somewhere." Wren was excited. "I can't wait to buy something!"

"Like what?" Tell asked.

"Anything!" Wren replied. "So long as I don't have to catch it, make it, or steal it."

"We can't buy anything until we trade our glass," Tell reminded her. "Not even water or food."

"I know." Wren nodded. "We'll go straight to Kun Anton."

Kun Anton. Their village traded with him every year, just as they had with his father. They'd heard so many stories about him over the years that it felt to Tell and Wren as if they already knew him. Tell searched farther into the city, wondering where the most powerful sorcerer in Halfway lived. He felt fear rising in him, even all the way up here. Which was what sorcery did—reach out and squeeze your heart. He swallowed hard, tamping down the fear . . . for now.

"It's more amazing than I imagined." Wren sighed dreamily. "And I thought I'd never get to see it." *Just because I'm a girl*, she thought to herself.

Tell seemed to read her thoughts. "Because of only one person," Tell added, meaning their mother. "It doesn't make sense. It's wrong."

One of the reasons people said that Tell would be chief one day was his clear sense of what was fair and not fair. He was never going to be chief now, but his sense of fairness hadn't disappeared, and Wren loved that about her brother.

"I'm glad you refused to live with Hammerhead," Wren told him now. "I'm glad I came with you. I'm glad we broke the rules. They're unfair."

"Yes," Tell agreed. "They are." He stood up. "Come on. We have to get down there before dark."

This time Wren didn't argue. They headed on down fast.

Paths and tracks joined and widened and joined again, converging on the city like rivers flowing into a circular sea from all directions. Tell and Wren faltered momentarily when their path merged with another, wider, more well-used path. When they stepped onto it, it felt as if they'd stepped into a current that could easily sweep them away.

"I just realized something," Tell said suddenly.

"What?" Wren asked. She'd been uncommonly silent, and so Tell knew she was as apprehensive as he was.

"What we've done so far, the journey down ... that was the easy part."

9

The closer they got to Halfway, the louder the city roar became and the drier their mouths felt, no matter how many sips of cold spring water they took. True, down there on the plain they were hotter than they'd ever been in their lives . . . but that was not why their mouths were dry.

"You do know where Kun Anton lives, right?" Wren asked anxiously.

"Of course!" Tell was glad his father had tested him doubly on this before he left. "Straight through the Mountain gate, right turn at the round house, left turn at the giant fig tree, a little way farther, then look for the big house with the black glass window next to a carved wooden door," he recited.

Wren should have felt more reassured, but she didn't. "I've wanted to be here all my life . . . but now I just want to get this over with," she confessed.

"So let's do that," Tell agreed, striding toward the walls, which looked much higher from down here on the plain.

But fifty yards from the gate, Rumble suddenly stopped and wouldn't budge, no matter what. Not with Wren pushing and Tell pulling, not after Wren tickled him exactly where he liked to be tickled, not when Tell tried bribery with their last chunk of salt cake. Rumble fixed an eye on them and snorted, as if they were being incredibly dense and had missed something basic. A mule's disdain is very clear.

"What's going on?" Tell asked, exasperated. "We're not supposed to go in now? After running us all the way down? I don't understand!" Tell was beginning to regret his promise not to beat Rumble. "You said Rumble listened to you; well, he isn't now!"

Irritatingly, Wren had started laughing. "I know why he stopped! I remember Mo telling me! Rumble likes to be brushed before going through the gate."

"Rumble's a *mule*!"

Wren shook her head the way parents do when their children do something beyond all understanding. "Yes, but he's secretly vain and doesn't want to look like a mountain goat." As she talked, Wren found Rumble's brush in the pack—three dried thistle heads nailed to a thick piece of bark. She ran it over the old mule's coat in long, crackling strokes, and he snorted happily.

"See!"

Tell rolled his eyes. But when he thought Wren wasn't looking, he straightened his clothes, combed his fingers through his untidy hair, and smoothed it back behind his ears. He didn't want to look like a mountain goat either. Wren never did, no matter what. Clean after the hot springs, dressed in rabbit-skin boots and a soft, faded blue tunic that had once belonged to her mother, she practically gleamed.

Freshly brushed and clearly feeling very handsome, Rumble now trotted perkily toward the Mountain gate, a massive wooden structure flanked by enormous, winged lions carved from pale stone, with eyes painted ruby red and elephant tusks for fangs.

Almost immediately, two enormous gatekeepers stepped out and barred their way with crossed spears so thick, Tell wasn't sure he could lift one with both hands. They were by far the biggest, most frightening men either Tell or Wren had ever seen.

"That's far enough!" roared the gatekeeper on the left.

The siblings stopped immediately and stood stock-still.

"What brings you to Halfway?" barked the gatekeeper on the right, looking them up and down with unfriendly eyes.

Tell didn't know what to say. "Uhhh . . ."

"Trade?" asked his sister carefully.

"Black glass," added Tell. "We're late."

"You'll be even later if you don't hand those over!" The

right-hand gatekeeper pointed a blunt finger at their bows and arrows.

"No weapons in Halfway!" yelled the left-hand gatekeeper. "No exceptions! Didn't they tell you?"

Of course! It was the first law of Halfway, made to prevent bloodshed. "I forgot," Tell confessed.

"You don't have to shout," Wren added politely. "We're standing right here."

"You'll get 'em back when you leave," said one.

"Unless you forget that, too," added the other.

As the guards laughed at their own bad joke, Tell unstrung his bow, shrugged off his quiver, and unstrung Wren's bow. Wren had tucked her short knife out of sight and decided not to mention it.

"You need a new string," Tell told her, clinging to things he knew as he put her quiver with his and wrapped all of it carefully with their bowstrings. He held the bundle out to the gatekeepers.

"What do we look like, servants?" yelled the right-hand gatekeeper, outraged.

The other gatekeeper gestured at a long, low shed just outside the gate. "Over there."

Tell ducked around the spears, took one quick, awed glance up at the Flying Lions as he walked right under their fangs, then stopped at the door of the weapons shed, where a sun-scarred old man stood waiting impatiently. When Tell handed the bundle over, the old man studied the bows, a look on his face as if he'd just eaten sour grass.

"Mountain yew?"

"Of course!" Tell answered proudly. Yew was the best bow wood.

"Who made them?"

"My father made mine. I made my sister's. Well, I made it for myself, but when it got too small for me, I gave it to her."

The old man grunted. Then his eyes lit on Tell's knife in the mountain lion skin sheath. Tell sighed and reached down to take it off. But the old man turned away.

"If you were a grown man, I'd take it. But you clearly aren't." The old man walked off with their precious bows.

Tell quickly hid his knife under his tunic and called after him, "Could you store them in a corner, so nothing will fall on them?"

The old man's eyes flashed with irritation. "Do I look stupid to you?"

Tell shook his head. "No."

"Do I look like someone who's never seen a bow before?"

"No. It's just that—"

"It's just that you mountain people think everyone else's a fool, that's what. You're the ones without a clue; it's the thin air you breathe. Affects your brains." The old man stomped into the weapons shed.

Tell peered through the open door and saw an amazing array of weapons stored there, many of which he didn't recognize. Pikes, spears, swords, ornate clubs, weighted nets, bows of every size and shape, knives that hardly looked like knives at all. He would have loved to spend the day in the shed, studying them all! But he had more important things to do, and so did the old weapons-keeper, who stacked his and Wren's bows next to some others in a corner.

Tell recognized every single one of them. They belonged to Curas, to the chief, the Mort brothers, Melk, all the men of his village. He saw Hammerhead's thick bow . . . and realized with a jolt that he had no idea what he was going to do when he saw the men or when they saw him and Wren.

"Go on, get out," scolded the old man. "You'll want to be wherever you're going before dark. It's not just scrawny wolves and the odd little snake you have to worry about down here after dark."

Tell returned to the gatekeepers and showed them his empty hands. The left-hand gatekeeper pointed up at a bundle of old clothes hanging from the top of the wall. "See that up there?"

Tell and Wren looked closely, then grimaced when they realized that the bundle of clothes was actually all that was left of a man. A grisly sight.

"Died slow, he did. Terrible noise for days," the right-hand gatekeeper explained cheerfully. "Know why he's up there?"

As Tell thought about it, Wren stepped forward. "He let a fire get away from him?" The second law of Halfway, which they both knew: all cooking fires, lamps, and candles had to be contained at all times.

"Yes! Be warned! He let a fire get away from him!" roared the right-hand gatekeeper.

"She's smarter than you are, boy!" yelled the left-hand gatekeeper. At that, the gatekeepers raised their spears and allowed Tell, Wren, and Rumble to walk past.

"And better-looking!" the right-hand gatekeeper called after them as he and his partner settled back into place, chuckling away.

Wren had the beginnings of a grin on her face. Now that it was over, she realized that she'd enjoyed their encounter with the gigantic gatekeepers. It had settled her nerves. She was done feeling overwhelmed. She was going to enjoy every moment, and as it happened.

"I bet we're the youngest ever to make the journey alone," she said to her brother.

"That's what Da said," Tell agreed, "and he didn't even know you were coming."

A sudden thought hit Wren. "Do you think the men will be at Kun Anton's?"

"Yes . . . and they're going to fall over backward when they see us," Tell said. Hammerhead most of all, he thought.

"Especially when they see me," Wren added. "They won't be expecting that."

"I wonder what they'll do," Tell mused uneasily.

"Only one way to know," said Wren as she pressed forward through the Mountain gate and into the Mountain quarter.

10

They were immediately engulfed by beggars and street hawkers selling everything from dewy-sided cups of cool water for the hot traveler, to dried meat and dried fruit, to yellow-throated songbirds in tiny wicker cages, and more. It was unnerving; they weren't used to so many people crowding in, with hair and skin of many different shades, wearing all sorts of clothes and ornaments, shouting at them in lots of different tongues. The idea of it had been exciting; the reality was overwhelming.

"Ignore them all," their father had said, so Tell now told Wren to do the same. Tell reached under his tunic and touched his knife. It was reassuring. Wren kept her head high, her nose at an aloof angle. Rumble walked more briskly than usual.

But the crowd moved with them, away from the gate. A hand reached out and pinched Wren's cheek. She shrieked and lashed out furiously, her composure shattered. Laughter rippled through the crowd. Tell whirled toward the nearest people, who danced away from him, jeering at his young fierceness.

All around them, the crowd came in close, then pulled back mockingly. The sport of it fed them, fueled by the idea of tormenting two of the People because they could and because they were children, Tell realized quickly. They'd never dare try this with any of the men, he thought angrily. Someone spat a big gob of green phlegm at Tell's feet. His anger rose, his eyes flashed, and his hand dropped to his knife. Blood was about to flow.

Wren knew that look on her brother's face.

"To Kun Anton," she ordered sharply. "*Now.*" She tapped Rumble, and he broke into a canter. They ran alongside him, breaking through the swarm, who jeered but couldn't be bothered to chase after them.

"They're too lazy to follow!" Tell puffed, outraged, as if that were a bad thing somehow.

"Good!" Wren shouted back.

But one was not so lazy. Unseen, one broke away from the swarm in the opposite direction, a ragged creature with hungry eyes and tattered sandals, who hurried away into the heart of the city with the air of someone who had just learned a precious secret and knew exactly what to do with it.

Once they were well clear of the throng at the gate, Tell

and Wren, breathing hard, tried to take in surroundings the like of which they'd never seen before and barely understood, despite all they'd been told. Without stopping—definitely not until they reached Kun Anton's house—they turned this way and that, almost in a panic, their pulses racing.

"Do you know where we are?" Wren asked urgently.

"No!" Tell replied, but Rumble kept moving, and so they stayed with him, trying to get their bearings.

There were people everywhere, in every direction, moving, yelling, buying what they needed, selling what they didn't. Individual voices and conversations by the dozen, until words and their meanings disappeared into the constant roar of Halfway. For Tell and Wren, who'd only ever known their small village, this was an avalanche of people, except real avalanches eventually stopped, and this one never did. It was what they'd heard from the hills earlier that day.

"So many people . . ." Wren almost sounded stunned.

"Too many," Tell declared.

And then, also . . . streets. They'd never seen a street before, only footpaths. But here, every street was paved, or cobbled, or foot-stamped dirt as hard as stone and lined with unbroken rows of mud-colored buildings leading to corners and more streets curving or zigzagging away to who-knew-where? Halfway seemed endless and yet tightly enclosed at the same time.

Houses and shops made of mud bricks plastered with mud leaned tight against each other. The ends of polished tree trunks protruded from the walls, holding up second and third stories. The only way to add space in Halfway was upward. Every building was higher than any they had ever known, with square or round or even arched holes for windows. The only color to be seen was on a few of the doors, but most were plain weathered wood.

Tell was used to nothing obstructing his view but clouds and mountains. He felt hemmed in. He couldn't see far in any direction. He felt as though he were trapped in a crowded maze of mud-colored canyons.

"Look for a round house!" he shouted.

"I am!" she shouted back, turning in a futile circle. "Let's just ask someone," she decided, and took two steps toward a woman carrying a dead bird by its feet. "We're looking for Kun—"

"Get away, you thieving little vermin!" spat the woman as she sidestepped Wren and hurried away, holding her dead bird protectively.

"I wasn't going to steal your wormy old bird!" Wren yelled at her back.

"There it is! The round house!" Tell called out with immense relief.

Ahead of them, at the end of the street, was a small, round mud hut, thatched with some kind of coarse grass.

The wall plaster had crumbled away in places, revealing the sagging mud-and-straw bricks behind it. It seemed deserted; anyway, it had no door.

"It looks really old," Tell decided.

"Maybe it's what houses here used to be, long ago," Wren mused. Since the Night Before hot springs, she'd been thinking more about things that happened in the past and how they rippled down to the present.

"We make a right—"

But Rumble had already made the turn onto a narrower, and blessedly less busy, street. This street was cobbled, and Rumble's hooves rang as he trotted along it.

"You know what?" Tell realized. "Rumble knows the way!"

"Of course he does," Wren replied proudly. "He's been doing it longer than we've been alive."

The narrow street quickly led to a wide square, which held the first green thing they'd seen since walking through the Flying Lion gate—an enormous old tree.

"That has to be the fig tree!" he said at last. Tell was mesmerized; he'd never fathomed a tree could grow so large and spread its branches so wide.

"And look, it has fruit! Lots of it." Wren licked her lips.

The tree was so old that some limbs were dead and gray. Most of it was lush and vigorous, though. Once a year dried, pressed figs from this very tree were brought back up the mountain as treats. Tell's mouth was already watering. The fruit looked soft and ripe. He'd never eaten a fresh fig. Would it taste different from a dried fig? He very much wanted to find out. He spotted an especially fat one, drooping heavily from its stem, low enough to pluck. But as he reached for it, he discovered that in Halfway, even trees have guards.

"Keep moving, little mountain goats! I can read your thieving minds. Don't even look at the fruit. It doesn't belong to you." The spry old guard had a nasty, knobby walking stick, which he waved menacingly.

Tell leaned close to Wren. "We'll come back after dark," he whispered.

"And don't think it'll be easier after dark!" the guard shouted after them. "The night guard isn't a sweetheart like me!"

Tell was astonished. The guard had read his mind! Clearly they had a lot to learn about Halfway.

They made a left turn at the fig tree onto an even narrower street, barely wide enough for them to walk abreast, keeping an eye out for a big house with a carved wooden door and a window of black glass.

"We must be close now," Tell said hopefully as they walked and walked.

But on this particular street, every single house was big. Bigger than any they'd seen so far, bigger than they knew houses could be! And every single one had a carved wooden door. Many had high walls extending beyond the buildings themselves. What's behind all those walls? Wren wondered. None of them had black glass windows next to the door. Tell and Wren slowed, confused. Overwhelmed.

"Maybe we passed it already?" Tell said at last, turning around to look back the way they'd come.

But Rumble just trundled on down the street. "Rumble knows," Wren said proudly. They followed gratefully.

"When we sell our glass, we're going to get you the best oats a mule can eat," Tell promised him. "And lots of it." It no longer felt strange to be talking to a mule. He now understood why Wren had done so all her life.

Five houses farther down, Rumble turned toward a huge house, by far the biggest on the street. Yes, it had a carved door, but Rumble led them farther down the wall surrounding it, to a high wooden gate.

"That's it!" Tell exclaimed. "We go straight through the gate into the courtyard." They'd heard about the courtyard; it was where the People slept while they were bargaining with Kun Anton over their black glass.

"Wait!" Wren blurted, reaching for Rumble to stop him. "There's no black glass window." In fact, there was no window at all, just a rough-cut slab of wood pushed into the window opening.

"It must be broken. Or maybe they're bargaining for a new one." Tell was ready to go through the gate and get behind the wall, out of sight. The mob at the entrance had shaken him more than he cared to admit. Wren looked at Tell uncertainly. "We go in through the gates and make a hard right. That's the most sheltered corner. Da told me. It's where he sets up," Tell insisted.

Wren looked at Rumble. The old mule was practically nuzzling the gates, clearly impatient. *Probably eager to get rid of the load on his back*, Wren thought, reassured.

Tell reached for the plank that kept the gate closed—actually had his hand on it—when a pebble whizzed through the air and bounced off the wood, inches from his hand. Another pebble followed the first, smacking him on the back of his head.

"Ow!" Tell whirled around, feeling his head for a welt. A girl stood across the way, in a shadow. Wren's age. Her clothes were absolutely filthy, and she had dark rings under her eyes and an expression on her face that Tell could not read.

"Was that you?" he demanded.

The girl nodded.

"Well, this is me." Tell stepped toward her.

"Tell, no!" Wren knew his temper. She slipped quickly between the girl and her brother. "That was stupid," Wren said to the girl.

"Maybe so," said the girl with an indifferent shrug.

Tell gaped at her. "Then why did you do it?"

She shot him a disdainful look. "To stop you from going through the gates."

"But why?" Wren shot back.

"Because if you do, you'll be killed like the rest of your horrible people," the girl said, her deeply shadowed green eyes growing even darker.

11

Her name was Rumi Anton. She was well fed, and her wavy hair looked brown in some lights, red in others. She wore leggings and a tunic made of such fine, smooth cloth that, even though it was dusty and dirty, Wren had to resist reaching out to feel it. They learned that she was Kun Anton's youngest child, the apple of his eye, and spoiled. A spoiled girl in such shock that she didn't know she was gulping for breath while words poured out of her as they stood in the street outside the gate.

"Yesterday, just before your men arrived with the black glass—we knew they were here; we'd gotten word from the gate; my father has runners and spies—ten Ropers arrived to bargain for the entire load. Their leader's name is Kennett; I heard him tell it to my father. My father let them in. Why wouldn't he? If you can sell something before you've even got it, you do. It's the best. No storage problems." Rumi paused briefly to draw in a deep breath.

"But it was just a trick. The Ropers were never going to buy anything. People call them Ropers because their hair looks like rope—not to their faces, of course! Just as your people arrived at our house, they took out these . . . these *strings*! They put them around my mother and brothers' necks, and Kennett said they would be strangled like chickens unless my father did exactly what he said, so of course my father did, which meant he greeted your chief like he always does and brought them all straight to the warehouse to unload, like he always does, but only after Kennett and the other Ropers had gone into the warehouse first . . . and got ready . . ."

Her story rushed out as if she'd been waiting far too long for someone to tell it to, someone who would understand and believe her. Her eyes were wet with waiting tears.

"Got ready for what?" Tell pressed.

"I don't know! I don't know anything! They took my mother and brothers into the warehouse too. I couldn't see from where I was hiding, but I heard a single shout when the warehouse door slammed shut behind them—then nothing."

"What do you mean, 'nothing'?" Wren realized that her hands were clenched into tight fists. They'd taken all the village men, too?

"The door's thick because of thieves," replied Rumi.

"Once it's closed, you can't hear a thing through it. I haven't been in there. I can't get in without knocking. . . ." Her voice faltered. "I'm scared to. I don't know what I'll find. No one came out, not even the Ropers. I've been watching since it happened . . . since yesterday."

Tell and Wren looked at each other in shock. The men of the village gone, just like that?

"Why didn't they take you?" Wren couldn't help but ask.

"I was already hiding. I have this place—it's disgusting; that's why I'm so dirty. Nobody thinks I'd ever go there, so—"

"You were hiding from the Ropers?" Tell interrupted.

"No, not them. Everyone thinks they're wonderful and amazing. Nobody will ever believe they did this." Her cheeks went red. "I was hiding from you . . . well, your people."

Tell and Wren gaped at her. "From us? Why?"

Rumi's eyes narrowed. "Because you're all wild animals, and you'd rather slit a person's throat than talk to them. That's what my father says. I always hide when you arrive. I'm glad I did." But as soon as the words were past her lips, Rumi bent double and began sobbing her heart out. "They're gone, they're gone, they're all gone but me! What am I going to do?"

Tell looked at Wren. He had no idea what to do. Nor did Wren, but her heart was more open. She touched Rumi lightly on her shoulder.

"We understand how you feel, but you shouldn't cry," she said.

Rumi jerked upright, face wet with tears and snot. "How can you understand?!" she demanded, wiping her nose on her sleeve.

"Because . . ." Wren paused. "We just do."

Tell did not falter. "Because we lost our mother two years ago, and our father is freshly blinded by a sliver of black glass and will most likely be dead in thirty days. Less, now. And if what you say is true, all our men are gone, too. Which means the women and children, and the old people, waiting up the mountain for them to return, will starve to death this winter without ever knowing what happened," he declared brutally. *"But you don't see us crying, do you?"* he nearly shouted next, betraying the emotion he thought he'd hidden.

"Why not?" Rumi matched his anger. "You should!"

"Because we've got more important things to do."

"Like what?"

"Like . . . finding out exactly what happened. And making those Ropers pay for it. It's our duty; we have to. And I want to." Tell's voice was hard, and so was his expression.

"Also, we need to sell our black glass," Wren added practically.

Rumi looked at both of them for a long moment, then nodded. "I'll help you."

"You? How?" Tell asked, unable to keep the scorn from his voice.

"Do *you* know how to sell your load of black glass so that you've got a few sous, and where to stable your mule and buy food and find a safe place to sleep? Of course you don't." Rumi's eyes sparked with contempt. "You think you're so tough. But without the rest of your people, you won't last two days in this city. Don't you understand? People without protection are bought and sold here. You're as valuable as your load of glass. More. Especially her. You'll be scooped up and sold to someone from a faraway place—if you're lucky. You need me, whether you want to admit it or not."

Wren looked from Rumi to her brother. He clearly did not like being bossed around by a girl younger than him. But Wren shot him a warning look and stepped forward.

"Yes," she said simply. "You're right. We do."

12

Rumi led them deeper into the city, keeping to the darkest, narrowest, twistiest streets. She tied a shawl over her head, as if she didn't want anyone to see her face. Or maybe she just wanted to keep the deep shock in her eyes to herself.

Tell and Wren didn't know it and wouldn't have admitted it if they had, but they were in shock themselves, trying to wrap their minds around what had happened. They assumed the worst; it was better to, and the People of the Black Glass routinely did. The chief, gone. The Mort brothers and Curas, their finest hunter, gone. Even Hammerhead, gone. All of them . . . gone. Those bundles of fur in the secret cave by the hot springs seemed even sadder now. Almost pathetic.

Flooded with feelings, their eyes down, Tell and Wren scarcely noticed anything except Rumi's feet just ahead of them—and that was the first of their many mistakes that day. They couldn't have found their way back to Kun Anton's house if they'd tried. Even Rumble seemed subdued, the picture of a plodding mule.

"We're at the Desert quarter now, just the edge of it," Rumi said over her shoulder.

"What's a quarter?" Wren asked.

Rumi blinked at the question. It was so obvious. "Halfway was started by four different trading clans from four different places. So it's divided into quarters. It always has been."

"But how do you know we're at the edge of one?" Tell asked. To him, nothing had changed. Everything looked the same. The street and the crammed buildings on either side of it looked no different from any others they'd seen. Mud brick plastered with mud.

"This street marks the difference—it goes all the way from the wall to the center. Not in a straight line, of course," Rumi explained impatiently. "On this side of the street, people live under the protection of the family who runs the Mountain quarter—our quarter. Good people. They love us. We make a lot of money for them."

Rumi gestured dismissively at the other side of the street. "And that's Desert." She sniffed.

"Why's it called Desert?" Wren asked.

"Because their gate and all the paths that come to it face a huge desert, five days' travel away. My father says it's the worst quarter—badly run by weak people."

Wren leaned close to Tell. "What's a desert?" she whispered. Tell shook his head—he didn't know.

They finally scraped down one last alleyway, past the back sides of shops and houses, and stopped at a gate set into a high wall topped with big, jagged shards of flint. Anyone trying to climb over it would be torn to shreds.

"You'll be able to sell your load here," Rumi told them.

"Our da never mentioned another black glass dealer in Halfway. Only your father."

"Because there isn't one," Rumi said simply. "But this man wants to be. He buys and sells precious stones of all kinds. He's tried to undercut my father many times. He never succeeds—he's just not smart enough. But he hates my father. He'll buy your load just to spite him. He's also a snake and he'll rob you blind if he can, so be careful. His name is Rold Roland, and one of his front teeth is green. Good luck."

"You aren't coming with us?" Wren asked, alarmed.

"I can't. He'll recognize me; he'll think this is a trick and he'll just throw you out. I'll wait for you right here."

"But—" Tell felt suddenly helpless, maybe his least favorite feeling of all. "How do we do it?"

"Do what?"

"We've never sold anything before," Wren admitted.

"How many sous is our load worth? What if he offers less? What do we say? What do we do?" Tell hated that none of his skills were of any help to him here.

Rumi blinked at them, astonished. Buying and selling had been a part of her life for as long as she could remember. It was as if they'd said they didn't know how to eat. Finally, she sighed, the expression on her face becoming serious and businesslike.

"What kind of load is it?"

"Da said he'd had a good year at the glass. Lots of big, clean slabs," Tell stated. Wren nodded in agreement. Their father had said it more than once.

"Then it's probably worth twenty sous."

"Twenty! But that's amazing!" A fortune, to the two of them.

"Calm down. Just because it's worth that much doesn't mean you'll be selling it for that much. You'll be lucky to get half."

Tell shrugged. "Half is good enough."

"I said you'll be *lucky* to get half. Rold Roland's going to take one look at you, fresh off your mountain, and, well, watch his hands—if he rubs them together like he's washing them, you're in trouble."

13

Rold Roland's soft pink hands never stopped rubbing together as he smiled at Tell and Wren. The carved stone rings on his fingers scraped and chattered against each other as he did so.

"Pray tell, why are you here instead of at that thief Kun Anton's? I need to know that little fact before we can do business. And, by the way, I have a nose for lies." Rold's left front tooth had an emerald set in it, but the tooth around it had died and turned black. It was hard not to stare.

"Come now. Don't be shy." He seemed delighted to have them there.

"We're outcasts," Tell confessed grimly. "We broke our law. They said we're too young for the journey, and Wren's forbidden to come down altogether—"

"Wren, what a pretty name." Rold Roland's rings

clacked together even more vigorously as he flashed his emerald tooth at her.

"And," Tell continued, steering the conversation away from his sister, "our black glass was claimed by others when our father died, so we ran away with it."

"Naughty!" Rold Roland scolded.

"Our father mined it, he died for it, he left it to us, so we're selling it," Tell said fiercely. "But we can't sell it at Kun Anton's."

"Because he buys black glass from the rest of our village, obviously," Wren added, the first words she'd spoken since they'd been shown into Rold Roland's chamber by a silent man with a strangler's huge hands. The chamber was designed to be impressive, and it was. Panels of gleaming, pure white stone covered the floor and walls. Chunks, slabs, slices of red, purple, black, and green stone were strewn about casually. Rold himself lounged on a padded platform, dressed in robes made of cloth as shiny as his polished walls. A big black-and-white flightless bird hopped and strutted around the chamber, dropping dark squirts of poop wherever it went.

Rold Roland flicked a sweetmeat of some kind into the air, and the big bird caught it before it hit the ground. "Nothing is obvious, my sweet. Nothing and never."

Rold looked back and forth from Tell to Wren, clearly gauging their story. They gazed levelly back at him. If there's one thing the People know how to do, it's lie. Especially to lowlanders.

"So, you're on your own, eh? Free as birds," Rold said, standing up from his padded platform. "Let's see what you've got for me. Maybe it's worthless."

"It's not, and don't bother pretending it is," Tell said. "We know black glass; it's our life. This is the best load to come down the mountain this season."

Rold Roland hid both hands in his voluminous sleeves. "No need to quarrel, young sir—not yet, anyway. Not until I see it."

Rumble was waiting patiently at the back, in the shade of the high, jagged-topped wall. Tell stepped forward to unload, but Rold stopped him.

"Let my man earn his keep for once. Look at the meat-hooks at the ends of his arms. Some say he has the strongest hands in Halfway."

Before Tell and Wren could argue, Rold added, quite firmly, "I insist. That way we all see everything together. It's how business is done down here." At the same time, Rold locked the backyard door they'd come in through and pocketed the massive key.

"For safety," Rold assured them. But Tell began to feel uneasy. Wren signaled him to stay calm as Rold's man began unloading the wrapped slabs of black glass. He was suitably careful.

"Unwrap one. Let's see what our young friends are

trying to sell us here." Rold's man peeled the grass matting away from a gleaming slab and held it up to the light. Rold touched it lightly.

"Hmm. Nice." He turned to Tell and Wren. "I'm sure you've got an inflated idea of what your load's worth. You probably think you should get, oh . . . around ten sous for it."

"Actually, we don't," Tell said evenly.

Wren, however, was outraged. "We should get twenty sous, at least!"

Their fierceness didn't upset Rold. In fact, it seemed to amuse him.

"You're like young wildcats! Panthers. But twenty sous? I'm sorry, it's not that special, and it has to be, at that price." And then Rold stepped closer. "Or do you have a few good pieces tucked away somewhere? Sorcerer-grade, perhaps?"

"No, we don't," Tell said smoothly. "But that's what killed our father, trying to get one." That was only half a lie. They didn't have the sorcerer's slab with them. It was the hardest decision they'd made since leaving the village; they'd entrusted Rumi with the sorcerer's slab. Tell had carefully inched it out of the pack frame and given it to her after tightening the wrapping.

"If you run off with this, we'll find you and gut you like a pika," he'd warned.

"If I want to run off with it, I will, and you'll never find me or your stupid slab, even if you look for the rest of your lives," Rumi had spat back. "Which will be short because you're obviously helpless here," she'd added.

Wren had had to turn away to hide her smile. She'd never seen anyone stand up to Tell so completely. And he clearly didn't know what to make of it.

As Rold's man unpacked the last of the black glass, Rumble sighed gratefully. Wren rubbed his back where the straps had worn the hair off his skin and told him gently how grateful they were and how much they loved him. The mule surely understood, too, for he whinnied softly.

Rold Roland's bejeweled tooth glinted in the afternoon sunlight as his smile widened. "She can make even a broken-down old mule feel like a desert stallion!"

Tell decided he really didn't like Rold at all. "Let's talk about the load. We want twenty sous for it. It's worth that, and you know it—and we also know it sets you up against Kun Anton, which you've never been able to do on your own."

A look of surprise flashed across Rold's face. "Where did you hear that?"

"It doesn't matter where. Pay us, or we're leaving."

Rold's unnerving smile returned. He flicked his eyes at his man and nodded.

"You know a lot, mountain boy. But do you know what I'm thinking right now?" Rold paused, as if suddenly noticing the afternoon light. "I'm thinking, what if I don't pay you at all? What if I just take your black glass? What will you do? Go running back to your nasty people? I think not. And . . . while I'm at it, what if I take you, as well. Both of you. Not my line of business normally, but you're much more valuable than your black glass, and in these uncertain times a man must be flexible. Yes. I think this is going to be one of my best days ever." He nodded at his man again. "Take the boy. I'll deal with the girl myself."

Quick as the thought itself, the man's huge left hand lashed out and closed over Tell's entire face. A high-pitched shriek echoed around the enclosed courtyard, but not from Tell. Rold's man reeled back, hand flopping uselessly, blood fountaining from his wrist.

Tell had cut it halfway through with one fear-charged, backhand slash of his father's blade. Every vein, tendon, and ligament was severed. Rold's man tried to stem the blood pumping out by crushing down on his wrist just above the cut with his other hand. He succeeded for a moment. Then his hand flopped over backward, opening the wound wider. His eyes rolled back in his head, and he fell to the ground, unconscious.

"Tell . . . ," Wren's voice sounded strange. Tell whipped around. Rold had a noose of fine cord around her neck, pulled tight from behind with one hand, a fistful of Wren's blue-black hair clenched in the other hand.

"Let her go," Tell growled.

"I don't think so," said Rold. His eyes bulged, and he

was panting. He was scared, and Tell knew full well that a scared animal was a dangerous one. Tell raised his father's blade.

"You're fast, boy," Rold hissed. "But this is a strangler's noose. It's getting tighter and tighter. If you attack me first, she'll be dead before you reach her."

In a flash, Tell realized something: in a place where weapons were forbidden, even a piece of string could be deadly.

At the same time, he and Wren exchanged a look. Wren could no longer speak, but she could just about whistle. She did. The noose tightened.

But it unleashed Rumble. He struck like a snake, both hooves smashing into the small of Rold's back, blasting him sideways, away from Wren. Breath knocked out of him, kidneys crushed, Rold stumbled, then fell, and began to crawl for the safety of his house. Tell was about to finish him off when he saw his sister stagger as if she'd had too much apricot brandy.

She was fighting to get her fingers under the noose. It was cutting deep into her neck, tightening with every movement, as if alive. She could no longer breathe. Tell tried to get his finger under the cord, couldn't.

"Don't move," he told her, and with a quick, expert push of the knife tip and just a hiss of pain from Wren, Tell sliced into his sister's neck just below her hairline and got the blade under the noose. One twist and the noose dropped away, severed. Wren gulped air, pointed toward Rold Roland even as blood streamed from the cut.

"The key!" she gasped, pressing her hand against the wound.

Rold was almost at his door, moving ever more slowly as the damage from Rumble's double kick caught up with him.

Tell rushed across the yard, vaulted their load of black glass, then Rold's man's unconscious body, but it was too late. Rold made it inside, yelling hoarsely for more guards, slamming and locking the door behind him.

"We have to get out of here!" Wren rasped.

"How? The gate's locked! And what about our glass?"

They heard heavy footsteps thundering from inside. Rumble whinnied once, flattened himself against the wall, whinnied again. Tell glanced from the mule to the top of the wall, then to Wren.

"We climb onto Rumble, then over the wall!" he shouted.

Tell cut loose the pack frame, leaped onto Rumble's back, and jammed the frame over the jagged flint on top of the wall. He scrambled onto the frame and found his balance.

"Wren!" he yelled frantically. "Come on!"

"What about Rumble?" Wren was equally frantic. "We can't just leave him here!"

The door to the house burst open. Two huge men who looked to be brothers of the one lying on the ground charged out. Rumble whinnied again.

"NOW!" Tell shouted. But Wren was stroking the mule, unable to leave him behind.

He had no choice. He reached down, grasped Wren's tunic, and hauled her upward.

"Rumble, no!" she screamed.

"We'll come back for him," he promised as he pushed her over the top of the wall. Tell tumbled down into the alley just as the two guards reached the wall. He pulled the pack frame with him so they couldn't follow them over the wall.

It was Wren's turn to haul him upright. The pack frame was shattered. Abandoning it, they hurtled down the alley, running as fast as they could, not even looking back to see whether they were being pursued. At the first cross street they came to, they slipped into an alley that curved away out of sight. They disappeared into the huge city, with no money, no food or water, and no one to turn to. Rumi was nowhere to be seen. She and their hundred-sous piece were gone.

In one brief, catastrophic moment, they'd lost everything.

14

Tell and Wren were famished, they were thirsty, they were exhausted, night was coming, and they were very aware that everywhere they turned, there were people watching them with unkind eyes. They kept moving, looking for the kind of quiet, safe place that didn't exist in the streets of Halfway.

"We need to stop," Wren panted. "We need to sit." Stopping and sitting was the first thing they were taught up the mountain. "We need to breathe."

"This isn't the mountain," Tell reminded her. "We can't just stop! We can't just sit!"

"Yes, we can." Wren sat down with her back to a rough wall. "See?"

Shoulders slumped, Tell slid down beside her. "I don't know why I thought I could do this. Nothing I know is any use down here."

They drew suspicious looks, but two obviously lost and defeated children held no threat, and they were left alone. For long enough, anyway, to breathe the way they'd been taught to—inhale for a count of four, hold for seven, out for a count of eight; do that six times—and calm their minds.

In their village high on the mountain, the children of the Black Glass were taught how to get lost as soon as they could walk. Or rather, they were taught how to never truly be lost, because in their harsh landscape, that usually meant being dead.

They learned straightforward things, such as looking for landmarks, memorizing their surroundings, backtracking footprints across hard, cold ground. They learned the movements of the sun and the stars. They were also given deeper skills, which the old men and women considered more important. They learned how being lost creates panic. How panic clouds thought. How stillness and breath tame panic and clear the mind. How clear thought means that you are no longer lost—even if you don't know exactly where you are at that moment. But that was in a tiny village, high up and far away. Down in Halfway, Tell and Wren were having a hard time applying those lessons. And though they were ashamed to admit it, they'd been in a state of panic and confusion most of that day.

"Okay, let's think it through," Wren began. "We don't know how we got here. We can't backtrack our footsteps." They were in a labyrinth they had threaded in panic.

Wherever they had been, their footsteps were invisible or already scuffed away by the feet of countless others. "We need to find a familiar landmark."

In every direction, all they saw were people moving in a maze of one- or two- or three-storied buildings. It was overwhelming.

But a clear mind is a powerful tool, and by the time a drunken man with a walking stick yelled at them to "Get out, you thieving little mountain vermin!" they knew what to do.

"We're leaving," Tell told him. "If you can point us to the Mountain gate, you'll never see us again."

The drunken man lifted his stick in a direction opposite from what either of them would have guessed. But they had no choice except to trust his knowledge of Halfway, since theirs was useless. They began walking fast, as if they couldn't wait to leave and never return. They were lying, of course. They had no intention of leaving Halfway. Not yet, anyway. Not without medicine for their father and the mule that had saved their lives more than once.

And, of course, revenge.

Tell and Wren knew only one route in Halfway—from the Mountain gate to Kun Anton's house. So when they reached the massive gate, they did exactly that once again. They turned around and walked back into the city, but for a moment Tell gazed wistfully out at the weapons store, where their bows were. He felt naked without his bow slung across his shoulders.

Though they took the same route they had earlier that day, they did so this time with much more basic goals in mind. All they wanted was a place to sleep and something to eat. They found food sooner than expected, for when Tell and Wren reached the huge fig tree, they went into action without hesitation. This was like hunting mountain jackrabbits together, only much easier.

It was nearing twilight, with plenty of shadows for cover. Tell darted to the tree and began picking figs as fast as he could until the night guard saw him and charged, yelling, stick raised to beat him.

As Tell danced away with both hands full, dodging the whooshing stick, taunting the guard to keep his attention, Wren loaded up with figs herself, then ran. Tell turned and ran with her. They were too fast for the guard. Mountain people can run like rabbits, for miles.

Panting and giggling, they paused on the way to Kun Anton's house to examine their loot. A double handful each of plump green figs, some soft as a baby's cheeks and already splitting slightly, they were so ripe. Wren lowered her face to her hands, smelling the fruit.

"Mmmm," she sighed. "They're going to be sweet!"

Cradling his share, Tell selected the biggest one and lifted it to his already-watering mouth.

"Wait!" Wren cried.

"Why?"

"Think about it! Here we are . . . in Halfway . . . and things haven't gone the way we hoped, but still . . . we have fresh, ripe figs, and—"

"Okay, I thought about it," Tell said, flinging the fig into his mouth and gobbling it with one delicious bite. His knees weakened from the sheer flavor of it. He was about to say something like "By the mountain's rich blood . . . ," but their traditional mountain curses didn't seem to make sense in Halfway. He just moaned in ecstasy and popped another fig into his mouth instead.

"Oh, all right," Wren conceded, and ate her first fig, trying to eat it slowly and failing.

The figs gave them hope. They ate as they walked. Tell liked the ones that were almost too ripe; it was like eating jam. For Wren, that was going too far. They traded their haul back and forth, and by the time they reached Kun Anton's darkened house, their stomachs were bulging with stolen figs, with not a single piece of fruit left between them.

Instead of opening Kun Anton's big gate, where Rumi had stopped Tell earlier with the well-thrown stone, Wren climbed onto Tell's shoulders. She curled her fingers around the edge of the block of wood that had replaced the broken black glass window and yanked it out.

Only children were small enough to shimmy in through that opening, which made it the perfect entrance to their eyes. Once they'd squirmed inside, they placed the wood back loosely.

The People of the Black Glass were thieves and proud of it. They considered stealing to be a form of hunting. Many of the best things that came back up the mountain every year were stolen, which was one of the many reasons others despised them.

Tell and Wren knew to move as quietly as air through Rumi's gigantic, luxurious house. It was silent, deserted. They had no thought of looking for a candle or a lamp. Light would give them away. And even in the dark, there's enough light to see if you look with your brain, your feet, your fingertips as well as your eyes.

They found the kitchen and a huge clay pot half-full of cool water. They drank gratefully. Drank again. The water seemed almost as sweet as the figs. They were used to hunger but not thirst. There was always water in some form up the mountain.

They were too tired to explore the whole house. That could wait for daylight. All they needed was a safe place to sleep. Stifling yawns, they found a small, windowless room piled full of scented cushions, pillows, and blankets. Perfect! They made the deepest, softest beds they'd ever known, sighing in anticipation of sleep as they lay down.

"I hope Rumble got fed tonight," Wren said sleepily.

Tell was about to reply that he hoped Rumble was

still alive, when they heard a sound down the hallway. A soft clink. They froze, listened. Heard the scrape of a shoe against a piece of furniture. Someone was in the house, trying to be quiet but failing. Not a mountain person.

Pulling out his father's knife, Tell rose to his feet and left the room silently, knife held low, gleaming tip raised and ready. Wren came behind him like a ghost, holding her own short knife.

Tell worked his way down the hallway just in time to hear a flint being struck and see the sudden flare from a small open flame, then the steady, rosy glow of an oil lamp . . .

. . . a glow that was heading toward him. Tell retreated a few steps, crouched behind a hallway chair, readying himself to strike. Wren ducked into a doorway.

First the glow, then the lamp at the end of a slender arm, then the person holding the lamp came around the corner. When Tell saw who it was, he exhaled in relief.

"Rumi," he said softly. "It's us."

Rumi inhaled sharply, stopped. Her eyes were black pools. The lamp quivered in her hand. "What are you doing here?" she asked, voice trembling.

Tell stood, sheathed his knife. "We've got nowhere else to go."

"What happened?"

"I—I heard a scream, and got scared, and ran home. I'm sorry . . ."

"Come in here," Wren said from down the hallway. "Don't show your light."

When Rumi saw the soft nest they'd made, she didn't have to be asked to join them. She needed other people around her. It helped her to not think about her family.

"This is just a storeroom," she told them. "There are better rooms to sleep in."

"But it has no windows, so we can keep the lamp lit," Wren said, ever practical.

"It's probably better for you if nobody knows you're alive," Tell added.

Rumi nodded, clearly exhausted. She began yawning and couldn't stop as she made up her own soft nest. Just touching the fat pillows seemed to make her sleepier. But she wanted to know what had happened at Rold Roland's. They quickly told her.

"We have no black glass and no mule. We have nothing—" Tell finished.

"Except for the sorcerer's piece. Please tell us it's not broken?" Wren asked anxiously.

Rumi lay down with a little whimper of relief. "S'not broken . . ." She was falling asleep in front of their eyes. She hadn't slept in days.

"And it's safe? Rumi?"

But Rumi was already out. Fast asleep, right under their noses. Tell and Wren studied her for a long moment. She was the first person outside their village they'd ever seen up close. She seemed totally different from them in all ways. They were lean and sinewy from all the running, climbing, and hunting they did every day of their lives. They were scorched by the merciless high mountain sun and scarred by the sharp rocks surrounding them. Rumi was slow of foot and had the smooth skin of someone who spent most of her days under a roof. Tell was certain she couldn't tie a knot to save her life . . . and yet she knew where and who to sell their black glass to. And for how much. And how to find her way through her bewildering maze of a city.

Wren sighed. Sympathy didn't exactly bubble through their veins, but terrible things bond people more than good things do.

"She's been unlucky," Wren said, looking at her brother.

"What does that make us, then?" Tell asked.

"Us? We're sleeping in a soft bed tonight with full bellies, and that's all I care about right now." She lay down and was asleep in an instant.

Even though he'd seen it again and again, his sister's talent for making the best of any situation, no matter what it was, still amazed him. He was beginning to realize that it was a skill just as practical as shooting an arrow or making a pair of boots. And he knew he didn't have it.

Tell lay back into a softness such as he'd never felt before. Sleep was tickling him but hadn't fully grabbed hold yet. There were too many thoughts swirling in his head. Too many fresh memories that were raw and painful to touch. Too many feelings that he didn't dare dwell on. Fear. Despair. Confusion. Doubt. Other dark, heavy feelings he didn't even have a name for. He hated them all.

He cast his mind back, trying to think of the last time he'd felt strong and sure and full of light. The memory was vivid. He knew it instantly. It was two years ago, almost to the day. While the men and women were down the mountain trading that year's black glass, he had spent every day out on the mountain, hunting. He had taken many birds and animals, but the real reason he was out there was to catch the first distant glimpse of the mule train returning. Only then would he lose the underlying anxiety, shared by everyone left behind on the mountain, that for some tragic reason the trading party wouldn't return. He wanted to feel the warm certainty that they were safe for one more winter, that their family was whole again, that there were treats wrapped and hidden for him and Wren in their mother and father's pockets and packs.

Tell remembered the surge of joy and relief when he first saw the cloud of dust that announced the mule train far down the mountain. The wonderful feeling—that lightness—lasted for almost a full day . . . until the mule train arrived without their mother.

Alone and safe in a room with two snoring girls and a lamp glowing with top-grade oil, Tell allowed himself to think of her—his mother. The way she had been gentle with him and Wren even when she was not gentle with others. It had made them feel special, and special to her. The way she seemed bigger than any room she was in, that at any moment, something unexpected would happen. The way she could find laughter in moments that were definitely not funny. The way she told wilder and funnier stories, her voice louder and louder, as the winter dragged on. He had once found her alone at the edge of a sheer cliff, looking down into the snow-choked valley below. When he joined her, she stepped back quickly, put her arm around him, and said:

"You know the best thing about this awful mountain of ours? We're high enough to see how big the world is. You'll find that out for yourself soon enough. I can't wait to see what you'll make of it."

As Tell sorted through memories, an outside door opened in another part of the mansion. Tell didn't hear it. But when it was closed hard, Tell did hear that.

His first reaction was very unlike him. He just blew out the lamp, lay down, curled up, and pulled a pillow over his head, shutting out the world. He lay there for a long minute . . . then threw off the pillow, stood silently, and drew his father's knife yet again.

Because, after all, the People of the Black Glass were taught to fear nothing and nobody from a young age. Sometimes, Tell decided, that was a heavy burden.

Without waking Wren or Rumi, Tell headed up the hallway, making not a whisper of sound. Which didn't matter one bit. Whoever was in the house was making enough noise to drown out any sound Tell could make.

Whoever it was, was in a room off the kitchen. Peeking carefully around the corner, Tell could see the flickering light from inside the room and a shadow moving. He heard the clink of clay jars, the creak of a basket, the sound of boots moving.

Tell pulled back into the shadows as a figure emerged carrying a basket full of clay wine jars and loaves of bread. Tell had to bite down hard to stop himself from reacting. The man was the tallest he'd ever seen. His face was cruel, full of sharp angles, and he was strong enough to carry his heavy, awkward load as if it weighed nothing. But what hammered Tell in the gut and wobbled his knees the most, was what he saw when the man turned away . . . a perfect, gleaming, tightly woven braid the color of dark honey that stretched from the back of his head all the way to the base of his long spine. And, yes, it did look like a rope: a living one.

Tell knew with full certainty that he was looking at one of the Ropers. Ropers who had taken the men of his village. Rumi's family, too. Anger rose in Tell, a lust for vengeance such as he'd never felt before.

The Roper headed out of the kitchen through another door into a different hallway. Without hesitation, Tell crossed the kitchen and fell in behind him, a slender, lethal shadow with a gleaming blade, ready to be buried right next to the tail of that perfect braid. Killing him was Tell's duty. He knew exactly where to strike. The Roper would be dead before he hit the floor.

Tell knew that he would need to make his move before the Roper opened the door to the outside. As he took the final steps to the door, Tell closed in, bringing his knife to bear.

Then something lurched in Tell's brain. Without thinking about it consciously, Tell dropped down behind a storage box and let the Roper leave the house with his life. Tell did not know why he had decided to disobey everything he had been taught. But he did know what he had to do next.

Tell cracked open the door silently and watched the Roper cross Kun Anton's courtyard to the heavily built warehouse. He followed in the dark, silently. When the Roper kicked twice on the thick warehouse door, it was opened from the inside. And in the moment it took the Roper to step through the door, Tell saw something that made him feel the way he had when the cutthroat trap had ripped him off his feet and left him dangling upside down in the air.

The man who'd opened the door for the Roper—Tell recognized him! He had known him all his life. It was Hammerhead.

15

Tell waited for Wren and Rumi to wake up before telling them what he'd seen. He'd needed the time alone to think about what it meant. But he was no closer to understanding when dawn came and the girls began to stir.

They inspected the kitchen as if they thought the Roper would leave tracks, but all he'd left was a hole in the bread and wine supplies. They shared a slightly stale loaf for a quick breakfast, while there were still loaves to eat.

"If Hammerhead's alive, maybe the rest of them are, too? And your family, Rumi," Wren said between chunks of nutty bread. "We *have* to find a way into the warehouse. We have to look for them, not just wait."

"You can't get into the warehouse unless someone lets you in. It was made that way," Rumi declared stubbornly. She found arguing easier than hoping. Hope felt dangerous and took away her appetite. She gave her share of the loaf to Tell and Wren.

When they tiptoed around the perimeter of the warehouse, they realized that Rumi was right: there was no way in. The door was a hand-width thick slab of wood, with no handle and no lock. The walls were solid stone—not mud. There were no windows, and the only air flow in and out came by way of cleverly made ventilation holes covered with netting next to the roof beams, fifteen feet off the ground. The roof was tiled with thick slabs of gray slate. Kun Anton's warehouse was a fireproof fortress.

"How can there be no handle on the door?" asked Tell, frustrated by something that made no sense to him.

"My father's very clever," Rumi told them proudly. "He pays two men to live inside the warehouse, one for day, one for night. They count his goods and open the door whenever he knocks. He has a special knock." Rumi raised her hand, was about to try a knock, then thought better of it.

"But what if one of them falls asleep? Or . . . dies?" Tell had to ask.

Rumi shrugged. "It's never happened. If it didn't work, my father wouldn't do it."

"We'll just have to wait outside for someone to open the door, like last night. And then sneak in," Tell decided, looking around for a place to wait in hiding.

"That's the worst idea I've ever heard!" Rumi exclaimed. "You'll be caught and killed."

"Do you have a better one?" Tell challenged. Rumi was beginning to grate on him.

"Actually, yes, I do," she said, glaring at him, her hands on her hips. "Turn your sorcerer's slab into money. You can't do anything without money here. My father always said, if you have something rare and valuable, get rid of it as fast as you can; it'll only give you a headache. He was right. I'm already sick of thinking about your glass."

"Well, *my* father said to find the most feared sorcerer in Halfway, because she's the richest, and sell it to her," countered Tell.

"That's true. But her? I'm not going anywhere near her, and nor should you. We can try another one. Any of them are rich enough to buy your glass."

"You know where a sorcerer lives?" Wren leaned in, intrigued.

"I know where the sorcerer in our quarter lives; she's called Mountain, because this is the Mountain quarter. Nobody knows their real names; they're secret."

Wren felt question after question bubbling into her brain: *What do the sorcerers actually do? How do they help Halfway? Why is there a sorcerer for each quarter? Where do they come from? Why are they all women?* And . . . and . . .

Tell took one look at his sister and intervened before her torrent of questions was unleashed. "She sounds perfect. Take us to her."

"And stay with us. Help us sell our black glass," Wren

pleaded. "All we did yesterday was lose everything . . . and Rumble."

"Your old mule?" Rumi asked. They hadn't told Rumi about Rumble—she'd fallen asleep too fast.

Wren could only nod. Just thinking of her mule made her heart ache. She'd woken hoping he was still alive. . . . She couldn't even bear to think about it! She knew she should've been just as upset about the men, but she wasn't. Rumble was a loyal friend and companion, and the men were not.

"Oh, don't worry," Tell said boldly, emphatically. "We're getting it all back, including Rumble. But first I'm going to cut every ring off that green-toothed creature's hands."

Rumi shot Wren a nervous look; Tell sounded deadly serious. Wren shrugged. "I think he needs something more to eat. He gets like this when he's hungry."

After another loaf of stale bread and some salted meat, they slithered out through the broken window and set off to turn their father's misfortune into sous.

They didn't take their sorcerer's slab with them, even though that's what they were trying to sell.

"We're not taking our glass into anybody's house," Tell had said decisively. "Not after what happened yesterday." So they left the perfect piece of black glass where Rumi had hidden it. When they had an agreement for it, they would fetch it, and only then.

This time Wren walked beside Rumi while Tell followed, trying to memorize landmarks on their route so that he felt less lost.

"I have some questions," Wren said to Rumi.

"There she goes!" Tell teased from behind.

"Pay attention to what you're doing," Wren shot back over her shoulder.

Rumi managed half a smile for the first time since they'd met her. Wren took that as permission to ask away.

"So . . . what do the sorcerers do, exactly?" was question number one.

"Ummm . . . they work with the family who runs each quarter, and always have. Halfway was built on sorcery. Except for when it rains, which is hardly ever, this plain is bone-dry. But, long ago, the first sorcerer pulled up water from deep inside the earth—lots of water. Enough to drink and enough to make as many mud bricks as you want, even now. And so four trading clans began building here. Building all this." Rumi gestured at the entire city. "Everyone knows that."

Wren was fascinated. "I didn't!"

Tell trailed close behind, pretending not to listen but fooling no one. It pleased him to realize suddenly that if it *did* rain often, they couldn't have built Halfway with mud bricks. It was an obvious thought and didn't change anything for them, but it left Tell feeling that he was starting to understand Halfway. A little. Which was a relief.

"Where do they come from?" Wren continued with her list of questions. "The sorcerers."

"Nobody knows, and they don't tell," Rumi answered uneasily. "They . . . keep that kind of knowledge secret. We never see them, you know. They stay inside their houses . . . or they walk the streets without being seen— people say they can do that. Only the ruling family talks to them, and then only the head of that family. But sometimes . . . things happen to people who've done something they don't like. . . ." Rumi looked around carefully, clearly on edge.

"How many are there?" Tell blurted from behind.

"Five. One for each quarter, and then . . . her . . . the one at the center of Halfway." Rumi's voice dropped close to a whisper. "She's the most powerful. She commands the others when Halfway is under threat. She—" Rumi shook her head, not wanting to say any more. "Nobody talks about her. They say she hears every voice in Halfway."

Wren twirled around to look at Tell, whose reaction was as surprised as her own.

Rumi stopped dead and pointed at a tall, narrow house down the street. "Something's not right." Rumi's voice had gone even lower. People were scurrying in and out of the huge front door of the house. "That's where she lives: Mountain. The sorcerer."

"What's wrong?" Tell asked.

"Nobody goes near a sorcerer's house. And they

definitely don't rush in and out of it like that." As they stood there, a man in fine clothes hurried up the street, straight toward them. Following Rumi's lead, Tell and Wren stepped aside as the man whisked past them, at almost a run.

"I know him!" Rumi exclaimed once he was past them. "He works for the family who runs our quarter. I've seen him with my father." Rumi shrugged apologetically. "I'm sorry, but I don't think we'll be able to sell your glass here."

"But we have to sell it! We've got nothing else!" Tell's head was spinning. He'd never imagined not being able to sell their glass. "Our father will die if we don't."

"We'll sell it," Wren said quietly. "To the one in the middle."

"No!" Rumi looked at her, aghast. "No, no, no. It's too dangerous. They say she's the cruelest of them all. They say she can fly. People go in, but they don't come out. Or they change. . . . A prince once tried to invade Halfway. She turned him into a baboon. It was before I was born, but I've seen the baboon. Every year they parade him through the city on a chain! He's old and gray now, and limps, but he'll never die!" Rumi's cheeks had turned pale.

"Rumi," Tell said, gently enough that it surprised Wren. "You don't have to go, but we do."

"We have no choice," Wren agreed.

"Take us as far as you can. We'll go on from there. But"—Tell turned this way and that, looking for a horizon that didn't exist—"right now I can't even tell where the center is."

Rumi crossed her arms, thinking, making a decision. They waited. When she looked at them, there was something like despair in her eyes.

"Why not?" Her voice was so sad. She turned on her heel and led them deeper into Halfway.

16

They were able to see the sorcerer's house from several streets away because it was the tallest in Halfway. All streets led toward it . . . or away from it. The house wasn't somewhat, or just about, or nearly in the middle of the city; it lay in the *exact* center. Each corner touched a different quarter of the city, which was no accident.

The closer they got, the emptier the streets were, until there wasn't a single person to be seen, anywhere.

"Nobody comes here." Rumi's voice trembled. Tell and Wren nodded, using all their mountain training to keep one foot moving in front of the other. Tell kept the feel of his father's last embrace in the front of his mind; it helped.

Of them all, Wren was the least afraid. Or anyhow, the most curious. Sorcery existed; they all knew that. But no one talked much about sorcerers, and here they were about to meet one. Or try to. There was excitement mixed with her fear.

Rumi faltered once they were directly across the street from the sorcerer's house. She shook her head, her eyes wide with terror. "I can't . . . ," she said.

It was hard to speak somehow. "Let's get this over with," Tell mumbled. Wren nodded and continued on, feeling that if she stopped, she'd falter too.

It was like wading against a river in flood, harder and harder the closer they got to the source, pressing at them from every direction. They pushed against it, and finally they stood at the sorcerer's front door, two lost and grimy mountain children down to their last chance. There was no bell, knocker, or handle, just a blank door in a blank wall. They banged on it with their fists, then with a cobblestone pulled out of the gutter. Nothing happened. Tell turned to Rumi, watching from across the street, and raised his hands in frustration. She just shook her head.

"Wren, let's go," Tell said impatiently. "We'll find another sorcerer."

"No, let's not," said Wren with a strange tone to her voice.

Strange, because the blank door was swinging open slowly all by itself. Through the opening, they could see blackness as deep as a moonless night.

If it were a cave mouth in the mountains, the siblings would never enter it. Only bad things could come from stepping into darkness like that.

"We have to go in," Wren said finally.

"Yes, I know." Tell turned around to wave goodbye to Rumi . . . but to his utter surprise, she was crossing the street toward them. She reached a hand out to him, and he grasped it, pulling her in against the unseen current.

They looked at each other, eyes bleak. They had nothing much left to lose.

"What else would I do today, anyway?" Rumi said, mostly to herself. She squeezed Tell's hand, and together the three of them stepped through the sorcerer's door. It closed behind them with a decisive click.

17

They stood trembling in the dark just inside the door. Rumi finally let go of Tell's hand and was about to speak when his finger touched her lips, keeping her from uttering a sound. He leaned in close and murmured, "Let your eyes get used to it."

As their eyes adjusted, the reason the sorcerer's house seemed as dark as night became apparent. The ground floor was empty, with no windows. Or furniture. Or servants. But it didn't feel empty. Something was present, something without shape or form, but definitely there.

Or perhaps it was just their imagination and nothing more, but the feeling of it paralyzed them.

Eventually they realized that there was . . . not really light in the far corner, but it was definitely less dark. Slowly, the threesome tiptoed toward it. Tell and Wren were silent.

Rumi did her best. Silent movement is something that has to be learned and practiced. Nearly halfway there, Tell thought he saw a shadow moving across the patch of not-darkness, and based on their indrawn hisses of breath, so had Wren and Rumi.

When they reached the far corner, they understood why it was less dark. A narrow stairway spiraled upward, built into a passageway in the walls of the house. The spiral was so tightly wound that it seemed to squeeze the light out of the air. But there was definitely some light—or less darkness—coming down from above. Just enough for them to see each other's faces and communicate wordlessly that, yes, there was no choice but to climb the spiral stairs, one behind the other.

Up in the mountains, Wren would dig spiral trench traps for some of the ground birds they kept for eggs, or meat if no eggs were laid, leading them with stale grain into a place where there was no room to spread their wings and fly back out. The spiral stairs reminded her uncomfortably of those traps and how she used to laugh at the panic and confusion of the birds before she snatched them up. She understood the cruelty of it now.

The top of the stairs was blocked by a heavy curtain. Only once they pulled it did they realize how much light the curtain actually blocked. Their eyes, having adjusted to the deep darkness below, were now completely blinded by a room full of bright light. They had no choice but to cover their watering eyes and wait until they slowly adjusted once again.

It wasn't until later that Tell realized the sorcerer had used light and dark and light again to defend her house in the simplest of ways, in much the same way the People of the Black Glass trusted the cold weather and the unforgiving terrain of their mountain landscape to defend their village. The trio had already been defenseless three times in the sorcerer's house. And all without sorcery, so far as they knew.

They opened their eyes in fits and starts, little blinks that allowed them, finally, to look around.

"What is this?!" exclaimed Rumi.

Windows on all sides filled the room with light. There was all the stuff of a house like Rumi's—tables, chairs, beds, carpets, pillows, a kitchen against a wall with a chimney for a cooking fire, urns, carvings, flat pieces of wood painted with pictures of strange striped and spotted animals they'd never seen, nor heard of. There were cabinets and wooden chests all over, without any walls separating them. But everything was arranged so that there were no straight passages anywhere. This space was a maze of light, shapes, and rich colors. Across the room was a rectangular shadow that looked like a doorway.

"Why would she arrange her furniture this way?" asked Rumi, almost aggravated. "My mother would never allow such a mess."

Tell, however, was seeing it quite differently. "Because it forces us to cross the room slowly, and we're exposed every step of the way. You could hide over there, or there . . . or there, and pick off anyone trying to cross," he said, pointing at various big pieces of furniture. "Give me my bow, and I could kill twenty men before they reached the other door."

Rumi almost seemed insulted by the idea. "That . . . that isn't magic!" she sputtered. "It's just . . ."

"What? Smart?" Wren suggested. Having sorcery and also being smart—maybe that was how you became the most feared person in Halfway, she thought.

They reached the rectangular shadow. It was the entrance to another narrow spiral staircase. This one led to a swinging door at the top. Then a small chamber and another swinging door. It meant that at all times there was at least one closed door. They soon found out why, when they went through the inner door.

Wren turned to the others, her face alight. "It's beautiful!"

And it was. From wall to wall and floor to ceiling, the whole third floor was a garden. It was warm and damp and full of plants neither Wren nor Tell had ever seen before. A room full of greenery like this was unthinkable on their mountain.

"I've never seen so many different plants in one place," Tell marveled.

Rumi hung back, less impressed. She'd seen indoor gardens before.

Tell and Wren examined flowers in colors they couldn't name: huge single blooms, tiny blossoms in bunches, flowers that erupted directly from the stems of the plants they grew on. Scents melded in the air, from almost too sweet to acrid and bitter. Tangled vines, small, dense shrubs, lush rows of bushes with tempting little berries, ground creepers. Wren let her nose guide her as she flitted from plant to plant like a butterfly. And, indeed, there were also butterflies: bright yellow and black, floating in the perfumed air. Somewhere, a tiny creature gave voice.

"What's that?" Wren paused.

"Some kind of bird," Tell guessed.

"It's not. It's a frog," Rumi said, recoiling from a flower she'd just smelled; it was bitter.

"A frog? What's a frog?" Wren asked as Tell declared, "I want to see it!"

"I thought we were here to sell your glass," Rumi grumbled, but she began to move toward the sound, a piping song that soon led them to the tiny creature. It was no bigger than Tell's thumb and bright blue and black. It just sat there, unafraid, as they bent close. Tell and Wren had never even heard of frogs, and this one was truly beautiful, but they had both learned from experience with their own small, brown mountain scorpions that tiny creatures that seemed unafraid usually took a deadly penalty from anyone stupid enough to touch them. They left the frog alone. And a question formed in Tell's mind.

He saw Wren reaching for a crimson berry. "Don't!" he warned.

"Why not?" she asked, her fingers inches from the bright fruit.

"Do sorcerers use poison?" Tell asked Rumi. Rumi was about to reply when she blinked hard and gasped. She had seen something past Tell and Wren. They turned.

A golden-yellow viper coiled around a thin branch at the level of their faces, not three feet away, black eyes fixed on them, forked tongue testing the air. Tell and Wren backed away.

"Yes," Rumi answered at last. "Sorcerers use poison." She looked around the beautiful room with fresh eyes and shuddered. "This . . . this is a poisoner's garden. I've heard of them, but I've never seen one."

"It's still beautiful," Wren mused.

A poisoner's garden. Tell felt a very long way from his simple mountain village. He felt, once again, that nothing he knew and nothing he was good at was of any use here. It was a feeling he was beginning to hate.

Again there was no direct path across the huge space. Again they found the entrance to the next spiral staircase, opposite the one they had just climbed.

"I don't like this house," Rumi said. "At all."

"I don't think we're meant to," Wren answered.

They climbed the staircase and found the best thing they'd seen in Halfway so far.

At the top of the stairs stood a wooden door divided into hundreds of small, irregular panels, no shape the same. Each panel held a perfectly fitted piece of black glass. Tell reached out and touched one.

"This is our glass," he stated proudly.

"She's even more powerful than I thought," Rumi said, sounding miserable.

"How do you know?" Wren asked, fingertips kissing the cool, smooth glass she'd known since birth.

"No one else could pay for a door like this. Not even my father."

"Good. So she can definitely pay for our glass." Tell reached out to push the door open, but it opened without needing his touch.

"Let's get this over with," Rumi implored. "We shouldn't even be here."

"Then why let us in in the first place?" Wren argued, walking into the room. Tell and Rumi had no choice but to follow.

This room was lavishly furnished and surrounded on all four sides by a wide outdoor terrace. Patterned rugs were scattered on the gleaming wooden floor, a dining table and chairs, sofas, and strange animal skins. Cupboards and shelves lined every wall, holding boxes of all sizes and materials, spaced with a few intriguing-looking objects like bones, skulls, and crystals. There were tables covered with boxes as well. "It looks like you could actually live up here," Rumi said. "Not like the rest of the house."

But there was no sign of the sorcerer. "Hello?" Wren called out.

"Maybe she's out there." Tell pointed toward the terrace door. Wren's hand was turning the door handle when a woman's voice cracked sharply in their ears.

"No. Not out there."

They froze, expecting that someone was standing right behind them—that's how close the voice sounded. But when they dared look, no one was there.

They looked in every direction, until, across the room, a woman in a plain gray tunic rose from a chair they'd already looked at and found empty just moments ago. There was not a shred of doubt that she was the sorcerer.

18

As slender as a piece of tight-woven cord, with exceptionally long arms and legs, the sorcerer had no hair. Her head was instead covered with tattoos, a dense pattern of lines, circles, and symbols in a deep indigo color. The tattoos were disturbing enough, but it was her eyes that mesmerized them. Yellow-green and as penetrating as the points of Tell's arrows.

Tell had once come face-to-face with a mountain lion. They had locked eyes. The lion had looked at Tell as if from a great height and from deep inside him simultaneously. Tell had been unable to move or even breathe much until the mountain lion looked away.

The sorcerer's eyes were like that. Far away and deep inside you at the same time. She stalked toward them, and their breath caught in their throats.

"So. Two mountain creatures and Kun Anton's brat. Names." Her eyes flicked to Wren first.

"I'm Wren."

"Tell."

"I'm, uh, Rumi. Rumi Anton."

The sorcerer came closer, her lion eyes darting from one to the other, top to bottom, as if measuring them for something. "Why are you here? What do you want from me? There's trouble in Halfway; we all know it. Are you that trouble?"

The three children looked at each other, not knowing how to answer. It was Wren who spoke first.

"We have a piece of black glass—"

"A sorcerer's slab," added Tell, eyes lowered.

"All we want is to sell it to you, then go home."

"What if I don't wish to buy it?" asked the sorcerer. She hadn't given them her name.

"You will," Rumi said confidently.

"My father said it's a once-in-a-lifetime piece," explained Tell.

"I've seen it," Rumi affirmed.

"You unpacked it?" Tell was shocked. So was Wren.

"Of course I did. Only a fool takes responsibility for a wrapped package." Rumi turned back to the sorcerer. "It's unmatched. It looks like smoke from a hot, clean fire."

The sorcerer gave Rumi a sharp look. "You sound like your father." Then she looked at Tell and Wren. "And what about *your* father? Why isn't he here selling the glass? Why you two children?" Her eyes narrowed. "Did you steal it?"

Tell was aghast. "From our father? No!"

"We're here, because, he . . . well." Wren looked to Tell to continue.

"When he struck the blow that cut the slab, it blinded him," Tell finished flatly.

"Your slab cost an eye?" The sorcerer suddenly seemed to glow.

"Not his eye—" Tell said fiercely.

"*Yes*," argued Wren. "His only eye. You know it did!"

"No," Tell insisted. "It cost his *life*. Where we live . . . our village . . . if someone gets badly hurt, they have to heal in thirty days, or . . ." Tell shook his head with grim finality.

Wren glared at him defiantly. "But we're going to buy medicine and go back and save his eye, so that he doesn't have to die. Our mother—she's gone." Wren lifted her chin. "That's why we're here. We don't want to be orphans. We went against our village's rules. We're not allowed down the mountain, but we . . . anyway—" Wren ended awkwardly; she was talking too much.

The sorcerer held out her hand, as if waiting for them to give her something.

"What?" Tell asked, confused.

"I need something of your father's."

"Why?"

The sorcerer ignored the question and kept her hand out. Tell set his jaw stubbornly.

"Give it to her. It's all right," Wren reassured him. She didn't know *why*, but she knew.

He clearly didn't want to, but eventually Tell pulled out his father's black glass blade.

Oddly, the sorcerer sighed heavily when he laid it in her hand. She headed across the room with it. She paused halfway, her back to them, until they realized they were supposed to follow.

On a table sat a plain wooden case, and this was where the sorcerer stopped. She set the knife down carefully and lifted the lid. Inside, nestled on a lambskin of the purest white, lay a slab of black glass. Her slab. Her sorcerer's glass. Who knew how old it was? No one else had successfully cut a slab in their lifetime, or their father's lifetime.

Rumi grunted critically. "Theirs is better. It's—" A look from the sorcerer closed Rumi's mouth.

She held up Tell's father's knife. "I need your blood on the blade. Both of you. Just a little."

Wren stopped Tell's reaction before it started by taking his hand in hers. "We need to," she said simply.

He furrowed his brow, not understanding Wren's calm certainty.

Wren held their clasped hands up between them. "I just know we do."

And before Tell could pull away, the sorcerer flicked the knife across the meat at the base of their clenched little fingers, leaving a neat crimson line joining sister and brother. Neither of them yelped or flinched. Mountain training.

The sorcerer grunted her approval, cut her own thumb with the other side of the blade, then lowered the knife onto the lambskin so that the edge of the blade touched the slab.

She gazed down, her lips moving with a silent evocation. The tattoos on her head seemed to glow, then come alive and writhe like snakes. It was terrifying.

The sorcerer pointed at the slab.

Tell's eyebrows climbed high. Rumi pressed in so that she could see too. They all leaned close as an image came into view in the black glass. It was like looking at a reflection in a pool, a gentle wind blowing across the surface. Then it was as if the wind stopped altogether, and the image gradually became perfectly clear.

"Oh!" gasped Wren. "There he is!"

Their father. In the glass. They could see him raising his mallet to strike the antler chisel. They could see the pitch-pine torch flickering behind him. It was as if they were somehow *inside* the vein of black glass, looking directly out at him . . . looking at something that had already happened. And they finally understood why sorcerer's glass was so precious.

"His name?"

"Seka."

"A good name," mused the sorcerer.

They saw him turn his head away as he should . . . then turn back, grim with determination, and look directly at the black glass. At them.

"No! You have to look away!" Tell couldn't help but shout. "How many times did you tell *me* that?!"

But their father couldn't hear, of course, and struck with all his might. There was a dizzying, tumbling movement in the sorcerer's slab. Then they were suddenly looking up from ground level at their father as he clutched his eye in agony and sank to his knees, mouth open in a silent scream.

"How can we see something that's already happened, and so far away?!" Tell asked, almost angrily.

Wren started to understand. Maybe. A little. "This glass here and the glass Da cut . . . they connect. . . . They talk to each other. Sorcerer's glass, it's . . . that means . . . that means . . ." Wren's brow furrowed as she tried to think it through. Tell shook his head, not following.

The sorcerer remained silent. Then a single drop of clear liquid fell onto her glass slab. It instantly went blank.

"Oh!" Rumi exclaimed. "I'm sorry." She was crying. "It . . . it made me so sad," she said as she wiped at her tears. "Your father did that for you, you know. Looked, when he knew he shouldn't. He wanted to cut the perfect piece . . . for you."

Tell and Wren hadn't thought of it that way. They glanced at each other and saw in each other the hurt that they felt in their own hearts—a deep, complex feeling that had no easy words to express it.

The sorcerer closed the case. When she looked up, her yellow-green eyes blazed. She was excited. Rumi knew the time was right.

"They want two hundred sous for their glass," said Kun Anton's youngest child. "No less." Tell and Wren stopped breathing. *Two hundred sous?!* A lifetime's worth. More.

"Where is it?" asked the sorcerer sharply.

"Hidden," Rumi said boldly.

"Fetch it," the sorcerer said, pointing at the door.

"Gladly. For two hundred sous." Rumi's entire pose communicated stubbornness.

"I have to touch it. If it speaks to me, I'll pay your price. If not, then goodbye."

"I think you already know it speaks to you," Rumi retorted.

Making the sorcerer angry seemed like a bad idea, and Tell quickly intervened. "Um . . . how do we know we can trust you? Yesterday, a man with a green and black tooth stole our entire load, except for this one piece—"

"And our mule," added Wren.

"And then tried to kidnap us."

For the first time, the sorcerer smiled. "You can't trust anyone, of course. You've learned that." Then her voice went low and much more frightening. "But you can trust this: if I really wanted to take your black glass, I could. And I would." She turned to Rumi. "You haven't hidden it as well as you think, little girl. It's not safe. Not from the likes of us."

The three children went silent. Tell felt for his knife, but of course it wasn't in its sheath. It was on the sorcerer's slab. He'd never felt more helpless.

"Maybe this wasn't such a good idea," murmured Rumi. Tell and Wren shared a look with her. They agreed.

"You really think it was your *idea* to come here? Something you *chose* to do?" The sorcerer smiled again, and the three felt utterly out of their depth.

"Here's what will happen," the sorcerer said in a way that meant there would be no argument. "I'll give you a hostage: someone I value highly. I'll keep one of you here. You can choose who it will be. When you bring the glass, we'll trade the hostages."

"When we make a sale," Rumi countered. "That's when we'll trade the hostages."

The sorcerer's eyes flashed. Rumi was clearly beginning to aggravate her.

"I'll stay," Wren said quickly. "Rumi knows where it is. Tell, you need to protect her."

"You won't need protection." The sorcerer nodded past them. "You'll have Cormorin with you."

Someone else was in the room. How? When? The trio exchanged alarmed glances and turned. Standing close behind them, having arrived without a sound, with his pale blue eyes cast to the side as if he were trying to avoid the whole situation, was the most unusual-looking boy they'd ever seen. He was older than Tell but not by much. He had flaming-red hair, a hooked beak of a nose, knobby wrists, and long, bony fingers, and his gray tunic sleeves were too short for his gangly arms.

"This is Cormorin. He's my apprentice and very valuable to me. You can kill him if I cheat you." Cormorin kept his eyes down but sighed copiously. "I know you can do it," she said to Tell and Wren. "Your knife told me so. You've killed already on your journey."

"No one has died," murmured Tell, shaking his head.

"Even though they should've," Wren added.

"The man with the big hands, yesterday—or should I say, hand?—he died last night." Tell stared at the sorcerer, amazed. She knew about that just from touching his father's knife? No wonder Rumi had asked so much for their glass.

Rumi interrupted his thoughts by gesturing at Cormorin. "I thought all sorcerers were women."

"Most of what most people think is wrong, most of the time," the sorcerer said dismissively. She shot Cormorin a look. "Be quick. There's trouble out there, enough for everyone."

Tell felt enormous relief when she indicated he could retrieve his knife. With a last look at Wren, he and Rumi left with Cormorin.

Wren stood waiting awkwardly as if she wanted to ask the sorcerer something but didn't dare.

"What is it? Ask, or let it go. I can't bear hovering."

"Well . . . ," Wren started. "It's our mule. His name's Rumble; he's a fine mule. He saved our lives. We had to leave him at a disgusting man's house yesterday. Rold." Wren's skin crawled just uttering his name. "The way he smiled at me, with that tooth . . ."

"Let me know when you get to the question. Then I'll know when to listen."

Wren blushed, embarrassed. "Will you help us get our mule back?"

"No," the sorcerer said flatly. "Get him back yourself if he's that important to you."

Wren met her intimidating gaze. "He is. And we will."

"There's food and drink behind that screen there," the sorcerer said, waving a long hand in that direction. "Find a way to be quiet. I have things to do."

"I have just one more question. . . . Then you won't know I'm here," Wren added quickly. "We know how to be still; it's how we hunt."

The sorcerer had already begun muttering an incantation, and her irritation was palpable. Still, she paused.

"Sorcerer's glass . . . Can the different pieces speak to each other because they all come from the same place? And then is our piece even more valuable because it cost my father his eye? Does that make it more . . . more powerful?"

The sorcerer looked Wren up and down for a long moment. Wren waited, eager for her answer.

"That's two questions, not one" was all the sorcerer said before she turned and walked away, leaving Wren disappointed. But not for long. She shrugged and went to find the food and drink. It was surprisingly plain, just unflavored oat cakes and water. But when there was food of any kind to be had, the children of the Black Glass ate it whether they were hungry or not.

19

Cormorin turned out to be good company and a welcome break from the intensity of the last few hours. Once away from the sorcerer's house, the apprentice walked jauntily and grew quite chatty, asking them questions about themselves—he'd never spoken to one of the People before—sometimes interrupting to point out curious little things about Halfway as they walked the streets back to Rumi's house: a street that zigzagged back and forth nonsensically (the result of an ancient and long-lasting feud between neighbors); an owl's nest (Cormorin had once seen the owl catch a rat, of which Halfway had many); a low house with a flat roof where fruit was dried (the best dried apricots in Halfway).

Cormorin knew the city far better than Rumi did, since she'd spent much of her life behind walls and indoors. And he clearly loved it. Tell could see that Rumi was enjoying their tour as much as he was, and he was surprised to realize that it pleased him. He knew firsthand how light moments could feel precious in times of darkness.

As they jumped over a puddle of water, he caught a glimpse of the three of them. Their reflections were something to behold. The gangly, flame-haired apprentice to the most powerful sorcerer in Halfway, a willful and wild mountain boy who had recently killed a man without knowing it, and the once-spoiled daughter of one of the wealthiest merchants in the city. A strange crew. Eyes followed them as they moved through the city, but there was nothing to be done about it, and they didn't care.

After Cormorin had pointed out a rickety stall that was the best place to buy cures for a toothache, Tell asked him where he might find a cure for blindness.

"What kind of blindness? How did it happen?" Cormorin asked.

By the time they reached Rumi's neighborhood, Cormorin had heard short versions of both their stories and was no longer smiling.

"I'm on my own too, so I know how it is for you. Or close enough anyway," he said after a sympathetic pause. His pale eyes looked into the distance, not at them, until he said: "You get used to it."

Rumi exhaled with a little huff of surprise. "You're . . . you're an orphan?" Just saying the word was hard for her.

"No," answered Cormorin. "Both my parents are still alive, I think. Somewhere."

Tell frowned, trying to understand. "I don't . . ."

"They sold me, when I was younger," Cormorin stated flatly. "For money to buy wine."

Rumi blinked hard. "They sold you to the sorcerer?"

"No. Not to her." Cormorin said it in a way that made it clear he didn't want to talk about that part of his life anymore.

"What's her name, anyway?" Tell asked.

Cormorin leaned in close. "No one knows it, not even me. It's best not to think about it."

Rumi leaned in even closer. "Is she always so angry?"

"No." Cormorin frowned. "It's been worse since yesterday."

Before Tell could press for more information, they reached Rumi's gates. Only later did Tell realize that Cormorin hadn't needed directions to get there. He'd already known where Rumi lived.

"I'll go and get the glass," Rumi said quickly. Tell was expecting to have to help her through the window, but Rumi darted across the road instead, jumped down into the drainage ditch, and disappeared. Tell and Cormorin crossed as well and peered into the ditch. There was no sign of her.

"Hm!" Cormorin said. "That's interesting."

Tell made a more careful survey of the ditch, then leaped across it. He looked back at the bank Cormorin was standing over. That was when he saw a weed-choked entrance to a narrow side tunnel that went under the street, straight toward Rumi's house. He pointed it out to Cormorin, who squatted down for a better look.

"Good thing she's small."

"She's . . ." He was about to say, she's irritating, she talks too much, she looks down on him and Wren, but he didn't. "She's been unlucky. . . ."

"Not for you," Cormorin said bluntly. "Luck has two faces."

"I suppose it does," Tell agreed. "So, what kind of luck do you have? What makes you a sorcerer's apprentice?" he asked.

"The right kind of suffering," Cormorin said gravely. "At least, that's what she told me when she brought me in. She said I'd already been stripped to the bone, which saved her the trouble of doing it herself."

Tell's face softened. "In our village, they tell us suffering makes us stronger."

"I bet that's always said by people who *aren't* suffering to people who *are*," Cormorin added dryly.

"Yes!" Tell exclaimed. "How did you know?"

"I'm an expert," Cormorin said with half a smile.

Tell knew that half smile well; it masked many things. "At least it was worth something—your suffering," he suggested.

Cormorin's half smile became a grin. "I never thought of it that way, but yes."

Tell was enjoying talking to someone who seemed as different from him as a person could be—but actually wasn't. He'd lost all his friends up the mountain over the last two years and told himself he didn't care. But talking with Cormorin felt good, which made him think that maybe he *did* care after all.

"We—my village—are proud of it," Tell told him. "Suffering, I mean. We don't change anything. We don't improve anything. We just get better at suffering. And, right now, I really don't know why—"

A rustling sound came from the side tunnel, and he paused. He and Cormorin crouched, alert for trouble. Weeds began shaking at the tunnel entrance, and then Rumi emerged, cradling the wrapped slab.

"It's still whole," she said, displaying it with relief. She hurried along the bank toward them. She was about to hand it over to Tell when a half-buried root seemed to come alive. It whipped out toward Rumi's foot, curled around it, and she stumbled hard, the sudden movement sending the sorcerer's slab out of her hand and into the air.

The grass matting peeled away as it flew. Naked for the first time since Seka had cleaved it from the vein, the perfect, gleaming glass spun through the air, about to hit the rocky sides of the ditch and shatter into a thousand useless shards, taking Tell and Wren's future along with it.

Later Tell tried to figure out what happened next, but he couldn't. Not enough to understand it. Rumi's scream was punctured by a word from Cormorin that sounded like the bark of a dog, and suddenly everything just . . . stopped.

The slab of glass hung in the air inches from the side of the ditch, holding the reflection of a small frog in midleap. Rumi was frozen in midscream. Cormorin's mouth was wide with whatever sorcerer's word he had uttered. The only thing moving as far as Tell could see was . . . himself.

He didn't need to understand why or how to know what to do next. He hurtled into the ditch and in three long strides reached the black glass. He grasped it gently in both hands.

The moment he touched it, everything unfroze. The frog leaped away. Rumi finished her scream and caught her balance, Cormorin the one staggering backward onto his rump. Tell, clutching the glass, swung toward Cormorin.

"How did you—"

"What did you—" came from Rumi simultaneously.

Cormorin held up a hand to stop them. "We need to get back." He looked sharply at the root that had tripped Rumi, now just an ordinary root again. "That wasn't an accident. Your slab is powerful, which means we're in danger as long as we're out here."

A high, thin voice rang out from down the street. "Are you children all right? Do you need help?"

They looked up. Someone was approaching. Someone slender and sinuous, like one of the weasels that hunted mice high in the mountains, the kind that killed many more than they could ever eat.

"Who's that?" Rumi breathed as she scooped up some matting to re-cover the slab.

"No idea," said Cormorin. "But I don't like them. So let's not find out." He began walking away so fast that Tell and Rumi almost had to run to keep up. When Tell took a quick glance back, he saw that the weasel person was now hurrying away in the other direction.

About to point this out to Cormorin, Tell saw that the young apprentice had become even paler than ever, if that were possible.

"Ohhh, I'm in so much trouble," the apprentice moaned.

"Why?"

"Because I'm not allowed to do . . . what I just did. She doesn't even know I can." Then he pressed his lips together and said not another word all the way back.

When Rumi shared a look with Tell, he realized they were both thinking the same thing; Cormorin was more scared of the sorcerer he lived with than anything out here on the street.

20

The sorcerer pulled out another lambskin, laid it on a table, and gestured for Tell to set the slab on it. Strangely, Tell had a difficult time letting go of his father's glass. He didn't know why. This was the moment he'd been waiting for ever since he'd had the crazy idea to come down the mountain. Wren understood completely.

"It's all right," she murmured, squeezing his shoulder. "It's why we're here."

Rumi, Cormorin, and the sorcerer looked on patiently. This felt like something big to all of them, somehow more profound than just the trade of a rare and powerful object for money to live on.

With a soft sigh, Tell leaned forward and laid down their father's final, and greatest, piece of glass on the soft wool much more gently than he'd ever been laid down as a baby. The sorcerer approached it warily.

Cormorin licked his lips, then said hesitantly, "I need to tell you—someone tried to destroy it. They had power. I did something that I—"

She stopped him with a raised finger. "Take them outside. Don't return until I say you can." Her voice was harsh, the tattoos on her skull bright, almost glowing.

Cormorin immediately headed for the terrace door, beckoning the others to follow, which they did without a word. The truth was, none of them wanted to be anywhere near the sorcerer at that moment.

The instant the door closed behind them, all the windows went dark, which stopped Wren from peeking in . . . which she was trying to do. Whatever the sorcerer was doing with their slab, it was clearly meant to be private. So Wren turned her attention outward. "You can see the whole city from here!" she exclaimed, trying to look in every direction at once.

"All four gates." Cormorin seemed almost proud. "Which is why this house is the most powerful place in the city. One reason, anyway."

"Was this the first sorcerer's house?" Wren asked. "The one who found water."

"Yes." Cormorin nodded. "The other four came much later."

Enthralled, Tell, Wren, and Rumi walked slowly around the terrace, pausing to look down when something specific drew their gaze: a loud lovers' quarrel at one side, two angry women chasing a boy holding a loaf of bread at the next. They were literally standing on the heart of Halfway. One voice would not carry this high. But thousands upon thousands of voices filled the air around them with a low rumble. There was also a surprising amount of greenery behind the walls; city people were still farmers at heart.

Wren looked at enclosed gardens enviously. What she'd give to be able to grow food and herbs as abundantly as the people of Halfway!

Then she sidled over to Cormorin. "Can I ask you a question?"

"Of course," he answered, leaning back against the terrace wall. He'd seen the view many times.

"Ho! You're in trouble, now," Tell said with a laugh. "It's never just one question with her."

Wren ignored her brother. "So, how does it work?"

"How does what work?"

Wren waved her arm across the city. "How do the sorcerers protect all this? What do they actually do? How is she"—Wren pointed inside—"how is she different from the others? Why is *she* the one at the center?"

Cormorin blinked, a little overwhelmed.

"I have more questions, but that's a start," said Wren reasonably.

Tell smirked. "Told you."

"Uhhhh . . . ," Cormorin stammered.

Rumi simplified things. "If an army came, could the sorcerers stop them?"

"A whole army? No. But their leaders . . . ?" Cormorin left the rest to their imaginations.

"Cut the head off, the rest of the snake dies too," Tell interjected. "We say that, up in the mountains."

Cormorin nodded in agreement. He and Tell thought in similar ways.

"We know there's one sorcerer for each quarter. Rumi told us," Wren continued. "Do they each do the same . . . thing?"

Cormorin looked very uncomfortable. Talking about sorcery was strongly discouraged, even for sorcerers. Or *especially* for sorcerers, maybe.

"You can tell us," Wren said reasonably. "We're just children. Who would believe us?"

Cormorin pointed in all four directions. "Forest . . . Ocean . . . Mountain. Desert is behind us," he said.

"Pfft!" Rumi scoffed. "Desert is behind in everything."

Cormorin continued quickly, wanting to get this over with. "Each sorcerer uses different, uh, tools—whatever they're strongest at. Uhhh . . . Forest is a shape-shifter and can pass through solid walls; Ocean—potions and poisons and so on. But this changes all the time; it's a living thing; it moves, it grows. New discoveries are made or bought or traded . . . or stolen."

Wren leaned forward, eyes blazing with excitement

and her new bombardment of questions. Cormorin held up a hand, trying to stop her. It was futile.

"And her?" asked Wren. "Is she called Center or Middle? What's her sorcery?"

Cormorin shook his head so sharply, his flaming hair swung across his face. "I don't talk about her. It wouldn't be wise. Or safe."

"I know the answer, anyway," Wren said easily. "It's *everything*. She can do all the different kinds of sorcery. That's why she's here in this house, at the heart of Halfway."

"I think we'll stop now," Cormorin said with a little gesture that carried even more weight than his words. Wren began to ask another question . . . but didn't. Or couldn't. Her eyes widened, and she glared at Cormorin. The apprentice sorcerer looked up innocently at the sky.

"You have to teach me that!" Tell exclaimed, astounded. "Name your price!"

Trying to hide a grin, Cormorin turned to Rumi. "Can you see your house from here?" he asked, very clearly changing the subject.

"I—I haven't looked," said Rumi. They went around the terrace in search of Rumi's house, then crowded to the railing between huge clay pots that held spiky desert plants with striped leaves. "Oh! You got these pots from my father. They came in last year."

"Yes, we did," Cormorin confirmed. "They were quite expensive."

"But not too expensive," Rumi countered. "Otherwise you wouldn't have bought them."

Cormorin laughed. As he and Rumi traced streets and landmarks they recognized from this vantage point, Wren noticed that her brother was no longer looking at the city but rather was gazing out at the rising purple shadows in the distance. Their mountains, far away. Their home, even farther.

He felt her eyes on him. "It's hard to believe there's anything up there at all." His voice was quiet. His eyes were somehow the eyes of a much older person.

"Are you missing it?" she asked.

Tell pondered, then: "Yes! I am!" he exclaimed, surprised by his own answer. "But I also hate it and couldn't wait to leave. It makes no sense." He sighed heavily. "Nothing makes any sense. I mean, look at where we are, right this second, up here."

"I know. It's amazing, every little bit of it!" Wren replied quickly. "If it weren't for . . . well, for everything . . . I'd love it."

"That's a big if," Tell said soberly.

"There it is!" Rumi pointed suddenly. "I can even see the courtyard. And our warehouse!"

"They say it's impossible to steal from you—the warehouse, I mean," Cormorin began.

Pride filled Rumi's face. "It is. My father had it specially made." Then she burst into tears. "I'm sorry . . . I'm sorry . . . ," she said between sobs. She hurried away crying and trying not to at the same time.

Cormorin looked at Tell and Wren in dismay. "I thought it would please her to see her house from up here. It's a rare view."

Wren patted his shoulder. "It probably does. She cries a lot."

It was Tell who went after Rumi, not Wren. When he caught up to her, he said decisively, "We're going into your warehouse tonight. I don't care how. We're going to find out what happened. Avoiding it does us no good."

Rumi swiped her tears with her sleeve. "I know," she said shakily.

Now he grasped her arm. "Rumi, listen, I need you to think about the warehouse. Try to remember everything you know about it. Everything your father told you about it. We need a way in. We need your help. Again. And maybe we can find out what happened to your family and our men."

Tell saw that Rumi had stopped crying. He waited until she looked at him with reddened eyes, then he continued. "My people—we lie, we cheat, we steal, even from each other. It's what we do. But we'd be in bad trouble without you, and I want you to know that I will never lie to you, and . . . none of those other things either. Just like I would never lie to my sister."

Rumi nodded, not trusting herself with words yet.

"I don't know what we'll find," Tell continued. "It's

most likely going to be terrible for all of us. But we need to know. Then we can plan our revenge."

"Revenge! Against the *Ropers*?" Rumi blurted. "They're too powerful! They're too—"

Tell cut her off. "Everyone thinks we have no power because we're children. That's a mistake. And it makes us even more dangerous than they know."

It was nearly imperceptible, but after absorbing Tell's words, Rumi squared her shoulders and tossed her curls back. Tell noticed; she would help them. Again. But instead of giving him ideas on how to get into her father's warehouse, she simply said, "I'm thirsty."

There was no water on the terrace, nor food. Wren was the only one who'd eaten or drunk anything lately, while waiting for them to return. She knew she should've felt at least a little guilty about it, but didn't.

"We can't go inside." Cormorin shrugged apologetically. "We just have to wait."

Tell and Wren were used to waiting and waiting again, to eat or drink. Rumi was not. Wren poked around in one of the clay pots and fished out a small pebble of quartz from under a spiky leaf.

"Put this under your tongue. It'll help."

Rumi shook her head in disbelief. "It's just a pebble."

"It's what we do in the mountains," Tell told her, rubbing it clean on his sleeve. "It keeps your mouth from getting dry."

Looking skeptical, Rumi took the pebble, put it under her tongue anyway, sucked it experimentally, and raised her eyebrows in surprise—it worked! She smiled her thanks; the first real smile they'd seen from her since they met. It lit up her face and made Tell want to find ways to evoke it again. As if reading that thought, Wren raised a knowing eyebrow. Cormorin, too. Tell ignored them.

Despite wanting to tease her brother, Wren knew she needed to take advantage of their situation while it lasted. "Earlier, your sorcerer said there was trouble in Halfway," she asked, cornering Cormorin once more. "What did she mean by that?"

Abruptly, Cormorin strode away, but then paused, back to them, until they realized they should follow—something he'd clearly learned from the sorcerer. He led them to the side of the house looking out over the Ocean quarter.

"That big blue house out there," he said mysteriously. They squinted, looking for it. "It's the only one. Blue is a very expensive color. No one else would use it on a house. It costs a fortune."

With his hunter's eyes, Tell saw it first. "What about it?"

"Oh! It's Ocean's house, has to be," said Rumi. "That's what you mean, right? Only a sorcerer could afford it."

"Yes, that's exactly what I mean. She was our strongest rival. She wanted to take our house for herself. They all do."

"You said *was*, not *is*," Wren pointed out, thinking that the house looked like a square of sky.

Cormorin looked as if he regretted bringing it up. Or maybe he regretted what he was about to tell them.

"Ocean was found dead yesterday, by her helper," he said quietly.

"That's a good thing, right?" Tell said. "Your strongest rival, dead?"

"No," Cormorin corrected him. "It's a very bad thing."

"But—why?" Wren asked.

"Oh!" Rumi exclaimed suddenly, loud enough to startle them. "Mountain! Oh!" She held her head in both hands. *I think she may be dead, too!*"

"What?!" Cormorin leaned out over the rail, peering in that direction. "How so?"

"We went there earlier today, to sell the glass. Her house was open. People were going in and out. That's not normal, is it?"

At that, Cormorin paced away, looking longingly at the door, as if he were about to swing it open and go inside, despite the trouble he'd get into.

Rumi bent close to Tell and Wren. "Sorcerers don't just die. They're almost impossible to kill. That's what they say, anyway."

Tell got it almost immediately. "So someone knows how to kill sorcerers!"

"Why would anyone want to?" Wren asked, shocked.

Cormorin swung back over to them, his face flushed, agitated.

"That's why she's so angry, isn't it?" Rumi concluded. "That's the trouble she talked about."

Almost as if she heard their conversation and wanted to stop it, the sorcerer emerged onto the balcony. A long string of discs threaded onto a knotted cord swung down from her hand. She held them out to Tell.

"Take them, and be gone. We have work to do here."

Tell's heart thudded as he took the heavy string. He'd seen one battered sous, once, in his entire life. This was a fortune.

"Count them," Rumi advised.

"We don't need to," he said.

"Yes, you do," Rumi insisted. "Count, or you're the fool. That's what my father says."

Tell looked helplessly at the string of sous and turned to Wren for help. She shook her head.

Rumi realized something. *You can't count?*

Tell shrugged. "Where we live, nothing much needs counting beyond our fingers and toes."

Rumi took the string from Tell, laid it neatly on the tiles, and knelt down next to it. Tell and Wren expected the process to take a while, but Rumi didn't count by ones. She counted groups of sous, and very quickly.

"Don't worry. I'll teach you to count. It's eas—" She stopped suddenly, looked up at the sorcerer. "You're short. We said two hundred. This is one hundred and ninety-nine."

"It's a better number," declared the sorcerer. "More powerful. Some protection for you. You'll need it. Now go."

Rumi stood up and set her jaw. "Not until we get one more sous from you."

"Little girl, little merchant girl, you'll learn the hard way that it's not all about—"

Tell scooped up the string of sous. "We'll take it."

"You're being cheated!" Rumi said hotly.

"No, we're not," answered Tell.

Wren agreed. "Whatever power there is in this number, it's worth one little sous."

Rumi folded her arms tightly, trying not to quiver. Taking less than the agreed-on amount went against every cell in her body.

"All right, then," snapped the sorcerer. "Tell me what the right number should be—and it's not two hundred," she challenged. "Tell me in the time it takes to—"

"Two hundred and eleven," Rumi said scornfully. "That's the next powerful number."

From her other hand, the sorcerer held out a short string of twelve sous, swinging it back and forth. Clearly, the sorcerer had expected this contest from the youngest daughter of Kun Anton. Surprised, Rumi counted them with a glance.

"Thank you," she said simply and graciously as she took them. Her father had also taught her that good manners should begin and end every trade.

"Cormorin, show them to the street." The sorcerer closed the door without another word. Their visit to the most powerful sorcerer in Halfway was very much over. And they still didn't know her name.

Once Cormorin had seen them off, he hurried to face the sorcerer. She was standing over the new slab of black glass, examining it intently. She didn't so much as glance up while Cormorin stood nearby, head bowed.

"What is it?" she asked eventually.

"Uh . . . I tried to tell you earlier. I used a command I'm, uh, not really supposed to know . . . to save that black glass," he confessed to her. He knew his face was as red as his hair. He could feel it. "I didn't think. I just did it."

"Which command? Don't say it. Don't say anything out loud right now. Not even here. I feel a presence."

So Cormorin thought the spell he used. Her eyes engulfed his, and after a moment she grunted, startled.

"Who caught the glass? You?"

"It was supposed to be me, but it wasn't. Tell caught it. I—I must've gotten something wrong." Cormorin bowed his head, steeled himself for punishment.

But all the sorcerer said was "The apprentice who doesn't learn more than he's supposed to is not much of an apprentice." She began to pace. "This piece of glass came to us just in time. It's no coincidence."

"There's more!" he blurted. She stopped. "They asked me to hold their payment for them. They don't want to carry that much money out in the streets. They only took the small string."

"So they trust you. And they'll be back. Good."

She stepped to the table where, earlier, they'd watched Tell and Wren's father in her old slab of glass. She picked up the case for the old glass, and Cormorin was instantly by her side. Carrying things was his job, not hers.

"Where would you like me to put it?"

"Wherever you want," she said. At first Cormorin didn't understand. So she added, "It's yours now."

Of everything that had happened to Cormorin so far that day, this was the most shocking. He backpedaled, genuinely afraid.

"No! It's too soon. You know it is."

"I agree, it's much too soon."

"I'm not ready!"

"Sometimes you don't have a choice. This is one of those times."

Cormorin stared down at the case in disbelief—his? Truly? It was hard to stay calm. When he looked up, she was gone.

21

Tell lined up the shot, and even though it was dark, the bow he'd rigged was small and weak, and the arrow was too short and tied to a piece of string, he put it right through the triangular gap between the rafter and the warehouse roof. It was a shot he could have made as a gap-toothed little boy.

Once it was looped over the rafter, they tied the string to the end of a length of rope, which they pulled up and over the rafter. Wren climbed the rope like a monkey on a vine. Hooking her leg over the rafter, she pressed her face close to the ventilation hole, listening intently while Tell and Rumi waited tensely below. After what felt to them like a lifetime, she got to work cutting a hole in the netting that kept birds, bats, and chipmunks out of the warehouse.

Rumi was astonished at Wren's strength and bravery.

She had no idea that what Wren was doing was normal for mountain folk. Tell could've done the same, but Wren was the better climber and still small enough—hopefully—to fit through the ventilation hole. Otherwise they'd have to get Rumi up there, and Tell didn't want to think about that.

At last Wren had a hole to her liking and fed one end of the rope down into the warehouse. Then, after nodding down at Tell and Rumi first, she grasped the rope and slid in feet-first. It was a tight squeeze, even for her; she had to puff out all her breath to get through. Tell and Rumi grasped the other end of the rope, Tell wrapping it once around his waist so that he could lean back against it, and just in time, because the rope went tight with Wren's full weight. But not for long. After a few moments, the rope went slack again. She was in! Kun Anton's warehouse was not impregnable after all.

And only children could have done this! Rumi thought to herself, remembering Tell's words on the sorcerer's terrace about their power.

They had bought the string and rope from a stall that sold nothing but string and rope on the way back to Rumi's house. These were the first things Tell and Wren had ever paid for, and the transaction thrilled them. Plus, Rumi had refused to pay the price asked and saved them quite a bit of money.

They'd spent the savings at a street stall, on the most

delicious meal they had ever tasted: small chunks of spiced meat cooked over carefully contained coals and laid onto thin squares of unleavened bread. "Poor man's pockets," Rumi called them before showing them how to fold everything together the way people born to Halfway do. They'd washed it all down with clay mugs of sweet lemon water, chilled by condensation.

As usual, Wren had been full of questions—when her mouth wasn't full, anyway. She'd asked where different people came from: A salt-bleached family without shoes came from the edge of a faraway sea—how could children have hair so white! Two small, silent people wrapped in glowing red and iridescent green feather capes came from a jungle full of birds. An enormous, profusely sweating man wearing nothing but furs came from a misty forest far to the north; it was clearly his first time in Halfway too. Interestingly, Rumi hadn't known where a gaunt man with a stringed musical instrument came from; she'd never seen anyone like him, either.

Wren also wanted to know what each of the nearby shops and stalls sold; Rumi knew them all. Pots, wool for weaving and knitting, soft stone for carving, dried and smoked meat. Tell made note of a stall that sold leather boots, promised himself he'd return. He asked about eye medicine, but Rumi couldn't help, so he decided he'd ask Cormorin when they went back for their sous. They'd deliberately avoided talking about the sorcerer or their new fortune. Not one peep. They weren't ready to examine what was swirling around in their heads after their visit to the mysterious center of Halfway.

After licking the crumbs and gravy off her fingertips, Wren had begged Rumi to take them past Rold Roland's house, just so they could hear Rumble's bray. Without knowing how they would accomplish that and too tired to ask, Rumi sighed and set off with a hint of a limp. Her feet were aching; she'd already walked more that day than she ever had in one day in her life, but she'd recognized the need in Wren's eyes.

When they reached the house, they peered up at the jagged pieces of flint atop the walls.

"Now what?" Rumi asked in a low voice.

"Cover your ears," Tell advised.

"Why?"

Wren licked her thumb and forefinger, pinched them together, and popped them in her mouth, then whistled so loudly that everyone on the street stopped in their tracks. Rumi winced, shooting her hands to her ears.

"That's how she calls Rumble down from the mountainside," Tell explained with a grin. "She has the best whistle in the village."

"Shhhh," Wren whispered. "Listen."

They did, intently, and despite the roar of the city, they heard the sound of a mule braying. It was faint, as if he was weak or shut away somewhere, but it was unmistakably

Rumble. Wren sagged with relief, rubbing her hands over her face.

"He's still alive!" she said, her voice quivering. Then she whistled again—two short notes, then a long blast that echoed around the houses. The answering bray seemed to have a little more spirit to it.

"We have to go," Rumi warned, glancing in every direction. "People are looking at us." She was right. People were beginning to show a lot of interest in them.

"What did you tell him?" Tell asked as they hurried away.

"That we hadn't forgotten him, and we'd be back for him," Wren said matter-of-factly.

"You can talk to your mule?" Rumi could scarcely believe it.

"Of course! And he talks to me." Wren was bouncing on her toes, she was so happy.

Rumi looked to Tell, who nodded. She just shook her head. The last few days of her life were too big and shocking for her to deal with. She decided not to try.

Once safely back inside Rumi's deserted house, Tell set about making a bow and arrow from whatever he could find. He took a crosspiece out of a massive chair made from tough, thick, dried reeds. He split the length of reed, then tillered it down with his father's knife to make a small bow. It wouldn't kill a mouse, let alone a man, but that was not its purpose. He fashioned an arrow from the handle of a long wooden spoon. It didn't need a point, but he put one on it anyway because an arrow without a point seemed unnatural. He didn't bother with feathers—too much trouble for such a short shot.

He also carved his special mark on the arrow. He did this automatically. Everyone in their village had a special mark for their arrows, to stop another hunter from claiming a kill he hadn't made. Tell's mark was three notches in a row, a hand's width down from the nock. He couldn't imagine ever shooting an arrow without it.

While Tell was at work, Rumi showed Wren around her home, and they both began to understand how truly different their lives were . . . right up until the moment they weren't.

"You had a room all for yourself?!" Wren had exclaimed, amazed.

"Yes, and my own servant," confessed Rumi, thinking that maybe all the people who saw her as spoiled were right.

"My brothers share a room, but it's a big one. Not as big as my mother and father's, of course—" Rumi suddenly paused and grew quiet, and despite blinking hard, even holding her breath, she still couldn't stop the tears from running down her cheeks. Wren looked away, more sympathetic than she would have been a few days ago. Rumi managed to stop crying quickly. "I'm going to learn how to not cry!" she said angrily.

"Well, I'm going to learn how to count like you do!" Wren replied, matching Rumi's determination.

"Yes, you have to," Rumi agreed. "Your people got cheated, both ways, every single time they came down the mountain."

Wren frowned. "What do you mean, both ways?"

"Everything you sold, you sold for half its value, and everything you carried back up cost double what it should have," Rumi explained. "Did you never ask yourselves why you were always poor, even though you have the only black glass there is?"

Wren was thunderstruck. No one, she was sure, had ever considered that painful question. So, if they'd just been able to count, they could've grown fat over the winter, instead of becoming as thin as grass stalks due to not enough food and too much worry? This was . . . this was . . . an outrage! And humiliating! Then a question occurred to Wren, but she hesitated, not wanting to set Rumi off again. But she had to know.

"Your father . . . did he cheat us too?"

Rumi's face reddened as she nodded yes. "Every single time. He said being easy to cheat was the only thing that made dealing with those—I mean, with your people—worth the trouble. I'm sorry," Rumi said, clearly feeling terrible, even though what her father had done was normal and expected.

Wren just shrugged. "Don't be. We stole plenty of things from you on the way out."

"What—you did?"

"Oh yes. Stolen things are much more valuable to us than things we paid for." Wren lifted her chin. "My father's boots 'fell off the back of a mule.' My mother had a feather pillow she loved from somewhere down here. One year, she brought me back a toy lamb made of wool, with eyes of blue stone. Even though it wasn't new, I was so proud she'd stolen it for me."

Rumi's mouth fell open. "Eyes of blue stone? That was mine! I looked for her for days! She was my favorite toy!"

"Oh. She was my favorite toy too. Well, and my only one." Wren didn't know what else to say. Each girl considered the other, trying to figure out how to feel about the stolen toy they'd shared. They couldn't. It was almost a relief when Tell sauntered over, newly fashioned bow in hand.

"It's time," he said.

"What are you going to shoot with that sad little thing?" Wren teased.

"Air," Tell replied. Brother and sister walked away, as casually as if they were going for a stroll in the yard. Rumi felt the exact opposite, but she did think to pick up a lamp and flint on the way out, to light their way.

They waited at the warehouse door for Wren to open it from the inside, Tell with his knife out, Rumi ready to strike the flint and light the lamp. The door swung open quietly from the inside. Wren leaned her head out and murmured:

"There's nobody here."

Tell eased the warehouse door closed behind them as Rumi lit the lamp, revealing a vast space full of goods of all kinds, neatly stacked and arranged in a grid of squares scored into the hard dirt floor. Some goods were basic: charcoal, salt, split logs, leather hides as stiff as wood. Others were worked by skilled hands: piles of rugs and blankets, kitchen pots, woven grass mats, tunics. Some things were exotic and exciting: stools carved to look like animals, shining boxes with pearly lids. Despite the grim task they were there for, Tell and Wren couldn't ignore what they were seeing in front of them.

"Look at this beautiful wood!" Tell exclaimed, running his hand along the top of a stack of rich, red-grained wood.

"That came in through the Forest gate," Rumi explained.

Wren spied piles of warm blankets, enough for many mountain villages. Then something she didn't understand— sacks full of orange-colored dried flowers. "What are those for?" she asked Rumi.

"They keep fleas and bedbugs away," Rumi told them. "You scatter them where you sleep. They're grown on the edge of the desert."

Wren bent close, then recoiled from the sharp tang of the flowers. "We could use a few sacks of these," Wren observed to Tell. By the light of Rumi's moving lamp, they saw mounds of charcoal from coarse to fine, stacks of massive clay pots exactly like the ones on the sorcerer's terrace, boxes of teas and spices, pink rock salt, and on and on.

They walked up one orderly row of goods and down another.

"Where does all this stuff come from?" Tell asked, amazed. "Who brings it here?"

"You've seen all the different people here. Traders bring it from all over—just like you with your black glass. The charcoal comes from the endless forests to the north. That pink salt . . . I think it comes from mines in the mountains—not your part of the mountains. White salt comes from people who live on the edge of the ocean. Clay pots—they come from all over. There's clay everywhere."

Tell suddenly realized that their entire life—a life of black glass—was just a tiny part of a much, much greater world, much of which came through this warehouse on its way to somewhere else. It was exciting, yet it made him feel small at the same time.

"And it all belongs to your father?" Wren asked.

"Yes. He buys anything he thinks he can sell for more, and he always does. He's very good at it." She fought the quiver in her voice and won.

"Let's see if we can find . . . something," Tell said with unexpected gentleness, walking more purposefully. Row after row, they saw nothing that shouldn't have been there, until, at a back corner of the warehouse, they came upon a big black pool of what looked like tar spread across the hard dirt floor.

"My father would never allow this!" Rumi said, appalled.

Tell squatted down. "It's blood. About a body's worth, I reckon."

The light in the warehouse began to shake and jump, and Rumi collapsed in a dead faint on the floor. Wren caught the lamp just in time. The last thing they needed was to start a fire!

"Did you really have to say a whole body's worth?"

"Well . . . it is!" Tell protested. But he knelt down beside Rumi to see what he could do for her.

Which was when they heard the thump of a door being flung open somewhere across the warehouse and the sound of heavy feet climbing up . . . stairs?

Wren blew out their lamp, and they ducked down low. Tell put his hand over Rumi's mouth to keep her quiet if she woke. Concealed behind bolts of indigo cloth, they barely breathed as they saw a light flare across the warehouse and the silhouettes of two men moving toward the warehouse door. As they walked between the piles of goods, Tell got a better look at them. The Roper with the honey-colored braid, who Tell had seen in the kitchen the night before, and Hammerhead, holding the lamp. Tell's heart felt as if it were being clenched by an invisible fist.

"Why don't I come into the house with you?" Hammerhead was suggesting. "Then you won't have to carry anything."

"And how do we get back in here if you come?" the Roper asked as if talking to a child. Not a smart child either.

"We prop the door open."

"No! You stay right here, at the door. Wait for my knock. I won't be long."

The Roper kicked the door closed behind him as he left. Hammerhead was clearly seething. But neither Tell nor Wren cared about his state of mind. Their eyes were fixed with horror on their rope dangling down from the ventilation hole, as plain a sign as any that Hammerhead was not alone in the warehouse. All he had to do was notice it, and they'd be well and truly trapped.

22

Luckily, at first it appeared that Hammerhead was only interested in looking for something he could steal—probably the reason he'd wanted to go into Rumi's house in the first place. Lamp held high, he stomped up and down between the rows of goods, becoming frustrated, knocking over boxes of herbs, kicking bags of nuts. Most of what Kun Anton sold was not easy to carry away. In his fury, Hammerhead kicked over a beautifully glazed clay bowl, just to make it shatter. A typical Hammerhead act, and exactly why he'd never been chief of their village.

Finally, he arrived at a pile of rock salt and grabbed a pinkish-white lump the size of his fist. Salt had value everywhere, or you could eat it. The trouble was, the salt was one pile over from the stack of indigo cloth, Tell and Wren's hiding place.

Which was when Rumi began to stir. Tell pressed a

hand to her mouth to still her. But Hammerhead clearly heard something. He whirled, eyes flicking up and down the rows of goods. He raised his lamp high and began stalking their way, silent, focused.

Tell's mouth went dry. He knew he'd have to take on Hammerhead, and he knew he couldn't. Hammerhead was many things, all terrible, and he was also very, very hard to kill. At least two men that Tell knew of had tried, up on the mountain. Their bleached and frozen bones told the way their stories ended.

Tell drew his knife, nodded to Wren to do the same. Maybe he could distract Hammerhead long enough for Wren to stick him with her knife? He knew his eyes were as wide with terror as his sister's. More than they had felt with the sorcerer or Rold Roland.

They were saved by their rope. Saved and condemned at the same moment.

Just as he was about to reach the bolts of cloth, Hammerhead noticed the rope. His big, broad forehead creased in a frown as he thought about what it meant. The fact that Hammerhead thought slowly made him even more dangerous; he'd learned to react to any situation with maximum brutality, no matter what.

He tossed the rock salt aside and veered toward the dangling rope, passing so close to Tell, Wren, and Rumi that they could have reached out and touched him. Or stabbed him. But Tell was paralyzed. He couldn't. He didn't dare. Nor did Wren. Their fear of Hammerhead began before they could walk or talk and had grown with them, every day since. That's a deep fear.

Tell swallowed, tasted humiliation, and pretended to himself that he was making a smart choice. But he knew in his heart that he was too afraid to move. He was a coward.

Wren looked down at Rumi and saw fear bright in her eyes. Then she looked back at Hammerhead and, for the first time in her life, saw one of her own people through the eyes of a stranger. Wren suddenly realized exactly why people hated them, feared them, cheated them, disdained them. In the way he walked and his grunting breath, Hammerhead seemed more like an animal than a person. Wren wanted to explain to Rumi later that he was by far the worst of them.

Hammerhead circled the rope, then yanked on it. Tell hadn't tied off the other end to anything, and the rope poured down through the ventilation hole. Which meant that the string came with it. Which meant that Tell's crude little arrow clattered around in the ventilation hole on the end of the string, caught for a moment, then flicked free, sailing to the ground almost at Hammerhead's feet.

Tell almost gasped out loud. He'd marked his arrow! Hammerhead would know he'd shot it as clearly as if Tell himself were standing right in front of him.

Hammerhead grunted as he stooped to pick up the little arrow. Suddenly, the sound of boots kicking the door echoed through the warehouse. By the mountain's sweet tears! Tell never thought he'd be grateful for the return of the Roper, but he was. Hammerhead was still intent on getting a better look at the arrow. He brought his lamp close.

But the Roper kicked again, harder, faster. Even Hammerhead couldn't ignore it. He lurched to his feet with a huff of frustration . . . and accidentally blew his lamp out.

"Hanging rock!" Hammerhead cursed as he fumbled to find his flint in the pitch dark, fumbled more to relight the lamp. The kicks grew louder and louder still, the fury behind them evident.

Lamp lit at last, Hammerhead scurried for the door. Tell and Wren both realized the same unthinkable thing—Hammerhead was afraid of the Roper.

"The blasted lamp went out," Hammerhead was explaining now. The Roper seemed to accept the explanation. He shoved a big basket of supplies at Hammerhead, took the lamp, and slammed shut the warehouse door.

Then he did something that shook Tell and Wren to the core. Viper fast, he slapped Hammerhead across the face, a ringing blow that made the most feared man in their village stagger sideways . . . and do nothing in retaliation. He just took it.

"When I tell you to stay at the door and wait for my knock, that's what you do. That's the only thing you do.

You don't go wandering around looking for something to steal, you light-fingered, light-brained mountain goat." He strode away with the lamp. If he'd seen Hammerhead's face as Tell, Wren, and Rumi did, he might not have been so quick to turn his back on him. But seething or not, murderous or not, Hammerhead followed obediently, the rope, the string, and Tell's marked arrow forgotten. For now.

Motioning for the other two to stay put, Tell crept after the men. The Roper stopped at a pile of woven grass baskets, reached down, and lifted a slab of wood hidden underneath them. Tell drew in a breath. The grass baskets were not for sale; they were there to conceal a trapdoor to what could only be a tunnel.

The Roper held the trapdoor up for Hammerhead, who disappeared down a flight of stairs, cradling the supplies. The Roper followed, letting the door and the pile of grass baskets settle back down onto the floor as he descended.

Tell couldn't believe their luck. They'd just been shown Kun Anton's secret tunnel. If you didn't see it for yourself, you'd never find it.

The tunnel pleased Tell. "It makes sense," he said as Wren and Rumi approached in low crouches. "No one would build a warehouse they could accidentally be locked out of."

"I wonder what else my father hid from me," Rumi asked aloud as they inspected the pile of grass baskets. "He said I knew everything there was to know about the business. He said I would be taking over when I was grown, not my brothers. Was that all a lie too?"

Tell and Wren had no idea how to respond.

"I wonder where the tunnel goes," Wren asked, changing the subject.

"Only one way to know," Tell answered, voice loud with bravado.

Rumi took two steps backward. "We're going down there?"

"You don't have to," Tell said. "But we do."

23

Rumi brought two more lamps from the house while Tell and Wren wedged the warehouse door open with a piece of wood.

Rumi had chosen not to go with them. Tell had explained how dangerous it might be and that they should be prepared to fight for their lives. She realized that she'd help them more by waiting at the house until they returned, and no one tried to talk her out of it. In truth, all three were relieved.

Not that it was easy for Rumi, alone at night in a house full of fresh memories of her family. There was bravery in that, too. Tell and Wren promised they would return as fast as they could. They understood all too well that not knowing was the worst torture.

"And what if . . . if you don't return?" Rumi asked, even though hating to.

"Go to Cormorin," Wren said. "Show him the trapdoor. Tell him where we went."

"But we'll be back," Tell told her. "Tonight."

Raising the door hidden under the grass baskets took all their combined strength, and even then they struggled to get it all the way up. So they decided to leave it propped open, rather than close it and have to lift it again on the way back.

The stairs down into the ground were thick, wide, and strong. When Tell and Wren reached the bottom, their lamps held high, they realized that this was no mole tunnel. It had been built by men who knew how to build tunnels; it was cut high and clean, big enough to carry any load through it, and the floor was packed firm. This was a wealthy smuggler's tunnel.

Tell turned to Wren. She nodded. She was ready. Tell blew out his lamp and handed it to her, freeing both hands. Touching the wall lightly to give himself the memory of it, Tell led them down the tunnel. The air felt stale and damp. It smelled faintly of the raw sewage that leached downward into the earth from every ditch in Halfway.

Wren was a mountain girl, used to air and space and light. Being underground sent a rattle of fear through her. There are times when being in control of your fear is essential. This was one of those times. Wren imagined crushing her fear under her heel as if crushing a brown scorpion, as she had been taught by the old women.

Tell, on the other hand, had been in the shaft where they mined the black glass many times, so he felt no fear of this one. But what they might find at the other end . . . that was another thing entirely. He thrust all such thoughts away, as if they were a deadly enemy and he was shoving them off a cliff to their death. The siblings were well prepared when life turned brutal.

The tunnel changed direction twice, to the left, then left again. The final section was the longest and dipped downward deeper underground, Wren almost treading on Tell's heels, she stayed so close to him. Once it began to rise and they could see stairs ahead, Tell decided to begin his calming breath—four in, hold for seven, eight out—as he always did close to prey when he was hunting.

They had no idea where they were or what waited for them. They didn't even know if they'd be able to raise the door at the top of these stairs. They blew out Wren's lamp. Shoulder to shoulder in pitch darkness, they felt their way up the stairs until they reached the big door lying flat to the ground.

"Just enough to see out," Tell murmured as they pushed upward.

But they couldn't lift the door by arm strength alone. They had to duck down, climb another stair, and push with their legs. The heavy door rose just enough to give them a chance to peek out.

They saw nothing—just deep shadows. There was light, but not much. Their noses told them the air was fresher, but they weren't outside.

But the sound . . . the sound they heard made their hearts thud. Tapping, scraping, the faint clink of small pieces of glass falling to the ground. This was a sound they'd heard while drinking their mother's milk, while learning to crawl, while beginning to understand who, what, and where they were. It was as much a sound of winter in their village as the howling wind.

Winter was when the People of the Black Glass gathered with their raw glass and made knives, arrowheads, and jewelry in preparation for the season to come. It was when they told stories from the past summer or rekindled unfinished arguments.

Tell and Wren knew that whatever else it signified, the sound of black glass being worked by hand meant that the men were still alive. But in what condition? Just as they'd held their grief at bay, so now they held back their relief until they could understand the situation.

Then they heard Hammerhead's familiar bellow. "Stop slacking, you light-fingered, light-brained mountain goats! We have to finish by tomorrow!" The equally familiar sound of Hammerhead's heavy hand thumping against flesh followed.

What was going on? Where was the chief? They had to find out. But there was one major problem: all the sound came from behind them. The tunnel door opened away from whatever was happening. They would have to shimmy out from under it if they wanted to see the men.

Which meant they would have to risk getting caught.

But they had to know.

Tell signaled to Wren that she should get ready to look. He moved to the center point of the door. Then, baring his teeth and inhaling a great lungful of air, he summoned every cell in his body to the task and lifted the door another foot by himself. He felt as if his bones were going to be crushed to dust by the weight.

Wren didn't waste time worrying about Tell. She slithered under the side of the door, knowing that if Tell's strength gave way, the door would crush her. But she didn't worry about herself, either. She was halfway out, then more, then slid back in with a fat chunk of firewood in each hand. She shoved the first chunk back under the edge of the open door until it could go no farther, then darted around behind Tell and did the same on the other side.

Then Wren took some of the weight, and they lowered the door. It dropped a tiny bit, then stayed open, propped up precariously on the chunks of firewood.

Tell slumped against the edge of the opening, muscles quivering, trying to pant quietly, which turned out to be incredibly difficult. Wren put her mouth to his ear.

"It's *another* warehouse. There's a pile of firewood just on the other side of the door," she whispered. "It's a good place to hide."

And then, once again, she wriggled under the edge of the trapdoor and was gone.

24

From her hiding place—a smaller pile of firewood than was comfortable—Wren took in a scene she could scarcely believe. It was intimately familiar and yet utterly wrong.

Exactly as they would up the mountain, the men she'd known all her life sat in a circle around a meager fire, working raw black glass into useful objects. But they weren't telling stories or teasing one another, as they would at home. They were slumped and silent, and far more alarming, they each had a thin strangler noose around their neck, each noose anchored to a big slab of cut rock behind them, with just enough slack for small movements. A circle of cruelty around a fire barely worthy of the name. And there was still no sign of the chief.

Something familiar jiggled Wren's brain, but she couldn't think what it was as Hammerhead's voice claimed her attention.

"Work faster, you mountain scum! We need to be done by daybreak!" Hammerhead stalked the edge of the circle, breathing heavily, peering at their work with unkind eyes. Tucked under one arm was a clay jug of wine from Rumi's house, which he slopped into a mug next to each man's place. After each slop, he'd take a slug for himself. He wasn't drunk yet, but he was working on it. Hammerhead and drink were a bad pairing.

One time, Wren remembered, Hammerhead had gotten hold of a gourd of apricot brandy and began destroying a hut rock by rock, yelling and screaming, chasing after anyone who came near, hurling the rocks at them. The entire village had had to run away up a steep slope of scree until he passed out in the middle of the half-destroyed hut. It was his own hut, so no one cared. But a drunk Hammerhead was to be avoided even more than the sober version.

As Tell joined Wren, Hammerhead paused over Curas, the village's best hunter, and watched him closely. Curas paused as well.

"Did I tell you to stop?" Hammerhead growled, a slur in his voice.

"I can't work with you watching," Curas replied quietly.

Hammerhead leaned down close to Curas's ear. "Get back to work. Now."

"Then move on," Curas said. He was a calm man, which was why he was a great hunter, but there was an edge to his voice that neither Tell nor Wren had ever heard before.

"Are you telling me what to do?" Hammerhead asked belligerently.

"I'm telling you what has to happen if you want me to keep making weapons for your new masters," Curas replied in an even tone.

Hammerhead let out a roar of anger and yanked hard on the strangler cord, cutting off Curas's breathing. Wren bit down on her lip to stop herself from crying out as Curas quickly turned blue. Hammerhead's anger turned to bewilderment as he realized what he had done.

But what happened next sent a rush of mountain pride coursing through Wren and Tell, for the first time since reaching Halfway.

Curas did not panic. Even as he was dying, he felt on the floor for the right shard of black glass. His fingers rejected two pieces before deciding on the one he wanted. That gleaming shard, he lifted to his throat and sliced deep into his own flesh to cut the noose, just as Tell had done for Wren at the green-toothed Rold Roland's house, only much deeper.

Curas sank to the floor heaving for breath, pressing his hand to his neck to stop the gushing flow. A strangler's noose doesn't work as planned on someone willing to draw their own blood to live.

Once they saw that Curas would survive, the other men tossed their tools and black glass into the fire and folded their arms.

"What do you think you're doing?!" Hammerhead's eyes darted back and forth in confusion.

"We're not working anymore. Not for you, not for them," said the older, thinner Mort brother.

Hammerhead stumbled into the circle. "They'll kill you all!"

"Guess who they'll kill first?" the younger, thick-set Mort brother said with a happy smile. "The whining cur who's been licking their feet and promising them weapons in a city without weapons."

Hammerhead sucked his lower lip as he thought his way through his new problem. He didn't like the conclusion he came to.

"I saved your lives, and you know it! Without me, you'd all already be as dead as the chief."

Tell squeezed Wren's arm. The chief was . . . dead!

"We'd rather be dead if this is our life," said a man renowned in their village for his bitter outlook on everything.

"They're going to kill us anyway, you fool," said his neighbor as he emptied his cup of wine and stole another.

"We just want to make sure you go first," jeered the smallest man in the village. "That'll be satisfaction enough."

Hammerhead met their resistance the only way he knew how. "I'll strangle you all! I'll pull every string around every neck if you don't go back to work right now!"

"Okay, so you'll die last," said Mort the younger with

a shrug. "It'll be horrible for you when they find you here alone with no weapons. They'll make it slow. They know you're an egg-sucking dog with knuckles for a brain."

Hammerhead lurched from one direction to another, almost walking into the fire, as thoughts tormented his brain. The men simply sat there, a circle of calm certainty.

"You think what I've done is easy? Working with them?" Hammerhead blustered.

"Easier than this," said a sharp-faced man called Toyot, who some felt was next in line to be chief. "Plus, it's what you've wanted all your life. To tell us what to do."

"You wonder why you've never been chief?" Mort the older asked, then answered himself. "You think it's just because everyone hates you? And we do. That's not the reason, though. It's because you don't know how to be a chief, and never will."

Hammerhead's confusion grew. "What does that have to do with anything?"

Curas sat up slowly, blood staining his shoulder. He downed the wine in his cup, jabbed a crimson-crusted finger at Hammerhead, and said in a newly raspy voice, "You can pretend all you like with *them* that you've replaced the chief. But not with us. We know you for what you are."

Hammerhead looked at the hard eyes fixed on him, all fierce with implacable willpower. He seemed to shrink physically.

"We *have* to go back to work." He gave one last try, his voice now a whine. "They said if we do well, they'll keep us on."

"What, as slaves?" asked quiet Melk, one of their da's best friends.

"I'll work with you," Hammerhead begged. "I'll help."

"Untie us first," demanded the sharp-faced Toyot. "We're not dogs."

"I can't! They won't allow it."

Curas stood up slowly, flexing his knees. He'd already untied himself the hard way.

"They'll blame me," Hammerhead pleaded.

"That's your problem," Curas said as he sliced the strangler's noose off two men, gave them the shard of black glass so that they could free the others. The freed men rubbed at their necks, their relief palpable.

"Let's get back down that tunnel," Mort the younger suggested as the last man stood, free.

"Not yet," Curas said calmly to them. "We don't know who's waiting at the other end, and we're unarmed. Those Ropers could just pick us off one by one as we climbed out." Curas thought for a moment. "They've never come back here before dawn. So, we make weapons in that time . . . but not for them. For us."

"We can't fight them! You haven't seen what I've seen," Hammerhead exclaimed, panicked. "They're bigger than us, they're stronger than us, they're smarter than us, there are more of them than us. They have a sorcerer on their side! We can't beat them."

"Not by doing nothing, we can't," Curas said. "So get to work. Being here has turned you into a coward."

So Hammerhead got to work, but not in the circle of the men. They refused to make space for him. He worked alone. This was how the process of being cast out began.

For Tell and Wren, seeing Hammerhead's humiliation was a wonderful thing. They were too young to understand that a humiliated bully is an extremely dangerous creature. They were deciding whether to reveal themselves or not, when Mort the younger stood up.

"Let's make a fire worth the name," he declared. "It's not our wood." He headed straight for the pile of firewood. Tell and Wren glanced at each other in alarm and shrank down as low as possible.

It almost worked. Mort the younger stacked chunks of firewood onto his left arm, picked up a final piece in his right hand, and was about to turn back to the fire, when he paused.

First he took in the propped-open door, and then his shocked eyes met theirs. After a long moment, Tell and Wren moved to a crouch, ready to stand up and reveal themselves, but Mort the younger shook his head urgently.

Noting their faces furrowed with confusion, he shook his head again.

"What are you playing at over there?" shouted his

brother from the circle. "Stop shirking, you lazy ferret!" The others laughed. Being free to die in a way of their own choosing had certainly raised their spirits.

Mort the younger mouthed one word. *Go.* Then, out loud, he retorted, "I learned shirking from you, my sleepy little bunny."

The men's laughter was cut short by the sound of a door slamming open at the front of the warehouse, followed by the flicker of torches flooding in from outside.

Tell and Wren could have dived—*should* have dived—into the tunnel right then, but they didn't. They lingered out of fatal curiosity as too many Ropers to count streamed in, torches held high, filling the warehouse with light.

The Ropers were as different from the People of the Black Glass as humans could be. They were tall and muscular, but the contrast went far beyond that. Tell had seen one of them already; he hadn't realized that they would *all* look the same as that one. Or as similar as different men could look, anyway.

They were clean-faced, their skin shining with oil, their long hair pulled back in tight braids hanging down the length of their backs—perfectly plaited hair the color of honey, of coal, of flame, hair so light as to be almost clear, bear brown, hazelnut brown, wood brown. Not a single Roper was bald. Unlike the People, who wore whatever they could get their hands on, the Ropers all wore the same clothing: tight shirts and leggings made of dark blue cloth. They looked, sounded, and moved as one. It was frightening, and impressive.

The man at the center of the wedge of Ropers had knuckle-size chunks of amber and smoky crystal hanging around his neck—the only one of them with any ornamentation. He seemed to be slightly older than the rest. This had to be Kennett. He noticed instantly that the tunnel door was propped open. He didn't say a word; he just pointed. With shocking agility, a Roper ran straight through the circle of mountain men, leaped over the fire, and sprinted for the tunnel door.

But Tell and Wren were closer and quicker. They scrambled for the opening as the Roper closed in on them. They skidded through the gap under the tunnel door, kicked away the chunks of firewood, and fell into the tunnel, the door slamming shut above them.

Moments later, they thudded onto the tunnel floor, winded but with no time to catch any breath. Almost immediately the door swung open above them.

Tell pulled Wren to her feet and reached his left hand to the tunnel wall as he had on the way in. They sprinted away into the pitch black, driven by the sound of heavy feet thundering down the stairs behind them.

Tell and Wren could never have outrun the Roper in a race on open ground. But in a dark zigzagging tunnel, driven by fear, they were able to increase the distance between them because the Roper chose to run holding his flaming torch, slowing him just enough to give the siblings the advantage.

They hurtled right, right again, then up the stairs, and into Kun Anton's warehouse. Leaving the door propped open had saved their lives. After the absolute darkness of the tunnel, the moonlight spilling through the high vents was almost blinding.

All their experience of working and hunting together came to bear in an instant. They automatically moved to either side of the open door and waited without a word until the Roper hammered up the stairs, his flaming torch leading the way.

Fear gives you strength. Anger gives you strength. Wren and Tell waited until the Roper's head and neck emerged, then slammed the heavy door down as hard as they could, adding their own weight to the blow. The edge of the door scythed onto the Roper's head. The flaming torch flew out of his hand and rolled away into the warehouse as he lay there unmoving.

"Is he dead?" Wren, gone pale, asked.

"I'll make sure he is," Tell said, drawing his knife. After seeing their men yoked to rocks with strangler cords, Tell didn't need to think twice about it.

He never got to strike the blow.

"Tell! *Fire!*" Wren yelled. He looked up just as a pile of fine cloth became a hissing mass of flames. The Roper's rolling torch had ignited it. Flaming bits of cloth rose and danced through the air in every direction, propelled by their own heat. Charcoal. Wood. Grass baskets. Carpets. Grain. There was fuel everywhere.

"Run!" Wren yelled. Dodging the flaming cloth, they raced for the door as pile after pile of valuable goods from all over the land burst into flames behind them.

"We have to get Rumi!" Tell shouted. They slammed the warehouse door shut, hoping to seal the fire inside, and bolted for their friend's house.

They pounded in through the courtyard door, down the hallway, and through the kitchen.

"Rumi! We have to go!" Tell yelled as they ran into the living area . . .

. . . where the slender, weasel-like person was waiting for them, wearing a smile that gave them shivers.

"Oh!" Wren gasped as they skidded to a stop.

"Wren. Tell." The weasel person had a high-pitched voice. "Haven't you two been busy."

Tell already had Seka's knife in his hand when a pair of massive arms clamped around him from behind and lifted him off the ground. The same was happening to Wren— she was engulfed from behind. The last thing Tell remembered was his precious knife shattering on the tiled floor. A violent flash of light exploded behind his eyes, and then everything faded into a deep red darkness.

‡ ‡ ‡ ‡

From her hiding place in the storm drain, Rumi saw Tell and Wren being carried away, their bodies limp. Flames reached hungrily upward through the ventilation holes high on the walls of her beloved father's warehouse. At that moment she didn't care whether the flames stayed inside the warehouse or surged out and engulfed the entire city.

There is a hard place beyond tears, and for the first time in her life, Rumi found it. Dry-eyed, she retreated into the drain, curled up, and fell asleep.

25

Tell's dream was an unpleasant one about being chased through endless dark streets by a horde of people, but he tried to stay in it anyway. Somewhere in his brain, he knew that if he didn't wake up, he wouldn't have to face the next horrible ordeal waiting for Wren and himself. Also, every time he moved his head so much as a twitch, pain spiked from temple to temple. So he lay as still as he could and willed himself back to sleep—not a difficult task given all they'd been through. He began to slide back down that delicious slope when a hand shook his shoulder, shook it again.

"Tell, wake up." It was his sister.

Tell groaned, buried his face in the bed, and tried to keep sleeping. For a moment it seemed as if he would be allowed to, but then an almost-forgotten scent filled his nostrils. For Tell, this was a scent that made sleep impossible.

The nutty smell of baked oats, the sweet perfume of honey, with tangy hints of dried fig . . . This was the smell of happiness. A honey cake. His parents would bring them back up the mountain as a treat. One each for him and Wren, and never more than that. They were expensive. Luxuries. And still the best thing he and Wren had ever eaten, because their honey cakes were further sweetened with relief at the return of their mother and father. They hadn't had one in two years.

Tell opened his eyes and, yes, Wren was dangling a honey cake inches from his face. He reached out, and she pulled it away, grinning.

"You have to see this!" she exclaimed. He sat up. "Look!" He looked.

On a low table against the wall past the foot of their beds, there was a wooden plate piled high with honey cakes. More than they had ever seen. More than they could eat. Beside the plate were a jug and two drinking mugs.

"I woke up and they were there." Wren couldn't stop grinning. "Like magic."

She bit into the honey cake she had used to rouse Tell, groaning as she chewed, at first fast, then more slowly as she realized that, for once, she didn't have to bolt her food, which was the way everyone ate up the mountain. She truly savored what she was eating for the first time in her life.

Tell walked to the table, grabbed a honey cake in each

hand, bit into one, then the other, then the first again, as if he couldn't decide which one to eat. When he sighed in ecstasy, honey cake crumbs gushed into the air. Wren laughed. At that moment neither of them cared who had captured them, where they were, or what their future held. . . . They had honey cakes.

Only when they were both chewing happily did they actually look farther than the plate with the honey cakes. Their beds were made of a lustrous dark wood, their bedding was soft and clean (though not as clean as before they had slept in them), and the walls were covered in polished plaster dyed a deep rose color. The floor was laid with mint-green tiles etched with intricate repeating patterns in white. The windows were high and only partially shuttered, letting in stripes of golden light. They had never seen such a room. Rumi's house was luxurious, but not like this. They had never even imagined such a room. How could they? All they knew was stone and slate and cold drafts and clothing so rough their skin was permanently chafed. The only place they'd seen that was remotely similar was the sorcerer's top floor.

Tell stopped in midchew. "Uh, Wren?"

"What?" She had just popped a last piece of honey cake into her mouth.

"What if these are poisoned?"

"Don't care," Wren replied, and reached for another.

Tell nodded in agreement and bit into his third. The

jug held sweet, sharp lemon water, perfect for washing the cakes down. They were on their second mug when they heard a sharp double rap on the door, just as it swung open.

The weasel person stood in the doorway, clad in fine sandals, trousers, and a tunic of soft-looking, flowing cloth. Behind them stood a wide man and an even wider woman with grave faces, dressed plainly.

"I see you like honey cakes," said the weasel person. With their mouths full, all Wren and Tell could do was nod.

"My name is Selt. I'm sorry we had to . . . use force last night, but it seemed prudent. You're unpredictable, dangerous children."

"Is this your house?" Wren asked after gulping a mouthful of lemon water.

"Would that it were," Selt said with a smile. Wren and Tell frowned, puzzled, not understanding the answer. "No," Selt explained. "It's not my house."

"Then—"

Selt held up a hand. "All your questions will be answered. But before that, you need to be made presentable. You're rather . . . smelly, to be honest. And your clothes, well, they'll just have to be burned."

Tell and Wren shrugged. Being smelly was normal. After a while you didn't even notice. But their clothes . . . When they looked down at the old, stained, coarse, tattered tunics they were wearing in this fine room, they suddenly saw them in a new light.

They were ashamed. Embarrassed. Feelings that were jagged and uncomfortable to them. Feelings they'd never had before.

Selt smiled sadly, seeming to understand exactly. "Paulik and Syrinna will take care of you. They'll let me know when you're ready."

"Ready for what?"

Selt didn't respond, turned to leave, then turned back and gave them a serious look. "There's something you two need to understand. Where you are now, this situation . . . it's a good thing for you. So, resist your feral natures. Don't try to escape. Don't run off into a city where your lives are in danger, more than you know. Oh, don't worry, no one will stop you. But you'll never be allowed back here, and you'll have thrown away the best chance you'll ever have at a life worth living."

Wren and Tell had a hard time understanding Selt's way of speaking. Selt used words they'd never heard before, or in ways they were not used to. Selt noticed their confusion and sighed.

"What did I just say to you?"

"We're lucky to be here?" Wren guessed hesitantly.

"Exactly." And with that, Selt swung around and left.

Tell and Wren exchanged wary glances. Nothing in their lives, so far, had prepared them for any of this. Paulik pointed a blunt finger at Tell and beckoned him forward.

Tell winked at Wren. "As long as there are honey cakes,

I don't care about anything else." He scooped up one more and followed Paulik down the hallway.

Syrinna pointed at the platter, inviting Wren to take another, but the girl shook her head.

"I can't eat another bite." As she trailed Syrinna out of the room, she added, "And I never thought I'd say that."

Paulik picked up Tell's tunic and dropped it into the fire that was heating the water for his bath. The man never said a word—in fact, he was completely silent—but he communicated very clearly with movement, gestures, and his eyes. He nodded toward the bath, and Tell climbed into warm water for the second time in his life.

The People of the Black Glass were almost never naked, due to the cold, but Tell didn't feel at all self-conscious. The silent man had a discreet manner that removed all that. As Tell luxuriated in warmth, Paulik selected the root bulb of a plant with wavy leaves from a pile of them. He snapped off the leaves, tossed them into the fire, and crushed the bulb in a stone bowl. Adding water to the bowl, he whisked it with a forked stick until the mixture began to foam.

With Tell looking on fascinated, Paulik gestured for him to stand and make a cup of his hands. He poured some of the foaming mixture into Tell's hands and mimicked him rubbing it on himself. The mixture didn't have much smell, but the foam and bubbles slid pleasantly across Tell's skin. Paulik gave him more and indicated all the places Tell should wash. When Tell was done to Paulik's satisfaction, he reached out his hands for the stone bowl. Paulik gave it to him carefully, and Tell upended it over his own head, gave the bowl back, and lathered his hair into a mass of foam. A moment later, Tell was yelping. Foam had gotten into his eyes. He dropped like a stone into the bath, scrubbing his eyes and wriggling like a frog.

When he came up, eyes stinging and red, a strange gurgling sound filled the bathing room. The moment Tell realized that Paulik was laughing, the big man stopped and clamped his mouth closed.

But not before Tell saw something that afterward he tried to talk himself out of seeing. Paulik had no tongue. Just a scarred stump in the back of his throat. Which explained why he didn't speak.

Tell dried himself in silence and dressed in new clothes: pants and a tunic made of a patterned fabric so fine that it whispered across his skin when he moved. Paulik pointed at a pair of slippers waiting neatly on the floor and looked on patiently as Tell figured out how to get them onto his feet.

Then he beckoned Tell across the bathing room to a big, flat, wooden case hanging on the wall. He opened the lid of the case, and Tell saw that the inside was lined with two perfectly fitted, very thin pieces of black glass. So thin as to no longer be black. Behind the black glass was a sheet of something that gleamed like light on water. Together they threw Tell's image back at him, and he saw himself clearly for the first time in his life.

He saw a hollow-eyed, tight-faced, intense creature in the shadowlands between boy and man. With a blade for a nose and a mouth that was too big. He raised his hand to his face, and so did the reflection. Then he scowled and strode away. He didn't need to know what he looked like. It was all too much. Paulik closed the case.

As Paulik led him out of the room, Tell paused. Just as they never apologized for anything, the People of the Black Glass never showed gratitude for anything. It was considered a sign of weakness. But after thinking about it, Tell lifted his arm, smelled his own armpit, and sighed happily, then walked on ahead. Behind him, he heard that gurgle again. But he did not look and decided he never would again.

Paulik next took him to a room lined from floor to ceiling with ornate, hand-pressed tiles. The floor was covered with patterned rugs, low sofas, and piles of tasseled cushions. He indicated that Tell should sit on one of the sofas, then left. Tell decided that the room made him dizzy, there was so much color and texture. Then a different doorway opened, and Wren entered, followed by Syrinna.

Tell's mouth dropped open.

Wren was transformed. She also wore pants and a tunic, but whereas Tell's clothes were patterned, Wren's were solid colors. Her tunic was sky blue, her pants a soft gray. The material had a slight shine to it from certain angles, so that when she moved, Wren seemed to glimmer and ripple with light.

"I . . . you . . . you don't look like you!" That was all Tell could manage.

"Same for you." Wren chuckled, delighted. "It feels . . . I don't know what. Different." Tell nodded.

Syrinna left, smiling to herself. Tell waited for the door to close behind her before talking.

"That man, Paulik . . . ," Tell began softly, "he has no tongue. It's been cut out. That's why he doesn't talk and never opens his mouth. Well, hardly ever."

"Syrinna didn't say a single word either!" Wren added. "Do you think she's also—you know?"

Tell shrugged. Wren took in the room. "And we thought Rumi's house was something!"

"I wonder where she is," Tell mused.

"I hope she's—"

Wren was interrupted by Selt's return. "Now, that's better! We'll get your hair cut later." Selt beckoned them. "Come."

"Where to?" Tell asked.

"To meet the person who rescued you. And, if I were you, to thank them."

Wren was tugging her tunic this way and that, intrigued by the way it changed color. "Rescued us?" she asked.

"From what?" Tell added.

"From yourselves, mostly." Selt walked out of the room, assuming that Tell and Wren would follow. And they did. There was no choice.

"You're not allowed in this side of the house without an escort," Selt told them, opening big double doors polished to a high sheen. They entered a circular room with a domed ceiling. It was filled with light from high windows, had rich, warm colors on the walls—dusky rose, faded orange, deep yellow, mint green—and big, square floor tiles as white as fresh snow. It was a beautiful room designed to create awe, and it did. They were both beginning to realize that, in a city made of mud bricks and plaster, color was found indoors. The wealthier someone was, the more color they had.

It took Tell and Wren a moment to notice the woman examining them from her place on a raised lounging sofa. She was striking and strong, with her glossy hair arranged in a gleaming knot above her head. Her slender neck glittered with a string of precious stones, a string of fingernail-size gold nuggets, and a string of amber lumps alternating with knobs of smoky crystal. Her tunic and pants lay close on her like a soft golden skin. She looked rich, powerful, and a little bit cruel.

"Isn't it nice to be clean and warm?" she asked. "And to wear clothes that don't scratch? And not be hungry, of course."

Only when she spoke did Tell and Wren realize who the woman was.

Their mother.

26

They had dreamed of seeing their mother again, many times. It's how people everywhere make loss bearable, if only for a moment. They had dreamed that she would stroll back into the village with a perfectly sound reason for being gone, and life would continue happily. Or they'd rescue her from cutthroats, and life would continue happily. Or they'd find her on a trail, mysteriously lost, and bring her home, and life would continue happily. Those were their childish dreams. But this? There was no way to dream this.

With their knees gone weak, neither Tell nor Wren could get their tongues to form words as they tried to compare the mother in their memory to the woman they saw in front of them. It was almost impossible, she was so different, so changed.

"Mo?" Wren breathed at last, barely able to utter the word.

"Don't call me that. Not down here," she said flatly. "Call me Lilit."

"But that's not your—your name is—"

"It's Lilit," she said sharply. "You need to get used to it. I won't answer to anything else."

In their dreams, they'd always imagined their mother being overjoyed to see them again. This . . . this seemed the very opposite.

"Da is . . . he's—"

"Let's not talk about him, either. There's no point."

"There is to us—he's the one who stayed!" Tell said angrily. "He got a sliver in his eye the day before everyone came down the mountain. He's blind!"

"Then you know what will happen next." Her tone was so matter-of-fact, it was impossible for them to tell what she was feeling or if this news mattered to her at all. "And that means there's no reason for you to go back up the mountain."

"He's not dead! Not yet! But the chief is!" blurted Wren. "And the men, they've been—"

Lilit, their mother, whoever this woman was now, stood up suddenly, stopping Wren.

"I don't want to talk about them. Nothing about that mountain has any interest to me, including the people. They're forgotten. That *life* is forgotten. Is that clear?"

"Including us?" Wren asked sharply. "Are we forgotten?"

Lilit wavered. "I tried. Oh, I tried. But I couldn't forget

you." Her voice, at last, sounded more like the one they remembered. "And now, by the fates, here you are in front of me, with nowhere else to go."

Tell felt her softening; he could see it. He could see the mother he remembered shining through the woman they'd just met. She gestured them toward her.

"Come," she said. "Come to me."

Come to me. It was all Tell had dreamed of these past two years—to hear those words. He felt as if he were melting too as he took a step toward her.

"No." Wren thrust her arm across her brother's chest. Then she met her mother's insulted eyes.

"What happened? Why didn't you come back? We've asked ourselves that question every day since. Too many times. Two. Years'. Worth!"

"Yes," Tell reluctantly agreed. "We need to know. We *deserve* to know."

Lilit rolled her eyes to the heavens. "I sent him a message. Your father didn't tell you?" They both shook their heads. "By the mountain's cruel skin! Did he think not telling you would mean it hadn't happened?"

"What hadn't happened?" Wren demanded.

"How did you end up here, in this house?" Tell followed.

Both were staring at her stubbornly, hurt shining from their eyes. Lilit looked away from their gazes as if looking away from a too-bright sun.

"Every time we came down the mountain to trade our glass, do you know what I did while the men were being robbed blind by that thief Kun Anton? I learned as much as I could about Halfway. I always knew I'd live here one day. I learned where real power lay; I learned who'd grown fat and lazy and who wanted more."

"How did you learn all that?" Wren asked.

Lilit pointed at her eyes, then her ears, and last at her rouged lips. "They take us for idiots down here. Sometimes that's useful. People say things they shouldn't when they think you won't understand." Lilit smiled bitterly, then continued.

"Two years ago, I slipped away from the other women in the marketplace. I came here. I knew this was the weakest ruling house, the worst quarter. I knocked on the door and offered them something they wanted, the most precious thing I had to give. . . ." She paused for a long time, as if thinking through a complicated series of events, then finally just said: "They liked my offer. I stepped in off the street without a second thought . . . and here I am."

"What did you offer them?" Tell asked, not liking the feeling in his chest, as if his heart had grown too big for it suddenly.

Lilit ignored his question.

"You didn't have to think about leaving us? Not for one second?" Wren's anger was written in her eyes.

"No, I didn't." She faced them directly so that they could

see the dark truth in her. "You see, I'd already decided to leave you. I'd decided to step off the Narrows on the way back up. I wasn't going to endure one more winter up there. I couldn't." She gestured at the room around them. "This is better than stepping off a cliff, don't you think?"

Tell and Wren had no way to answer her question. They said nothing.

"Should I apologize? Maybe so." She tossed her head haughtily. "Oh, I know the People of the Black Glass never say they're sorry; they mistakenly believe it's a sign of weakness. But down here, where it's civilized, we do. So here it is, the first apology of your lives, and I mean it: I'm sorry. I know I left you without a mother and with many unanswered questions . . . but I'd do it again. For me, there was no choice."

No choice for her? Maybe. But Tell's and Wren's faces showed the deep hurt they held, because of that choice. With a jarring thud, Tell realized that his idea of his mother was painted with the best memories of her but not all the memories, not the whole of her. And the whole of her was hard to consider.

"What did you offer them?" Tell pressed. "Why did they take you in?"

Again, Lilit waved the question away. "Now I have a chance to fix things with you, as long as you understand that I'm not the person you remember. To repeat: down here, I'm Lilit, and Lilit only. Down here, I'm nobody's mother." Then she reached all the way to the heart of what she was telling them.

"You see, I told everyone that I had no children, because that's what they wanted to hear. And, more importantly, because I thought it'd be easier to forget you if I did. And so that's the way it has to be." This was all said in such a casual tone, she could have been talking about giving away a pair of worn shoes.

It was more than Tell and Wren could deal with. They had to stick to simple things that made sense to them.

"Is this your house, then?" was all Tell could think to ask.

"I'm working on it," said Lilit with a little smile, the first they'd seen.

"What does *that* mean?" Wren asked.

"Enough. It's time to talk about you two. Try not to lie too much; I know more than you think." She raised a perfect eyebrow. "I know you entered the city by yourselves, two days behind the men. Which means you made the journey down by yourselves, which means you broke every rule there is to break, which means you can't go back. Why?"

"Not every rule," said Tell. "I had permission to come."

"From your father?"

"Yes. I can go back. And I will," he swore. "A father's word is law."

"Only in an isolated, ignorant, practically unpopulated mountain village," Lilit said, disdain clear in her voice.

"We came down to sell his black glass and find medicine for his eye," Wren told her defiantly. "We're going to save him! We don't want to be orphans. We don't want to go and live with other people. We didn't even know you were *alive*!"

Lilit turned to her, arching one of her fine eyebrows once again. She never used to do that up in the village, thought Wren. "And he gave you permission to make the journey, too? That surprises me."

Wren's silence was the answer.

"So you can't go back," Lilit surmised.

"She didn't want to live in the chief's house," Tell explained. "His wife—"

"Would've pushed you off a cliff as soon as she got the chance," finished their mother.

"That's why I—" Wren started to say.

"Why you took a one-way journey down the mountain, just like me. Only at a much younger age and by yourselves. Which is impressive." Lilit surveyed them, pleased. "I'm proud of you both. I'm sure it wasn't easy."

She then stepped closer, and for a moment the mother they dreamed of and the woman in front of them were one and the same.

"You're safe now. And I promise you, I'll make sure that me leaving the mountain . . . and leaving you . . . turns out to be the best thing I've ever done for us." Her hands reached out for them, but she didn't quite make contact, as if waiting for their permission. Tell looked at Wren. Whatever they decided, they would decide together. Wren nodded.

At that very moment, Selt entered, moving urgently, crossed to Lilit, and murmured softly in her ear. Lilit turned to Tell and Wren and pointed to a small door at the back of the circular room.

"Go with Selt. I have an important visitor. I'll see you later."

The moment for them to touch their mother for the first time in two years was clearly over.

As they passed through the small door, they heard the double doors open. Through the narrowing gap of the small door, Tell peeked back and saw Kennett, the leader of the Ropers, enter the circular room. Then the door clicked shut.

But not before Tell saw his mother open her arms and embrace the man whose actions threatened to wipe almost everyone they knew off the face of the earth.

27

"Life is full of surprises, yes?" Selt said as they retraced their steps through the vast house to their room. "I suppose your heads are spinning."

Wren nodded. It was all she could manage.

"Mine's been spinning since we came down the mountain," Tell admitted. "I thought she was dead. I really did." He put his chin to his chest, unable to continue.

"I suppose she is, in a way," Wren muttered thoughtfully. "Since we're not allowed to call her that. Mo."

"She has no choice," Selt said quietly. They'd reached their room, and much to their surprise, Selt came in with them, closed the door, picked up a honey cake, and took a bite. "I can't resist these; they'll be the death of me."

"A great way to die," said Tell, scooping up a honey cake for himself.

Selt swallowed. "Here's the plan for you. Once you

learn a few rudimentary manners and grooming and such, you'll be presented as Lilit's very capable niece and nephew, down from the mountains. Then a decision will be made."

"About what?" Wren asked.

"Whether to keep you in the household and, if so, what training you should each receive, where you might be most useful based on your talents and such. It's a great honor just to be considered and definitely a measure of Lilit's influence. She's been working hard to make this possible ever since you were seen entering the city. It's a chance at a comfortable life for you. And maybe more than just comfortable. This is a time of change, and therefore opportunity."

Tell and Wren barely breathed, they were listening so carefully. Selt shot them a sly look.

"I'm telling you this because I've followed you around Halfway, off and on, for the last few days, and it's clear that there's no end to the trouble you're willing to walk into. I want you to be able to think about this situation ahead of time and get used to it, because I know what your first reactions will be, and they'll be the wrong ones and will consign you to a life of misery."

Tell jutted his jaw stubbornly. "You can't know what my reaction would be!"

Selt smiled. "You'd get angry, you'd say that no one's going to tell you what to do or decide your future for you no matter who they think they are, then you'd stomp out, and if someone tried to stop you, you'd do your best to make them regret it."

Tell's face burned. Wren burst out laughing. "That's exactly how he'd react! Even worse if he's hungry!"

"Okay, Selt," Tell said, "if you're so clever, how would Wren react?"

"Yes!" Wren said eagerly. "What would I do?"

"You'd ask the wrong questions at the wrong time," said Selt.

"You're right!" crowed Tell. "That's what she'd do."

"No," said Wren. "I'd ask the right question. Just one."

"Which is what?" asked Selt, intrigued.

Wren made them wait as she thought about it. Then she nodded decisively. "I would ask who owned this house. Not who lived here. Who owned it."

"And why would you ask that?" Selt's eyes danced with curiosity.

"Because that's who the most powerful person would be. No matter where they sat or what they wore, that's where the power would be, and that's who decides everything in the end." Selt nodded thoughtfully. Or, impressed.

"I've learned some things since getting here," Wren said smugly. "From Rumi, mostly." And from her mother, though Wren barely dared admit that, even to herself.

Selt grunted and left without another word—but not without a quick, appraising glance back at them before disappearing down the hallway.

Tell took yet another honey cake. "Want one?"

Wren nodded, and he tossed it over. After a bite, Wren held the honey cake at arm's length. "You know what's strange?"

"Yes! I do know what's strange! *Everything!*" Tell practically shouted. "Cutthroats! Rumi! Ropers! Sorcerers! Apprentices! The chief is dead! Our mother is . . . Lilit? What kind of name is that, anyway? She didn't seem happy to see us. And that's not all—"

"That's not what I was going to say," Wren said, stopping Tell's tirade. She held up what was left of her honey cake. "Once you know you can have as many of these as you want, they don't taste as good. Not like the ones they brought back for us up the mountain."

Tell took the final bite of his honey cake. Savored it. Shook his head. "Those were always stale. These are better."

Sometimes it was easier to argue about small, unimportant things when everything else was totally overwhelming, but an argument about honey cakes was forestalled by the door opening.

Selt was accompanied by Paulik and Syrinna. "There are shoes under your beds. Put them on. We're going for a walk."

The biggest houses had high walls around their entire properties, and Selt led them out of a small side gate cut into the smooth ochre wall, guarded by a man as gnarled and as still as a tree trunk. Anyone on the street immediately moved away as they approached; it was as if the street belonged to them alone. Wren gestured at Paulik and Syrinna, walking two paces back. "We're not going to run away, you know."

"I should hope not," said Selt.

Tell looked back at them. He wondered if they were married. That would be a very quiet household, he thought.

"Tell me what you know about Halfway," Selt asked out of the blue.

Wren replied first. "No weapons, no fires, no fighting, trading only, four gates, four quarters, four ruling families, four sorcerers—"

"Five," corrected Tell. "One in the middle, the most powerful one."

"The sorcerers protect Halfway somehow," Wren elaborated. "But they also fight each other for the house in the middle."

And that was the extent of their knowledge about Halfway. Or, as much as they were willing to admit. They turned a corner to see yet another wall just as long as the first.

"Yes, there are four ruling families," said Selt, fingertips trailing along the wall.

"What do they rule?" asked Wren, putting her fingertips to the wall as well, copying Selt, as if some fresh wisdom would result in it.

"Many things. Practical things. Some would say boring things, but they're not. Streets, ditches, rules and laws, making sure trade is fair, making sure Halfway is a city worth living in."

"Well, they're not doing a very good job," Tell said, wrinkling his nose. "Every ditch smells of . . . you know what."

Selt laughed. "That's the smell of wealth."

"How can that be?" asked Wren.

"That smell means people, and without people, there is no wealth," answered Selt.

Tell and Wren had to think about that one. Then Wren suddenly said, "Ha!" and stopped, forcing the others to do the same. "I know what you're doing," she said triumphantly.

"Oh, really?" Selt's lips pursed in many different ways, this time to stop a smile.

"Yes! You're making a point," said Wren.

"And what point am I making?"

"What quarter is this?" demanded Wren. "It's impossible to tell. Everything looks the same."

"You see? She asks a lot of questions," Tell confided.

"I noticed." Selt nodded. "This is the Desert quarter."

Wren smacked her hand against the ochre wall. "This wall belongs to the family who rules the Desert quarter. You're making us walk all the way around it to impress us and show us how big the house is, so we understand how rich and powerful they are. But it's a waste of everyone's time."

"Why so?" Selt asked, a bit sharply.

"We knew that already, just from a plate of honey cakes. Who has more honey cakes than anyone can eat?"

Paulik and Syrinna gurgled with tongueless laughter behind them. Tell made sure not to look. Selt glanced away for a moment, with the beginnings of aggravation. Wren had that effect on people sometimes, Tell knew all too well.

"The family's name is Belton; it's an ancient family, one of the original four," Selt said at last. "The head is Ikarus Belton, and when he dies, which will be soon, he'll be succeeded by his son, Alin. You'd do well to learn their names and utter them with respect."

Tell and Wren shrugged, as if to say, *All right, we will.*

"What's our moth—" Tell caught himself. "How did Lilit get *here*? She said she offered them . . . those Beltons . . . the thing they wanted most!" Every time he thought about it, Tell felt his heart beating faster, and not in a good way.

"Ah." Selt smiled. "Lilit is a person of great vision and intelligence, as I'm sure you know. She's fearless and has an instinct for power. She's become indispensable to both Ikarus and Alin."

After a pause, Wren said, "I see," flatly.

"See what?" asked Tell.

Wren shook her head angrily. "It's going to be easier calling her Lilit now."

"What are you talking about?" Tell felt a dread he didn't understand.

"The old one, the father, the one who owns everything—she's his *wife!* That's how she got inside these walls; that's what she offered them. She didn't just leave our family—she joined someone else's." As Tell absorbed that information, Wren looked sharply at Selt. "Am I right?"

"Actually, you're not. Lilit's much too clever to marry anyone; then her power would be diminished, maybe even forfeit."

Tell felt a relief he didn't fully understand, and he thought Wren would too. But he was wrong.

"Then she offered them something even worse!" Wren persisted.

"In some ways, you're correct," Selt said softly. "She offered them an *idea*—a very dangerous one, but a way to more power. Everything here is always and forever will be about power."

"But they're already powerful!" Tell protested. "And wealthy!"

Selt looked up and down the street warily, then said, "In my experience, power and wealth only create the hunger for more."

There was an awkward silence along the high ochre wall, which spoke of wealth and power, as they thought about what their mother had done to become part of it, broken only when they heard the sound of impossibly heavy footsteps approaching from around the corner. It sounded as though a giant were coming. Selt held out a hand to still them as the source of the footsteps swung into view.

Three Ropers appeared, casting an intimidating shadow across them all. They carried no weapons, but their lock-step stride and the implacable judgment of their gaze were weapons enough. Tell and Wren had to summon every ounce of mountain training not to react. Had these men been in the warehouse? Would they recognize Tell and Wren if they had been? Tell was suddenly very glad for his recent transformation at the hands of Paulik. A sideways glance from Wren told him that she was thinking the same thing.

They also noticed that Selt, Paulik, and Syrinna did nothing as the Ropers passed, their braids swinging back and forth aggressively. Not a look, not a change of expression. They just stood there.

"Who are *they*?" asked Wren with feigned innocence once the men were safely gone. "Are those the Ropers we've been hearing about?"

"They're soldiers," said Selt evenly. "We don't call them Ropers. They don't like it."

"Well, why do they walk like that?" she asked.

"It's what soldiers do."

"Where are they from?" Tell pressed.

Selt looked at them with careful eyes and spoke in a careful tone. "They're from a far-off land where power is taken by force rather than earned; they're all that's left of a defeated army. Now, you may think that since they were defeated, they amount to very little. Just the opposite. They've lost everything, they have nowhere else to go, they're desperate, and they smell blood here. Be very, very wary around them. There's nothing they won't do."

"If they're so dangerous, why are they allowed in Halfway?" asked Tell. He couldn't stand it when things made no sense.

Selt smiled thinly, as if the question had a sour taste. "This quarter—our quarter—became uncontrolled as Ikarus grew old but wouldn't step aside for Alin. The streets weren't safe, not even in daylight. People left for other quarters. Houses stood empty. The marketplaces shrank almost to nothing, which meant the flow of money shrank almost to nothing.

"Then, one day, men like those you just saw strode in through the Desert gate and paid House Belton a visit. They had nothing to trade, they said, but they could make these streets safe again if the Beltons gave them permission. Which they did. And now . . ."

"Now House Belton can't do without them," Tell said.

"Yes," Selt admitted. "House Belton can't do without them."

Tell and Wren thought about this. Then Wren turned her attention to Selt. "And who do *you* work for?" she asked, making sure she asked sweetly.

"That's an interesting question." Selt was starting to look at the two with new respect. And wariness. "Today I work for you. Lilit asked me to take you into the markets and buy you whatever you wanted."

"If we're living inside these walls, there's nothing we need," Tell pointed out, and Wren nodded in agreement.

"It's not guaranteed you will be," Selt countered.

"We know," said Wren. "We understand."

"Then you should also understand that I need to be able to tell Lilit that I made you welcome today on her behalf." Selt looked quite serious. "Help me with that. What can I do that would please you, Wren?"

"Oh, that's easy," said Wren without a moment's thought. "Get our mule back."

"Your . . . mule?"

"Yes, his name's Rumble. He saved our life, and we love him."

"I used to beat him, like everyone else," Tell confessed. "But I stopped."

"He was taken by a man called Rold Roland," Wren continued. "He has a disgusting black tooth with a green stone in it, and he lives behind walls with sharp stones on top."

"He lives in this quarter," Tell added. "On the edge of it."

Selt looked at Paulik and Syrinna, who both nodded. "We know who he is," Selt said.

"Well, he stole our father's black glass and tried to kidnap us," Tell continued. "He was going to sell us. I'm going to cut off his fat fingers and take his rings. He'll never rub them together again."

Tell said that as a statement of fact, not as bragging. Selt smiled bleakly. "And you? Other than cutting off Rold Roland's fat fingers, what would please you today?"

Tell was about to ask for medicine for Seka's eye, but an even more urgent need overtook him suddenly. "Take us to Kun Anton's house, where you found us. We have a friend there."

"Rumi Anton? That's who you were looking for last night."

"Yes," said Wren. "She's helped us a lot. But she's been unlucky, too. She's hiding there."

"We want to make sure she's all right," Tell said, glancing around to make sure they were alone on the street. "But you can't tell anyone. We don't think anybody should know she's alive."

"And why is that?" Selt asked with growing interest.

Tell and Wren told Selt a shortened version of their ordeal while standing in the ashes inside the warehouse, looking at the hole in the ground that led to the tunnel. The stone walls were still there, but that was all. Most of the roof had caved in. Even the stairs down into the tunnel were burned. Rumi's family had lost every last thing in the warehouse. The house was unscathed, as were the surrounding properties, thanks to the way the warehouse was built. But Rumi? She was nowhere to be found. Tell had even dropped into the ditch on the street to shout her name into the storm drain.

They started with the moment Rumi tossed a stone at Tell at her gate. They ended with seeing the men making tools. They left out all mention of killing the Roper. They said they had no idea how the fire started.

Tell definitely did not bring up seeing their mother—Lilit!—embrace Kennett, the leader of the Ropers. He hadn't even told Wren yet, and until she knew, no one else could.

Selt's response surprised them. There was a flash of fear behind it. Grabbing them both with strong hands, Selt pulled them close.

"Speak of these things to no one else! Tell no one you were living here when the fire started. You'll be hung from the wall just for that, and they won't care that you're children. You need to stay behind our walls, and you need to forget your friend Rumi. She's doomed. The only lives that should concern you from now on are your own."

That flash of fear they saw in Selt? It was fear for them.

28

"I know where Rumi is," Tell declared later that afternoon. When he got no response, he looked over to see that Wren was already fast asleep on her bed, even though there was still plenty of light left in the day. Tell thought about waking her, as she'd done to him earlier with the honey cake, but it took too much effort. Even thinking about it took too much effort, so he flopped over and fell asleep. Being safe and warm and full of food had allowed exhaustion to flood in and overwhelm them.

The big meal they'd just eaten in the kitchen hadn't helped matters either. Selt had left to attend to other business, and they were seated at a table in the corner by a kitchen servant, where they could marvel at the sheer amount of food, cooking charcoal, and cooking tools available. "How much can one family eat?" wondered Wren.

They were given a series of delicious and sometimes

startlingly small dishes neither of them had ever heard of, let alone tasted. The only thing all the food had in common was that it was cold. It took Tell and Wren most of the meal, and discovering a bite mark in one of the chops, to real- ize that they were eating food from the night before, from the main part of the house; the part they weren't allowed into without an escort, even though their mother lived there.

As they ate at the table in the corner and watched cooks, laundry maids, and cleaners passing back and forth, some carrying bed pans exuding the smell of wealth, something began to dawn on Tell and Wren. They were not going to be seen as the niece and nephew of a powerful member of the household.

"We're going to be servants!" Tell hissed.

"If we're 'presentable enough,'" Wren added icily.

A look passed between brother and sister. It was a look that would have worried anyone who knew them even a little. Luckily, the only people who saw it were Paulik and Syrinna, and they couldn't talk even if they had something to say. When their meal was over, they escorted Tell and Wren back to their room and made it clear they were to stay there until called.

For the second time in a day, Tell tried to resist waking, tried to stay inside a dream he was having. This dream was a good one. He was high on the mountain with his father.

They were stalking a fat little rock jumper deer. Seka indicated that the rock jumper was his to take. The air was clean, and the light was rosy, Tell's bow felt supple in his hands, his feet were sure, and his eye was keen. What he needed to do and what he could do were the same thing, and that simple certainty made him feel strong in a way he hadn't for quite a while. The internal warmth from hunting with his father gave him strength too.

But having his earlobe pinched hard by Selt caused the dream and the feeling to disappear in an instant. His eyes flashed open angrily, and he was awake.

"Lilit has time for you now," Selt announced.

"Guess what? We have to wash and dress in *different* clothes," said Wren. "Again." There were two bowls of water on the table for washing. New clothes were folded neatly at the foot of their beds.

"Why?" Tell asked grumpily. "She knows what we look like."

"She's seeing you through the eyes of others," Selt explained. "When you don't know someone, all you can first judge them on is how they look. So, what you wear and how you look down here is very important. It says a lot about you."

"But anyone can wear whatever they want," objected Wren. "That doesn't tell you who they are."

"That's true. But people here think it does. So it does," said Selt firmly.

‡ ‡ ‡ ‡

Though not as grand as the round room they'd first met her in, Lilit's chambers could have contained their entire home up on the mountain, with room to spare. Lilit proudly pointed this out to them as she dismissed her maid. She also had a room for meeting visitors, with chairs and a carved bench to sit on, as good as anything Wren had seen in Rumi's house. As with the kitchen, Wren wondered how many things one person actually needed. But when it came to clothes . . . an endless supply, clearly. Lilit was wearing a tight tunic that seemed to be made from the same dark blue cloth the Ropers wore. A small necklace of amber and crystals adorned her neck, like Kennett's. Seeing it made Tell's stomach sour.

Lilit indicated the bench they were to sit on. Her movements were abrupt, a little jerky. Her face was drawn. She was trying to hide the fact that she was tense, but they knew her too well.

There was yet another plate of honey cakes on a table in front of them, so fresh that they glistened. Their mouths watered at the scent, but neither reached for one. They didn't want to show any kind of weakness. Lilit looked them up and down for an uncomfortably long time, then lowered herself into a chair across from the bench.

"It's good you're both handsome and strong. And you

clean up well. All you need are haircuts, and you'll at least look the part."

"Look the part of what?" Wren asked. "What are you talking about?"

"I thought we'd have more time, but we don't. Things have changed since yesterday."

"What things?" Wren asked. Lilit was making no sense.

"Selt told me you know whose house this is."

"Yes. The family in charge of this quarter," Tell said. "Desert."

"Ikarus Belton," added Wren.

"And his son, Alin," their mother finished. "Two of the most powerful men in the city. You'll be meeting them tomorrow, and if all goes well, you'll have a position in this house—"

"And if it doesn't go well?" Tell interrupted.

Lilit leaned forward aggressively. "It will! It has to! Very soon, the only safe place in the city may be behind these walls."

Tell and Wren scowled. They were beginning to hate the way people didn't say what they meant in Halfway. Lilit thought before trying to explain.

"I can't say anything more, but you have the luck, whether good or bad nobody knows yet, to be here at a time of great change. And change is always dangerous. But if you come out on the right side of it, the light of heaven will shine down upon your head."

Heaven? Their mother had never talked about heaven or anything like it when she lived up the mountain!

"So, you're lucky to be here, too," Wren suggested.

Lilit seemed to find that funny. Or anyway, she smiled. "I've worked too hard and done too much to want to call this luck. But yes, I suppose I'm lucky. Whatever the outcome, I'd rather be here than anywhere else. I want you to remember that. Whatever happens, remember me here, not up that godforsaken mountain. This is the life I chose for myself."

"And now for us," Tell said quietly.

"Yes, by the fates, for you too—hopefully. But there's not much I can do if you fail tomorrow. So be polite—meaning, answer the questions you're asked, and don't talk back. Be respectful—meaning, stay where they put you, and keep your eyes on the floor. Be grateful; show that you know how lucky you are to be here and not on that horrible mountainside."

Tell and Wren shared a stubborn look that Lilit recognized instantly.

"I know that look," she said. "What is it? Spit it out."

"We're going to be servants, aren't we?" Wren's question was really more of a statement.

"Have you not been listening to me?" Lilit's voice rose dangerously; she really was on edge. "A storm is coming, a violent one. The only shelter will be behind these walls. It doesn't matter what you have to do to be here."

"Will we have to carry pots full of other people's poo?" Tell asked.

"If it means you can stay, then yes; and you'll carry them gladly. And thank me for the chance to do it."

Wren chuckled.

"What?" asked Lilit sharply.

"You'd never have said that up the mountain, *Lilit*."

Lilit's eyes blazed. Wren knew that the way she'd said her name angered their mother, because it was intended, and heard, as an insult. Which pleased Wren enormously. Then Selt entered and gave Lilit a nod. Their mother pulled herself up tall and looked at them down her sharp nose.

"I've done much worse than carry night pots to get here, but it's been worth it. I have real power. I've chosen my own future." She shot to her feet. "Come and see what I mean. Perhaps it will change your view of me."

Lilit led them through the house, muttering furiously. "How can people who were, are, and always will be *nothing* feel so superior to others?"

"It's the thin air. It affects our brains," Tell said cheerfully. "That's what the weapons-keeper at the gate told me."

Wren cackled. They were both enjoying this. It was a small measure of revenge, but at least it was something.

Selt stood in front of a plain double door, which Lilit flung open. "There!" And in front of them lay a huge interior garden surrounded on all sides by the house. A sheltered, hidden garden. Trees laden with fruit Wren and Tell had never seen before grew in every direction, most of them mature and healthy. But there were also newly planted saplings, where there was room for them. Wren thought of their sad, stubborn little garden plot up the mountain and how much she and her mother had struggled to grow anything in it; there was no comparison.

In pride of place at the center of the garden grew a stout old oak tree, beautifully shaped. A tree that had clearly witnessed generations of Beltons. Tell spotted a branch that would make a fine bow and wondered how much trouble he'd get into for harvesting it. No doubt a lot.

There were also meticulously tended rows of vegetables, spice bushes, and edible and inedible flowers. This was the very opposite of the poisoner's garden in the sorcerer's house. Wren wondered who did all the work and when she could meet them. Gardening questions were already lining up in her head, starting with finding out the names of everything she could see.

"Where is he?" Lilit asked Selt, who indicated a corner of the garden. Lilit led them in that direction until they could hear a rhythmic crunching sound from behind a big bush. Wren's face lit up, and then she was bounding past everyone else and around the bush, where she could barely believe what she saw: a small, old, ugly mountain mule gorging himself on pomegranates.

"Rumble!" She threw her arms around his shaggy neck.

Rumble raised his head for an instant and seemed to grin, showing his worn-down yellow teeth stained crimson with pomegranate juice. Then he reached his dripping muzzle toward another luscious fruit.

With Tell grinning and Lilit and Selt both looking on pleased, Wren groomed Rumble with her fingers, rubbing his ears until the old mule groaned happily. Then, with a cry of anguish, she spied the fresh, crisscrossed lash marks on his back. Rumble had had his share of suffering too. Wren stroked the marks, as if to smooth them away. Rumble gurgled gratefully between mouthfuls.

"How did you get him back?" Tell asked Selt.

Selt handed Lilit a small bag. Lilit held it out for Tell. Tell took it cautiously. "Open it," she said tenderly.

Tell undid the string and tipped ten stone rings out onto the palm of his hand. They gleamed in the late-afternoon light. Ten stone rings and a blackened front tooth, with a round green stone set in the middle of it. Tell almost dropped it all in shock. There was still a smear of blood around the blackened root.

He could feel Lilit watching him. He managed to say, "He deserved it."

"I told you," she said, her voice soft. "I have real power."

Tell tipped the rings and the tooth back into the bag and held it out to Lilit. She pushed it back toward him.

"It's yours," she said. "The beginning of your own fortune." And for a moment it seemed as if Lilit was going to pull him into an embrace, but she just leaned closer so that she could talk into his ear.

"I can still be your mother, in secret. I know you want that. Do well tomorrow, and your new life will begin. Everything you learned on that godforsaken mountain: all the skills, all the ideas you think are normal—like putting people out on the ice—those are your weapons down here. These people, they're as soft as those figs you and your sister stole."

Tell was startled by that piece of knowledge, just as Lilit intended, judging by the twitch of a smile on her lips.

"Do as I say. Help me when I need it. In a time of change like this, a strong and decisive young man like you—there's no limit to what you can be."

Tell didn't know what to say or how to feel about what his mother had just whispered. But he had no chance to decide as an angry braying echoed in the garden, followed by a yelp of pain.

A stable hand had arrived to take Rumble back to the stables at the far end of the garden and paid the price. Struggling not to laugh out loud, Wren easily led Rumble away from the pomegranate bush and coaxed him down the path, handing the nervous stable hand the halter once the old mule was moving.

"If you want Rumble to do something, you have to ask him, and then wait until he agrees," Wren advised. "Otherwise, well . . . and never hit him. It doesn't work."

After one last scratch behind Rumble's ears, Wren returned, grinning happily. Her teeth were stained crimson too. She held out a ripe pomegranate to Tell. There was a split in the skin, and a row of seeds gleamed shyly inside it, like rubies. "These may be better than figs," Wren declared.

"You can't eat them inside," said Lilit. "And not in those clothes."

Wren looked down at herself. Her beautiful tunic was stained with drops of crimson juice. "Oh!" she exclaimed.

"I think I'll stick to figs," Tell decided.

"There's work to be done. I must go," Lilit said. "Get a good night's sleep. I'll be presenting you first thing in the morning." Then her dark eyes landed on Selt. "You'll be needed later. It's going to be a busy night."

Lilit strode away gracefully through the beautiful garden, her head high, her tunic brushing against rows of flowers, leaving a trail of fallen petals behind her.

"What do you think?" asked Wren, wincing as a thin black glass blade wielded by Syrinna sliced through her hair. What used to be a wild tangle growing down past her shoulders was now going to end neatly halfway down her neck.

"Well, I know I hate this," Tell grunted as Paulik shaved the hair at the back of his neck with another black glass blade.

Black glass was still sharper than anything else in the

known world. Not that the People ever thought to cut their hair with it, up the mountain. They just tied it back and forgot about it.

"No, I mean . . . her. This house. What's happening tomorrow. What do you think?"

Tell gave a sideways look toward Paulik, indicating to Wren that they shouldn't talk about it here. Paulik gently placed his hand on top of Tell's head and turned it back into position to continue cutting. There was a fresh abrasion on the tongueless man's biggest knuckle. That's the knuckle that usually makes the first contact with a face when throwing a punch. Or with a tooth.

Selt sauntered in, circled them both, clearly pleased. "What a transformation! You'll be kept on because purely you're both so beautiful."

Paulik and Syrinna were also very pleased with their handiwork and kept stepping in to lop a stray hair here and there, until Wren and Tell waved them off and backed away.

"That's enough for one day!" Wren protested.

"And I do not want to see myself again," Tell told Paulik, who grinned but, thankfully, did not laugh.

Selt followed them into their room and closed the door. Wren flopped back on her bed.

"I don't know why I'm so tired. We've hardly done anything today."

"It's the tension in the air," Selt explained. "Don't worry

about tomorrow. It's just a formality. As long as you look the part—and now you do—they'll lose interest in you right away. They're concerned about much more than two mountain children at the moment."

"But what does that *mean*?" Wren asked doggedly. "Lilit keeps talking about it, but she doesn't really *say* anything."

"It's better you don't know any more than you do, which is already far too much. Just keep out of the way." Selt's voice lowered. "But don't stop being the feral creatures you are just yet. Stay ready for anything."

Tell shook his head at Wren. "Have you noticed that nobody ever says what they mean in this place?"

"Yes, I have. It's terrible."

"I have something for you, Tell, and then I must go." Selt pulled out a slender, leather-wrapped bundle. "It's to replace the one that broke."

Tell unrolled the soft leather, and his breath caught in wonder at the object revealed. It was clearly a knife, with a handle made of rough deer antler. But the blade . . . the blade wasn't made of black glass or any other kind of stone; nor was it forged out of the crude bronze they'd seen here and there, which was soft and useless and couldn't hold an edge. This blade gleamed a dull silver and tapered to a point narrower than black glass could ever bear, no matter how pure or how perfectly worked.

Tell turned it over and over again. "What is this made of?"

Selt looked pleased. "I don't know. It's the only one I've

ever seen. I bought it from a faraway traveler who'd run out of money. He'd bought it from someone else, even farther away. It's not as sharp as black glass, but it's sharp enough and much stronger."

Tell ran a scarred thumb along the edge of the knife. "What are those words, again?" he asked.

"What words?" Selt's eyebrows furrowed.

"When someone does something good for you? What are the words?" Tell's brow was furrowed as he tried to remember.

"Ah. Yes." Selt's eyes softened. "The words are 'thank you.'"

"That's right." Tell picked up his new knife to test its balance, until Wren elbowed him.

"You need to *say* them," she said. "The words."

Startled, Tell looked to Selt, who nodded gravely.

"Oh. Right. So . . . thank you," Tell said for the first time in his life.

"It's my pleasure," Selt replied, then gave them each a little bow before leaving.

"I like Selt," Wren said. Tell grunted agreement and continued to caress his new knife, engrossed. His sister was focused on something more, though.

"Now can we talk?" she asked irritably. Tell looked up and nodded.

Wren took a breath, squaring her shoulders. "First, do you like it here?"

Tell deliberated for a moment, then: "I saw her with the leader of the Ropers this morning. What's his name?"

Wren's eyes narrowed. "Kennett. Where did you see them?"

"He came into that round room as we were leaving. She . . . she put her arms around him."

"I don't like that," Wren said quietly.

"Nor do I," said Tell. "In that warehouse, do you remember? We heard the men say they were making weapons for the Ropers. And Hammerhead said they had a sorcerer working with them. And . . . Lilit . . . says it's going to be a busy night. Why? What does that mean?"

"Everyone's scared—that's all I know," Wren observed.

"Oh, also," Tell added, "I think I know where Rumi is."

"Selt said we should stay behind these walls."

Tell stood up, tucked his new knife into the sheath on his belt. "You know what? I'm sick of people telling us where to be, and what to think and say, and what to wear, and what to do or not do—no matter who they are." He grinned bleakly in a way that showed Wren the face of the man he might become, if they lived long enough. "And no matter how many honey cakes they put in front of us."

Wren stood as well. "And we all know how much you like honey cakes."

29

Getting out of House Belton was easy. They simply left through the side gate. As Selt had said, no one tried to stop them, or even gave them a second glance, not even the two night guards at the gate. But navigating the streets of Halfway in the dark was a different thing altogether. The task was hard enough in daylight. At night it was almost impossible for two children who'd known nothing but a naked mountainside a week ago. There were lamps in alcoves here and there and light coming from barred windows, but most of the streets and alleyways were just long pools of different kinds of darkness.

Also, it was as if Halfway had two entirely different populations, one for day and one for night. The night people were much more dangerous and aggressive. People turn nasty when they think they can do things without being seen or identified, Tell and Wren discovered. They had to draw their knives twice, the second time standing back-to-back, ready to strike, before the group of drunken men taunting them realized that the price of their sport might be too high and moved on.

"All those fine words about Halfway being peaceful and nobody fighting, that's just rubbish!" Tell said disgustedly.

"You mean it's just the smell of wealth," Wren corrected snidely as they arrived at Kun Anton's house, out of breath.

They didn't bother with the house, except to look for a lamp. Once they had one, they waded into the tragic ashes of the warehouse and jumped down into the tunnel.

"I was right!" Tell exclaimed, holding the lamp high.

Rumi's small footprints were clear in the fresh ash, leading bravely into the pitch black of the tunnel. They were the only ones; her trail was a sad evocation of awful events.

"She must've been very scared," Wren fretted as they followed her footprints into the tunnel. In unspoken agreement, Wren and Tell made sure they didn't step on the footprints. And once they'd passed, the side-by-side tracks made it look as if the three of them had made the journey together.

The stairs at the other end were still there, the door propped open. Tell and Wren waited silently for many moments until they were sure no one was hiding behind the propped-up door, waiting to slam it down on them. Though they were sure there was no one in the warehouse, they still came up out of the ground like ghosts.

The area where the men had been held captive was deserted, though the circle of flat rocks they had been tied to and the ashes of the fire in the middle remained. Moving through the warehouse toward the door, Wren grabbed Tell's arm.

"I know whose warehouse this is!" she whispered.

"What do you mean?" Tell murmured. Murmurs are softer than whispers.

"These flat slabs of rock. Where else have we seen them?"

"Rold Roland's house! In that room with the big bird." Wren nodded. "This is *his* warehouse?" Wren nodded again. "But Rumi said they were enemies. This means . . . they weren't?" Tell exhaled angrily. "*Everything's* a lie in Halfway!"

"Oh! Do you think Rold Roland's got Rumi?" Wren asked suddenly.

"No, I don't," Tell assured her. He reached into his tunic and pulled out the bag Lilit had given him. "Bring the lamp closer." He poured the stone rings and the blackened tooth with its inset emerald into his palm. The emerald twinkled lusciously in the lamplight.

Wren guessed what the handful meant. "Lilit did this to get Rumble back?"

"Well, Selt did. And Paulik. I meant to show you, but I didn't want to spoil your time with Rumble."

"It wouldn't have. They whipped him! An old mule!

I hope they're all dead." Wren stalked toward the door. Not for the first time, Tell had the thought that his sister was a lot more ruthless than he was. A lot more like their mother.

Like Kun Anton's, the warehouse here was separate from the house. They were far across the yard and around the corner from where they'd jumped the jagged wall that first day in Halfway. Looking for the gate, they found something very sad . . . but not wholly unexpected.

In a secluded corner, they found five freshly dug graves. There had been an attempt to conceal them, but dug-up dirt always takes more space than the hole it came from, especially when a body is added to the hole.

"Five?" Wren said at last. "Rumi had two brothers, her mother, and her father. That's four. Who's the . . . ?"

Tell knew the answer. "Most likely the chief." He squatted down near the last mound and touched it with his fingertips. "We'll never know for sure unless we dig them up."

Another dreadful thought caused Wren's heart to thud. "Do you think Rumi found these? Do you think she knows?" They looked around for her footprints, but the dirt in that part of the yard was too disturbed to read.

"We have to tell her." Tell sighed. "She's going to cry."

"How can we tell her? She's gone," Wren pointed out. "But yes, she's most definitely going to cry."

"There's only one place she could be." Tell felt sure. "At the sorcerer's. And that's where we're going."

"Tonight? Now?"

"We also need to get our money," Tell added reasonably. "If we have to run, we'll need it all."

Wren nodded. Knowing they had two hundred sous of their own *had* made her feel safer and stronger, she had to admit.

Rold Roland's empty property held one last surprise. As they opened the gate to leave, they heard footsteps hurtling toward them out of the dark. Already on edge, they dove to one side as the big black-and-white flightless bird sprinted past them and out through the gate.

They watched the strange, half-tame creature hurtling into the dark city in a panic.

"That bird—it's like us," Wren said as they set off on the long walk to the very center of Halfway once again.

"I hope it has better luck than we do," Tell said wryly.

"What do you mean? We're still alive, and we're fat with honey cakes."

Tell grunted and picked up the pace.

They reached the sorcerer's house quickly because they ran most of the way. It helped that it was the tallest house in the city. It also helped that the closer they got to the center of Halfway, the fewer people there were on the streets. The last few blocks were totally deserted. In fact, there was not a living creature to be seen, nor a light in any window. The silence was unnerving. It was as if the sorcerer's house was actively radiating dread, the way a banked fire looks quiet but gives off intense heat. As before, the closer Tell and Wren got, the stronger the need grew to turn around and go the other way. By the time they found themselves at the handleless front door, they were using all their mountain training to keep from bolting back to the safety of House Belton.

"Are you sure we should be here?" Wren asked, wiping her sweaty hands on her fine new tunic.

"No," Tell said, and meant it, as he banged on the door with a cobblestone. The street echoed with the sound of his blows, but the door did not open.

"It opened for us last time," whispered Wren.

Not this time.

"We've lost our money—again," Tell spat. "We should never have trusted Cormorin; he's a sorcerer as well! We're fools. Now we have no choice; we have to go back to House Belton. Hopefully they'll let us in." He backed away from the door, when Wren grabbed his hand.

"Wait." Her hand moved like a striking snake. The brief burn of the cut on his palm from her black glass dagger was such a surprise that Tell couldn't stop a yelp from escaping his lips.

"Mountain thunder! Why did you do that?!"

"I don't know," Wren admitted as she cut her own hand. "But she needed our blood on black glass to see Da, so it must have some kind of power."

Wren pressed her bloodied blade flat against the door, then nearly fell forward when the door disappeared, becoming a hole in the side of the house. The blackness of the tunnel they had just left had been dead, inert. . . . This blackness was seething and horribly alive.

Wren stepped inside, Tell at her heels. The hole became a blank door again the moment he was inside.

The People of the Black Glass had no set ideas about a god, or heaven and hell, or anything like sin . . . which was lucky, because if they did, they'd all automatically be sinners, consigned to hell. But they were superstitious, and they did believe in sorcery, fate, luck, a vague afterlife of comfort and plenty to make up for their life of suffering and privation. Anyway, some of them did. Others believed in nothing but a keen eye and a sharp blade.

As Tell and Wren stood in the darkness of the lowest floor of the sorcerer's house, a sense of dread began to rise in them, becoming so intense that they could hardly draw breath.

"It's just sorcery," Tell hissed, moving forward toward the spiral stairs.

"I know," Wren panted.

But when they were about halfway across, they saw movement in the corners: small creatures skittering back and forth, then seething out of the darkness toward them.

"House demons!" Tell gasped. From an early age, all

the People of the Black Glass learned to fear the gnash-
ing little house demons that caved in roofs or caused fires
to leap out of fire rings and burn babies. They were only
knee high, but they had sharp, clacking teeth and malevolent eyes. Tell had always been afraid of them. "How
does anyone here know about house demons?!"

"It's *sorcery*, remember!" Wren scolded as they forced
themselves forward.

But Tell felt their nasty touch on his heels, and he
leaped ahead, dragging his sister with him.

"It's. Not. Real!" Wren yelled.

But at the spiral stairs, it became very real. As they
reached the first step, lightning crackled downward out of
the spiral darkness, forked into two branches, and struck
them. Their hearts stopped working. Unable to move
or breathe or even think, they crumpled to the ground.
Everything faded to black, and as Tell lost consciousness,
his last fragment of thought was *So glad it's over.*

30

But it wasn't over. Someone called their names faintly, from far away. "Tell! Wren! Wake up! Wake up now!" That voice, they recognized it. Then came the sound of a hand smacking flesh hard, again and again, echoing closer. Tell realized fuzzily that the flesh being smacked was his own cheek. At first he didn't feel it. Then he did. It stung!

"Ow!" he yelled. Rumi looked down at him for a moment, then turned away to slap Wren's face. Cormorin's face appeared next. His blue eyes were wide with fright.

"You weren't supposed to be able to do that!" the apprentice said shakily.

"Do what?" Tell asked groggily.

"Get into the house. And it should've killed you outright. Ugh! We're going to have to strengthen the spells."

Tell groaned and rolled onto his side just in time to see Wren's eyes flutter open and Rumi sit back on her heels, lowering her hand. Tell wondered if he looked as stunned as Wren did. He knew there was something he had to do, right away. He'd promised.

"Rumi . . ." Tell hesitated. Rumi turned to him. "We found . . . I mean, we think we saw your—" He stopped as soon as he saw her face. Her eyes were dark and bruised. Her cheeks, which had been plump and glowing just a few days ago, were almost gaunt. She was not yet an adult, but she looked older. Their eyes met. In suffering, they recognized each other. She nodded. Yes, she had seen the graves. All Tell could do was nod in return. And not a tear fell.

"I saw them take you away," she said, her voice almost devoid of emotion. "I thought you were dead. Where have you been?"

Tell tried to think of the right way to answer her question. "We found our mother" was enough.

"No . . . ," Wren countered weakly. "She found us."

Cormorin reappeared holding two tiny cups. "Drink this. You'll feel better."

They were in the maze of furniture on the second floor of the sorcerer's house. "Where is she?" Wren asked. "The sorcerer."

"Busy," said Cormorin.

"We've learned some things. . . . They might be important. We don't understand what they mean, but she might."

"You can tell me. She'll hear what she needs to hear."

Cormorin looked older as well, and not in a good way. Tired, tense, grim, and pale. Like all of them. He told them bluntly that the top floor of the house was forbidden to them. They sat at a table, the two-hundred-sous string coiled between them. Tell pulled it tight, so that the coins lay in a straight line.

"Keep that tied around your waist," said Rumi. "Out of sight."

Tell lifted his tunic and did as Rumi said. "We need to buy winter food for our village—for the women and children, anyway. The men are gone."

"What do you mean?" asked Rumi. Tell and Wren had a hard time meeting her eyes. There was such deep pain in them.

"At the other end of the tunnel, that warehouse you came up in . . . We found them, uh, was it just yesterday? They were captives. They were being forced to make weapons out of their black—"

"What tunnel?" Cormorin asked.

Tell glanced at Rumi. "There's a tunnel between Rumi's place and a thief called Rold Roland."

"*What?! That was Rold Roland's warehouse?!*" Rumi leaped to her feet, shock and outrage on her face. "But they're enemies! Rold Roland and my father are *enemies*! He said so all the time. Called him a viper in the grass."

Cormorin's eyes flicked from face to face, trying to understand.

"I don't think they really were enemies," Tell said as gently as he could. "I think maybe he worked for your father."

"Having people think you're enemies when you're not can be very useful," mused the apprentice. "We do it all the time."

"Well, whatever Rold Roland was, he isn't anymore. Show them," Wren said to Tell. Tell spread the rings and tooth out on the table. Wren reached out her forefinger and separated the blackened tooth from the rings, flipping it over so that the emerald winked up at them.

Rumi sat down hard, as if her knees couldn't hold her any longer. "All dead." She sat still for a long moment, her eyes far away. "Everyone's dead."

They expected her to start crying, but that Rumi was gone forever. Finding the unmarked graves of her family had made sure of that. Suddenly, she lunged across the table, face inches from Tell and Wren.

"I want to be part of your revenge." Her voice was a rasping, trembling hiss. "I'll do anything. I don't care if I live or die. I just want to hurt them, Kennett especially. It's all I want. It's all I have left."

Tell rubbed his face. "Things are all tangled now. . . ." He faltered when Rumi's eyes speared him.

"How?" she asked sharply. There were no tangles for her.

Wren tried to explain. "It turns out our mother is . . . well, she's helping one of the families that run Halfway—"

"Which one?" Cormorin and Rumi asked simultaneously.

"The Beltons, in the desert quarter."

"Ugh," Rumi exclaimed. "They're awful. Bullies."

"And weak," Cormorin added. "The worst of the four families by far. The old man's clinging to power; they couldn't even keep order in their own quarter."

"Well, they're stronger now. They're using the Ropers," Tell told them. "We've seen Kennett at the house. Their leader."

"You've been inside House Belton?" Cormorin now sounded shocked.

"Yes. All the honey cakes you can eat."

"That explains your nice clothes, and . . . your hair," Cormorin said.

"Ah, so it's your turn to be spoiled now," Rumi said quietly.

"Not exactly. Not yet," said Tell. "We're going to be presented to the Beltons in the morning."

"That could be useful," Cormorin mused.

"And if we're lucky—" Tell continued.

"According to our *mother*, who told everyone she has no children," interrupted Wren bitterly.

"They'll let us carry out night pots for them," Tell finished, waving his hand in disgust, as if waving away the smell of the night pots.

"*If* we're lucky." Wren sneered.

Rumi shook her head disdainfully. "And you're willing to be servants for the family working with the Ropers, who killed your men . . . and killed my family and buried them in unmarked graves? To . . . to be with your *mother*, who left you and pretends she *isn't* your mother? That's what you're going to do?"

The silence following Rumi's harsh words was profound, yet nobody heard the sorcerer arrive. Suddenly, she was standing over them, and she was terrifying. Incandescent with rage. The tattoos on her skull were so alive they seemed to rise into the air, a writhing halo. Her yellow eyes glowed. This was a sorcerer at full power.

Cormorin's eyes widened. "What is it? What happened?" he asked.

The sorcerer made a sound like a growl, deep in her throat. "Yesterday Mountain, the day before Ocean. Now Forest is dead—killed by sorcery-strengthened weapons made of black glass. Three of us in three days. Their light gone out, their power no more, their quarters unprotected." Her eyes paralyzed Tell and Wren. "I *knew* you were trouble."

"So now there are only two sorcerers protecting all of Halfway?" Rumi blurted.

"Only one," Tell said.

"What do you mean?" Cormorin asked.

"Only you," Tell said to the sorcerer.

She was at his side in a blink. "What do you know?" she hissed.

"We—we heard they have a sorcerer on their side," Tell nearly stuttered.

"It has to be Desert," Cormorin said instantly. "It's all coming from the Desert quarter. All of this."

"Desert? Feh! She's the weakest of us," said the sorcerer. "Beware the weak. There's nothing they won't do."

"You're the last one!" Wren realized. "They're coming for you tonight—that's what she said."

The sorcerer's tattoos roiled across her scalp. "*Who* said?"

Wren took a step backward. "Uh . . . our mother. She's part of it, in some way. She's—she offered them an idea, and they let her in, two years ago."

The sorcerer smiled, and it wasn't a pretty smile. "Beware the weak," she said once more.

"She isn't weak," Tell said.

"Those around her are, which means she is too," the sorcerer snapped. Then she swept her arm in front of their faces as if sweeping them away.

"You need to leave immediately. Now that I know who I'm up against, I can hold my house for a night. But it will be too dangerous to stay. Go back to—" The sorcerer stopped, cocking her head as if listening to something only she could hear. Then:

"Go to House Belton, stay there. Cormorin, you too."

Cormorin leaped to his feet, and the others needed no urging. They were on their feet instantly, eager to be anywhere else.

"Take your glass," the sorcerer ordered. Cormorin raced off to get it.

"Do we have to leave through . . . that, downstairs?" Wren asked the sorcerer.

"No." The sorcerer shook her head. "There's another way out. This house isn't as simple as it appears."

The four of them swept silently through the empty streets, Cormorin holding the black glass case in his arms.

"Why House Belton?" Tell asked. "Wouldn't Rumi's house be safer?"

"I don't know," Cormorin replied. "But it's important, or she wouldn't have said it." They saw movement up ahead and ducked into a dark alleyway.

As they hid in the shadows, hardly daring to breathe, they heard pounding footsteps and then saw four Ropers flash past the mouth of the alley, feet striking the cobblestones loudly. It was disturbing to see the glint of black glass in their hands and on their spear points. The mountain men had made those.

"We should warn her," Wren whispered once they were out of earshot.

"You already did," Cormorin assured her. "Don't worry. She's more powerful than they know."

"So are they," Tell argued. "They captured our men. That's not easy."

"Nor is her power, I promise you. We need to keep moving," urged Cormorin. "It's not safe out here."

They peeled out of the alleyway and hurried down the

street. The darkness at the center of Halfway seemed to fold in behind them as they disappeared from sight.

Getting back into House Belton proved more difficult than leaving, but the ochre walls were no match for mountain children. Using Cormorin as a ladder because he was the tallest, Tell boosted Wren onto the top of the wall while Rumi held the apprentice's black glass case.

While Wren ran silently along the top of the wall, the others kept pace with her on the street until she reached the side gate, swung down, and opened it. They were inside the walls before the two guards had even blinked the sleep out of their eyes.

"We won't tell if you don't," Wren whispered to the guards as they led their friends into the vast house. They saw no one. The halls were empty.

"Anyone for honey cakes?" Tell asked as he opened the door to their room.

But it wasn't honey cake waiting for them; it was Selt, who regarded them with eyes full of sadness, all affection gone.

"I don't know why Lilit thought you'd do as you were told," Selt said, sounding so disappointed that Tell and Wren felt a pang of something totally unfamiliar—guilt.

"We had to make sure Rumi was safe. We told you that," Tell explained.

"Well, she very much isn't. Not now. Not here." Selt's

eyes stopped on Cormorin. "Nor are you, apprentice. You're neither invited, nor welcome." Then Selt focused on Tell and Wren.

"I've tried to protect you from yourselves. But I can't anymore, not without endangering myself. When I leave this room, my decisions will concern my own survival, first and last. You can no longer count on me."

"But—"

Selt held up a hand to stop Wren. "What happens to you tomorrow is up to you alone." Selt turned and left, closing the door quietly on the four of them.

31

To protect Rumi and Cormorin, Tell and Wren waited sleepily in the hallway outside their room. Glowing motes of dust danced hypnotically in the steeply angled morning light. Wren's head drooped, then popped up again, as she fought sleep.

Cormorin had slept on the floor, Rumi had curled up with Wren and slept like someone who'd been given a sleeping herb. Tell and Wren had tossed and turned, disturbing dreams leaving them exhausted—the aftermath of the lightning strike in the sorcerer's house, maybe.

When Cormorin had hauled himself up from the hard floor at dawn, he'd twisted himself this way and that, his lanky spine cracking loudly, waking them all.

"I was thinking," he'd declared, far too early for anyone else to think. "If the trouble comes from inside this house, it might actually be useful to have you here. That's why she wanted us to come back." Half-asleep, the others just blinked at him.

He'd went on. "People think sorcery is about spells and poisons and black glass and such, and it is. But it's also about knowing things: little things, big things, hidden things. That's what she tells me every day." The others rubbed their faces. It wasn't clear that they'd processed a word he said.

"Just . . . just do well this morning," the sorcerer's apprentice had finished up. "For your sake and ours." Tell groaned, Wren groaned, and they'd both headed for the washing bowls.

Now, as the pair waited for Lilit outside their room, they grew increasingly nervous, which annoyed them.

"I don't want to do this," Tell finally admitted.

"Let's breathe," suggested Wren. Tell nodded, and they began in unison, doing cycles of calming breath.

They were as ready as they could be, given the circumstances. Rumi had helped them look their best. She told them she hardly recognized them. They no longer looked like mountain children but rather, the spoiled servants of a wealthy family, which stung, as it was intended to do. Then she made Tell wash his face again.

Before they'd left the room, Tell had asked Cormorin if he could use his black glass to find out where their men were buried, so they could at least tell their families up the mountain. Cormorin agreed to try, which meant giving up more blood, and as they waited outside their door, they held their hands high to stop the bleeding from their third shared cut.

"My hand looks like one of your arrows," Wren realized, showing Tell the three parallel cuts.

"You know, we should leave while we can, buy supplies, and head back up the mountain," Tell murmured, after making sure that the door to their room was completely closed.

"We *have* to do this," Wren insisted.

"No, we don't."

"For me," said Wren.

"For you?" Tell looked at her exhausted face, framed by a haircut that made her look like she was . . . from here. "Is this what you want?"

Now she just looked desperate. "I have no choice. You can go back up the mountain. I can't. I *have* to stay here."

"No, you don't," her brother argued.

"By the mountain's sharp teeth, Tell, I'm an *outcast*! And have been from the second I entered the Narrows. That's the rule."

"Not always," Tell said calmly. "Things are changing, whether they like it or not. And that includes the rules." Wren disagreed. Tell was adamant. "If you want to see Da again, you can and you will. I promise you."

"It's funny," Wren said quietly. "Finding her . . . Lilit . . .

makes me want to see Da more, not less." Tell felt the same. In truth, finding their mother in her new life, with her new name and home, made them appreciate the simple life they'd had up the mountain, even though they'd hated it much of the time. It was all very confusing.

The sound of approaching footsteps brought them back to the present. They exhaled, drew in a deep breath, stood up straight, and waited for their next ordeal.

When Lilit came around the corner, it was clear that she hadn't slept much either. Her eyes were red-rimmed, and no amount of kohl could hide that. Her features seemed sharper, as sharp as the black glass she'd turned her back on so completely. Her fine clothing seemed to be particularly close-fitting. She looked . . . dangerous. And beautiful. She examined them with judgmental eyes—the eyes of others, as Selt had said. She nodded curtly, then pointed at the knife on Tell's belt.

"No weapons. Leave your knife here."

After tossing his knife and sheath back into the room, Tell followed Lilit and Wren. *Why do powerful people always just assume you'd follow them?* Tell thought sourly.

"I wish we could put this off," said Lilit when he'd caught up. "But it's too late for that."

As they swept through the vast house, servants seemed to melt away to the sides, so they never had to pause for anyone. The only pause came from Lilit herself. In a wide hallway, in front of the doors to the round room, she stopped suddenly. There was a look on her face they'd never seen before. Doubt.

"Yesterday . . ." Her voice was very low. They could hardly hear her words. "Yesterday I told you that the only safe place in this city would be behind these walls. And I was sure of that . . . then. But now I don't know whether I'm protecting you or putting you in the direct path of danger."

"What has happened to you?" Wren whispered harshly. "We used to be able to understand you. Now you talk in riddles, like everyone else in this city."

Lilit looked exasperated. "You don't know it—nobody knows it—but there's a war raging out there, a war for this city. A war for the future. It should be over, but it isn't. I was sure we'd win easily, but we haven't. Not yet. And if we don't"—Lilit's smile went nowhere near her eyes—"let's just say that stepping off the path at the Narrows may have been the better choice after all."

"Maybe we should all just leave!" Tell suggested. "Right now."

"No, we're past that point." Lilit drew herself up tall. "They're waiting for you." She stepped between them, laid a hand on each of their shoulders. "Remember, I'm your aunt. You're my dead brother's children. Your mother lost her mind last winter. You're looking for a new life down here, where it's warm."

And with that, Lilit pushed the two children she

couldn't acknowledge through the double doors, into the round room where they'd first met her just a few days ago.

The room was filled with people, all of whom stopped in midsentence to look at them. This was clearly not a day for children. To a man—and they were all men—their eyes were unkind and impatient.

That is, except for the eyes of Ikarus Belton, the head of House Belton, ruler of the Desert quarter. His eyes were vacant. Dressed in a loose tunic colored the deepest, richest purple, he was propped up on a sofa, staring out at nothing, with a servant hovering just behind him, ready to catch him if he toppled over. He was there in body only, and it was a body about to fail.

On the next sofa over was his son, Alin. Middle-aged and plump, the spoiled little boy he used to be was still evident in his face and posture. Alin's eyes were hollow with lack of sleep and full of tension, just like Lilit's. It had been a bad night for everyone.

When Tell saw Alin, his mind went instantly to the sorcerer's words. "Beware the weak."

"I'm sorry for the interruption," Lilit sang out. "We agreed we would do this now."

Alin sighed petulantly and waved back the men around him with a flick of his wrist. "So this is them," he said, managing to sound disappointed.

"Yes," Lilit answered politely. "My nephew Tell and my niece Wren."

Tell and Wren dared not look at each other. They had no idea what to do, so they did nothing.

"You've gone to a lot of trouble for two . . . orphans." Alin's words were casual, but his eyes were not. They were dagger sharp on Lilit.

"To our benefit," she said smoothly. "They're strong and clever and not spoiled."

Alin looked unconvinced. He pointed at Tell. "So . . . what can you do that's strong and clever?"

Tell hesitated. What was he supposed to say? Lilit nudged him.

"Ah . . . I'm good with a bow."

"Bows are forbidden in Halfway. What else?"

"I'm pretty strong."

"For your age, perhaps." Alin's already-bored eyes shifted to Wren. "And you? What can you do?"

"Whatever I have to," replied Wren sweetly, an answer that Tell envied greatly.

Alin looked Wren up and down for a long moment, then shook his head emphatically. "No, you look like someone who does whatever she *wants* to." Alin's eyes fixed on Lilit's again. "Not unlike your . . . aunt, here. Who you bear a striking resemblance to, by the way."

"She's my late brother's child, so she would," Lilit responded calmly.

"Are you?" asked Alin, swinging his legs off the sofa suddenly. "Are you Lilit's *brother's* child?"

"Yes, I am," said Wren. Never had their ability to lie been put to the test so clearly. As always, the best lies were mostly made up of truth. "My father lost his sight mining black glass, and because, after thirty days, he was still blind, his friends took him up to the glacier and gave him apricot brandy." Wren paused, as if fighting emotion. "When he'd drunk enough of it, he went to sleep on the ice and never woke up. That's just the way it is, was, and always will be, up there. Then our mother lost her mind and threw herself off a cliff. Our life in the mountains is over." She kept her gaze level and clear. "Aunt Lilit is our only living relative. We have to start over, down here."

Alin nodded sympathetically, as if he understood their pain. But his next words weren't sympathetic in the least. They were delivered to Lilit.

"This is a mistake. I shouldn't have let you talk me into it. It isn't a good time to be taking in new people. I'm sure my father agrees." Tell and Wren could feel Lilit stiffen. Alin addressed his father.

"You agree, don't you, Father?"

Ikarus Belton said nothing, did nothing, was nothing.

"He agrees," Alin declared. "It is so." With an air of victory, he said to Tell and Wren, "Next year, maybe. Come back then by all means—if we're all still here." And then he flicked his wrist again, this time dismissing them.

Lilit's sharp inhale next to them, usually the harbinger of an extreme reaction, gave them a moment's hope. But then . . . nothing. Their mother exhaled and murmured, "It is so."

She placed a hand on their backs. "Come." Tell and Wren shrugged, determined not to show that they cared in any way. They had taken two steps toward the double doors when they heard a rattling moan behind them. Then a rising tumult of shocked voices. "Father, no," gasped Alin. They swung around. Ikarus Belton was halfway to his feet, held up from behind by his frantic servant. His eyes were no longer blank.

"Father, sit down, please," Alin begged. But Ikarus Belton bucked against those around him until he'd pulled one frail arm free. He raised that arm, shaking and palsied, as everyone else looked on in astonishment.

With enormous effort, Ikarus Belton aimed a finger at Wren, the tip of it dancing and circling. He turned his head to Alin and emitted a passionate moan.

"The girl . . . you want her to stay?"

With supreme effort, Ikarus Belton managed a gurgling half nod.

"It is so," said Alin, his voice flat with acceptance.

"Ikarus, what about the boy?" Lilit couldn't stop herself from asking.

But there was no answer. Suddenly spent, Ikarus Belton sagged back in his servant's arms and was lowered gently onto the sofa, where it was as if a shutter had come down across his being. No one there once again.

When everyone had settled down, Alin addressed them. "Ikarus Belton has spoken for the girl."

"And . . . ?" Lilit prompted.

"But not for the boy," said Alin with finality.

Wren opened her mouth to say something, but Lilit spun her and Tell around. "I'll see them to their room," she said as she pushed them toward the doors, her face almost purple with rage.

"You'll see the boy to the street," Alin corrected her.

32

As soon as they were through the doors and out of earshot, Wren whispered, "Alin doesn't believe we're your niece and nephew."

"He has doubt, and that's good enough," Lilit snapped.

"He doesn't like you," Tell said plainly.

"He does when it suits him," Lilit replied darkly. She put her arm around Tell. "Don't worry. I'm not abandoning you. I have a plan for you. It's already in place. I have someone who knows the worth of mountain people and will take you in."

"We'll be split up?" asked Wren, trying hard to keep a tremor out of her voice.

"Not for long," Lilit said. "Not if things go according to the plan."

"Except earlier you said they weren't," Tell reminded her.

"Come with me," said Lilit, picking up her pace. "There's

no time to waste. Things are moving very quickly right now."

The defeated looks on their faces spoke a thousand words. They followed her, heads down.

Lilit had a guard in front of the door to her quarters. She gave him a questioning glance, and he nodded. Then she swept them past him, into her quarters.

"Come and meet a true friend of mine." Then she added, to Tell, "He's agreed to take you in. I've told him all about you."

It took everything Tell and Wren had not to cry out when Lilit's "true friend" rose to meet them, saying, "If you two are here, things did not go well in that round room."

It was Kennett. Tell felt furious at himself for not expecting it. Kennett was older in the morning light than he'd seemed in a darkened warehouse. Wren observed a few threads of gray in his brown braid, but somehow that made him seem even more formidable. The gray made him seem wise and substantial. His green eyes were steady, his shoulders strong. Unlike the two Beltons, he was a leader by character, not birth.

"This is Kennett. He's the leader of his people—a great leader. He's working with . . . with the Beltons to change Halfway," said their mother, in admiring tones they'd never heard from her.

"Not such a great leader," Kennett said to Lilit. "I lost four fine men last night, and gained nothing."

Lilit touched his cheek while he placed his hand over hers. "Not in vain," she told him softly.

"We'll find out tonight. It's all of us or nothing. One big push." Kennett spoke as if neither Tell nor Wren was there. Or as if they were already on his and Lilit's side.

Tell's fury grew. He didn't dare look at his sister.

Their mother was in love with the man who'd destroyed them all, and he seemed to be in love with her. Even though all marriages were arranged up on the mountain, love sometimes happened, and Tell and Wren knew what it was.

"Well, it's not all bad. Wren's staying here with me," Lilit said, addressing Kennett's first comment. "And Tell needs . . . he needs someone he can follow."

Did Kennett recognize them from the warehouse? This was Tell and Wren's greatest concern. He gave no sign if he did. He simply nodded at Tell.

"You're welcome into my care, Tell," said Kennett. "Though I can't promise it's safe." He looked at Lilit again. "We'll know soon, one way or another." He turned back to Tell. "Come, boy. There's a lot to do before nightfall."

"Say goodbye to your sister," Lilit urged Tell. "Just for now."

Tell and Wren looked at each other miserably. They'd fought so hard to avoid this moment, and now here it was anyway and it seemed they could do nothing about it. Their heads were swirling with things they wanted to say, but none came out.

"Stop this," Lilit said sharply. "There's no time for sentiment."

At that, Tell and Wren let their faces become blank, unreadable.

"Save some honey cakes for me," Tell said, voice devoid of all emotion.

"Not likely," Wren replied, just the same.

And with that, they parted, almost numb with shock.

Back in the hallway, Tell turned to Kennett. "I . . . I need to fetch my knife. I wasn't allowed to take it into the round room."

"I can give you a knife," Kennett offered. "One you'd recognize; it's made of black glass."

"Mine was a gift from my father," Tell said quietly.

Kennett placed a hand at the base of Tell's neck and then pulled him around to face him. From a distance it might've looked like a friendly gesture, but it didn't feel friendly to Tell.

Nor did Kennett's eyes.

"Thanks to your mother—yes, I know who you really are—I probably know more about you people than anyone else in this city. So, I realize you're all vicious little liars and thieves. But right now I need the truth. Your life depends on it, boy."

Summoning up all the strength he had in his body and spirit, Tell stood his ground. "The truth about what?" he asked.

"Was that you in the warehouse?" Kennett's eyes were relentless.

Tell lifted his chin defiantly. "Yes, that was me."

"Did you kill one of my men?"

"Yes, I did," he said simply.

"How? I need to know exactly. He was a great fighter."

"I waited for him to come up the stairs in Kun Anton's warehouse and slammed the door down on his neck."

"By accident?"

"No. He was chasing me. It was all I could think to do."

Kennett tightened his grip on Tell's neck and looked into the distance, thinking. Tell gritted his teeth to hide how much it hurt.

"I should strangle you right here and stuff your scrawny body down a drain. Nobody'd ever know. I'd tell your mother you ran away the moment you got outside. She'd believe that about you." Then Kennett made some kind of internal decision and looked back at Tell. "But I won't—not today. Do you know why?"

Tell shook his head as best he could, still refusing to show even a grimace.

"Your mother said you have greatness in you. I see it, and I want it. If we succeed tonight, you'll join me, because everyone always wants to be on the winning side. And if we fail, it won't matter." Kennett released Tell's neck with a rough shove, which hurt more than anything else had, but Tell still refused to show pain. Kennett's mouth curved in the beginning of a smile. He was pleased by Tell's toughness.

"Where I come from, we live our entire lives for days like this. Good or bad, these are the days that define us."

Tell nodded.

"Go and get your knife. Meet me at the side gate." In three long strides, Kennett was halfway down the hallway. "This is a day that will define you as well," he called after him.

Tell raced for his room, head clogged with too many thoughts. When he burst through the door, what he found was chaos.

Rumi was sitting astride Cormorin, slapping his face, something she was getting good at. Her cheeks were flushed with fear, and the room smelled like the aftermath of lightning. Cormorin's nose gushed blood, and his eyelids fluttered uncontrollably. The beds and floor were covered with jagged shards of black glass. The wooden case that held Cormorin's sorcerer's glass was shattered into splinters.

"What happened?" Tell gasped.

"I don't know," Rumi answered shakily. "He made me hide under the bed. He tried to do something with his black glass, and it blew apart when this . . . this thing, like a shadow, flew out of it and attacked him. It's gone now, but . . . he won't wake up."

"Rocks and landslides! We need to leave right now,"

Tell said as he found his knife and strapped it to his belt. "There's someone waiting for me, and I don't think he'll wait long before coming after me."

"We can't leave without Cormorin!" Rumi cried out.

"We're not going to." Tell grabbed a blanket off his bed, shook the shards of glass off it, laid it on the floor.

"Help me roll him onto the blanket."

He and Rumi squatted and began rolling the floppy, lanky, red-haired apprentice onto the blanket. In midroll, Rumi stopped suddenly.

"Oh, I need to tell you!" she exclaimed. "He found your men."

"Where are they buried?" Tell was in no position to mince words.

"Nowhere," said Rumi. "They're still alive."

Tell blinked once at the news, thought for a moment, then stood up. "Open the door."

As Rumi did that, Tell gathered the end of the blanket and dragged Cormorin out of the room. It was easy sliding him across the tiled floors.

"This way." Tell took off at nearly a run, heading for the kitchen, with Cormorin sledding along behind, banging into the walls here and there, still unconscious.

"Where are we going?" Rumi hurried along beside him.

"To the garden. We'll leave through the stables," Tell said, panting, as they hurtled around a corner and ran into Paulik, who was blocking the hallway. Tell and Rumi stopped, hard, and Cormorin moaned as he slid into the wall.

"Paulik . . ." Tell hardly knew what to say, so simply blurted, "We're leaving. Bad things are happening in this house. Let us by. Please. You'll never see us again. You should take Syrinna and go too."

Paulik looked up and down the hallway, then, to Tell's amazement, turned to face the wall and covered his ears.

"Thank you," whispered Rumi as they hurried past him. "Thank you so much."

"What will I be doing here?" Wren asked unhappily. They were in Lilit's sumptuous chambers. Her mother was changing into yet another set of clothes for some reason. She pulled out a tunic that was quite plain, put it back, pulled out a less plain one, deep green in color.

"You'll become a servant in Ikarus Belton's quarters."

"Ugh." Wren couldn't suppress her reaction. She inspected her mother's belongings as they talked. A tiny portion of what she could see, if sold, would feed their village for a year.

"It won't be for long. He could die at any moment. He almost did, right in front of you."

Wren thought for a moment. "And Alin?"

"Alin needs me, and he knows it."

Wren fingered the necklaces—at least a dozen— hanging from the thumb of a polished tree branch shaped like a hand. "Is that why he doesn't like you?"

"Clever girl. And, yes, that's one of the reasons."

"And because you and that Roper—"

"*Kennett!* Learn his name. It's important to you."

Wren continued. "Did Alin expect you to be his wife after his father died? But now you—"

"You need to stop asking so many questions."

"But I want to understand."

"Questions are for little girls. Questions are dangerous. They give away what you know or don't know, and the answers are usually lies anyway." For just a moment, Wren saw the mother she used to know, the mother who challenged every idea, every rule, every custom of their village. "You can understand more by looking and listening and using your brain, and nobody knows what you're thinking. That's a very powerful thing," Lilit said, less unkindly. "Learn it, daughter. Learn it well."

33

Rumi looked down her nose at the wheezing, well-fed man in front of her and sniffed as if smelling something rotten. "My name is Rumi Anton. I'm the daughter of Kun Anton, and my father could buy and sell you before breakfast if he wanted to, so if you know what's good for you, you'll treat my friend with respect." It was a good thing that Kun Anton's death was not yet news in Halfway. Otherwise his name would've held no weight whatsoever. Rumi pointed imperiously at Tell. "He has the sous for what you sell, and that's all you need to know." She motioned to Tell. "Show him!"

Rumi had already taught Tell how to show his string of sous without giving anyone a chance to count it. It involved holding the coins in a coiled bunch, showing the bunch for a moment, then putting it away fast. Evidently it worked, because the wheezing man signaled the guard to open the door and let them into the holding area.

"Be sure to tell your father I've gone out of my way to accommodate you," he sniveled. "It's unheard of to allow children in here."

"Don't think of us as children," Rumi suggested in a commanding manner. "Think of us as money."

"Of course, of course," he said as they entered. "I think of everyone as money." Which was literally true.

Of all the terrible things Tell had seen in his life so far, this was by far the worst. It made him feel sick in heart and stomach. With his string of sous concealed, they had walked for hours, all the way to the far edge of the city, to a place Rumi had heard rumor of but had never been. The people market. It stretched along the inside of the high wall, using it as a barrier to escape and to hope.

This was a business built on cruelty, maintained with cruelty, and obviously very profitable, so not likely to change anytime soon. All along the wall behind palisades of pointed tree trunks were desperate people whose lives had collapsed catastrophically, and the stench of their despair mingled with the smell of wealth as Tell and Rumi walked along the ugly fence, looking through gaps for the men of Tell's village.

Cormorin had found the men as Tell had asked, by using his new sorcerer's glass and their blood on Wren's black glass dagger. Rumi told Tell that Cormorin was pleasantly surprised to discover that his methods and spells had actually worked. He'd confessed to Rumi that he barely knew how to use the glass and by rights shouldn't even have it. Then, stupidly, he'd tried to merge his glass with the sorcerer's, to find out what was happening at her house. That was when his glass was blown to fragments by whatever had come through it. By whatever had attacked him.

Cormorin had slowly come back to consciousness as, together, Tell and Rumi carried him down the street after sneaking away from House Belton through the stables. But he could barely talk. Rumi had summoned a cart, had Tell pay part of a sous for a ride into the very center of Halfway. It amazed Tell that you could pay someone to take you places.

By the time they'd reached the sorcerer's house, Cormorin had improved enough to use a slurred spell to open a door available only to him and the sorcerer. The sorcerer was waiting for them as they entered, visibly concerned.

"I think he tried to ... to help you," Rumi told her quickly as she and Tell held Cormorin upright. "Something like a shadow flew out of his glass and it ... it's gone. Shattered."

Unexpectedly, the sorcerer laid her hands on either side of Cormorin's face and felt his head, almost tenderly.

"What a fool," she murmured. "I thought it was her,

trying to attack me again. I stopped as soon as I felt him, but . . ." The sorcerer pointed to a chair where they could set him down. They were in a lower part of the house they'd never seen before. It was furnished simply. Tell liked it.

"Thank you, both of you," the sorcerer said. "Now, you have to go. I need to help Cormorin and then prepare for tonight."

"They're very worried in House Belton," Tell blurted out. "They expected to win easily last night."

"They have no idea how close they came to doing just that," said the sorcerer quietly. "Four of those Ropers gained entrance with black glass weapons. That shouldn't have been possible. And they were just a distraction. I was attacked by one of us: Desert. Treacherous creature. She's much stronger than she used to be. So are her attacking spells. She's somehow found new powers, ones I didn't recognize. I drove her off, but I couldn't destroy her."

"They're attacking again tonight, all the Ropers," Tell told her urgently. "Kennett—their leader—he told our mother, in front of us."

It was then that he'd realized with a sudden internal lurch that he'd chosen sides without ever thinking it through. He wondered if Wren had done the same. He wondered if she'd chosen the same side. Not being together was even harder than he'd feared.

The sorcerer sighed. "Desert's a fool, killing three

of her own kind. Every time one of us dies, all become weaker."

"What does that mean?" Rumi asked.

The sorcerer smiled bitterly. "Sorcery is the sum of all sorcerers. It used to be much more powerful than it is today. It was everywhere. *We* were everywhere. There were different schools; it was *alive*." There was genuine sadness in her voice.

For Tell and Rumi, this was like hearing secret lore. Even Cormorin pricked up his ears, as if this was new to him, too. They waited for more.

After a long silence, the sorcerer nodded to herself; she'd come to a conclusion about something important. "I can't fight her sorcery and all the Ropers, not when they have weapons of black glass and a sorcerer's protection."

"But . . . the stories say you defeated whole armies!" Rumi cried out, dismayed.

"Who do you think started those stories? We did." The sorcerer chuckled, as if remembering fond moments. "We did horrible things to a few leaders and made sure their armies saw the results. It always worked."

"Yes, like turning that prince into a baboon!" Rumi exclaimed. "I've seen it!"

"It's just an old baboon," the sorcerer confided. "I have someone who brings me baboons." Tell grinned bitterly. Lies. Halfway was built on lies.

The sorcerer stood at a window and looked out, like

an ordinary person. "Once, we were honored. Respected. Now we're loathed, driven from place to place, driven out. They kill us when they can. The world that's coming . . . or is already here . . . there's no place in it for us."

The sorcerer walked toward them. She looked tired. "This day was always going to come; Halfway is too rich and too soft. Too tempting." She already seemed duller, less alive, in Tell's eyes.

"Maybe it's time to pack up and leave this city to its fate." This was addressed to Cormorin. He struggled to his feet.

"Wherever you go, I go" was his reply.

Tell and Rumi stood there uneasily, not sure of what to do or say.

"You two are welcome to come with us, if you like," the sorcerer offered. "And your sister."

"Where will you go?" asked Rumi.

"Far away," the sorcerer said with a shrug.

Rumi took a deep breath. "I'd like to be far away from here. I'll come."

Tell was nodding. Nodding as if agreeing. But he surprised them by saying, "Wait. What if you had men to match the Ropers? What if all *you* had to do was fight the other sorcerer . . . whatever fighting means to sorcerers. Could you win?"

The sorcerer studied Tell. "Where would you get these men? And why would they fight for me?"

"Oh, they wouldn't fight for you—they'd fight for revenge," Tell assured her.

In the people market, Tell could barely lift his eyes from his feet, the sights were so horrifying.

"Don't show that this affects you!" Rumi scolded in a whisper. "They'll ask for more because they know you want to leave as fast as you can. And we can't pay more. We don't have enough sous as it is. Buying people is expensive."

But it was hard not to be affected, especially for someone used to the air, light, and freedom of the mountains.

And they couldn't find the men. Anywhere.

"Maybe they've been sold already," Tell said in despair. "We should go."

"Never assume anything," Rumi had said. "Always ask." Like the spoiled merchant princess she used to be, Rumi beckoned a heavily muscled and scarred guard, waited impatiently with her hand on her hip for him to reach them.

"We were told you had men of the black glass. We don't see them. Are they sold?"

The guard grinned, showing a mouth that had lost every other tooth, with more soon to follow. He pointed off to a far corner of the people market.

"They had to be set aside. They're dangerous to the others. It's not good for business, fighting among the stock."

As Tell and Rumi reached the isolated area, Tell's legs suddenly stopped working, because of what he could see over the crude spikes of the fence. The brave, tough, fearsome men of his village were barely recognizable, they'd been beaten so severely: faces grotesquely swollen, teeth missing, scalps blood-matted, ears raw. They were bound in such a way that they could only sit hunched over and only look downward at the foul dirt. They had been crushed by forces they didn't understand, and it showed in their faces. They were barely there, barely present.

In spite of insisting that Tell show no emotion, Rumi had to slap a hand over her own mouth to stop herself from crying out. She turned to Tell.

"They're never going to be able to fight," she whispered hoarsely.

Tell nodded, her words mirroring his own thoughts. His eyes suddenly flooded with scalding tears. He hadn't cried since he was a baby and couldn't remember that far back. He stopped almost immediately, his shame turning to fury. Rumi tried to comfort him with a touch, but he didn't want comfort and spun away. Rumi understood all too well.

He turned back to her, shaking with fresh fury. "You said you wanted to help."

Rumi nodded. Tell untied the string of sous from his waist and whipped it around Rumi's, tying it with a bowman's expert touch.

"Get them out. Say whatever you have to, promise

whatever you need to, use everything your father taught you. But by the mountain's broken back . . . get them out!"

Rumi's pain-darkened eyes held his, wouldn't let him go. "How will they fight?" she asked with all the gentleness she could muster. "How are they going to help us get revenge?"

Tell thought carefully before replying. "Maybe our revenge is to survive. We survive for those who haven't. And then one day, when they've forgotten we even exist, we strike back."

"Wait here," Rumi ordered decisively. She turned on her heel and headed for the merchant's quarters. Tell watched the purposeful way she walked now. Had he and Wren changed as much as Rumi had in the past few days? Maybe so, he decided, but not as suddenly, not all at once. He realized that she was actually a very strong person.

And then a strange feeling tickled at Tell. He realized that he very much wanted to find out who Rumi would become. He wanted to be there when she was grown up and to know her, as unlikely as that possibility seemed to be right then.

While Tell was puzzling his way through these strange ideas, a faint, rasping voice came from a hunched figure at the other side of the fence.

"Tell? Is that you?" It was Curas, his voice mangled, Tell guessed, by the deep cut he'd given himself to escape the strangler's noose.

Tell made sure no one was looking, then moved as close to the fence as he could. "Yes, it's me."

"Why are you here, you rock-headed fool?" Curas rasped. "Go back up the mountain. Gather the women and children. Bring them down low, find a way to survive the winter. Go!"

"We'll all go together," Tell said in a low voice. "We're getting you out of here."

Curas somehow twisted himself around; Tell could see the crusted, scabbed scar on his throat through a gap in the fence. "You?! How?" Curas asked.

Suddenly, a big stick smacked against the pen wall right where Curas's head would be. Tell whirled, his hand automatically going to his new knife. It was the guard, his face brutal.

"Don't talk to the stock," he said. "It's a rule."

"How do I know if I want to buy them if I don't talk to them?" Tell asked quickly.

"You're not buying them for conversation." The guard sneered.

Almost without realizing it, Tell instantly became like all the rich and powerful people he'd been exposed to since reaching Halfway. His fine clothes and well-cut hair completed the illusion. He looked at the guard with utter disdain and lifted his chin.

"Listen here, you," he barked. "My partner's busy nego- tiating for these men right now. As far as I'm concerned, they're already my property, so I'll do whatever I want with them. My business is *not* your business." Tell gestured the guard away. "Leave, or I'll make sure that wheezy man back there knows how you treat the people who line his pockets. Who knows? You might just find yourself on the wrong side of this fence!" Tell's eyes narrowed speculatively. "I'm sure you'd fetch a good price."

Much to Tell's astonishment, it worked. The guard groveled and skulked away fast. Tell exhaled a mighty breath of air. And he wasn't the only astonished one.

Curas's voice rasped in wonder from the other side of the fence. "Lightning and thunder, boy!" he exclaimed. "Where did you learn to talk like that?"

"I—I've been around too many rich people, I think," Tell admitted. Then he squatted so that his face was level with Curas's. "Will you and the other men will be able to fight tonight?"

"Fight who? And with what?" Curas's eyes sparked with interest.

Before Tell could answer, Rumi was at his side, breathing hard, either with exertion or anger, the people merchant chugging up behind her. "We've got a bit of a problem," she announced.

"It's not a bit of a problem," the merchant panted. "It's a huge problem."

"And that is . . . ?" Tell asked, as if no matter the size of the problem, it was of little concern to him.

"You have twenty-two men in here and money for only eighteen," the merchant explained.

"Twenty," said Rumi crisply.

"Eighteen," the merchant responded angrily. "And that's after she's already ground all the profit out of me. There's no doubt she's Kun Anton's daughter."

"Look at them." Rumi swept her arm across the pen. "They're damaged. You'll never unload them. That has to be reflected in the price."

"It is," snapped the merchant. "Anyway, the damage is only temporary. These are all superficial wounds."

"You wouldn't think they were superficial if it were you wearing the damage," Rumi shot back angrily. Tell could see that this had become personal for them both. He needed to intervene.

"I want to go into the pen and examine them," he said to the merchant, trying to summon the arrogant tone he'd used earlier.

"I'm afraid that's not possible," the merchant said quickly. "It's for your own safety."

"What's unsafe about men trussed like piglets?" Tell stared him down. "You can stay outside if that's what worries you. I have no fear of men like this. The door—open it."

The now-obsequious guard did so, and Tell walked in among the men, doing his best to look like a rich princeling, all the while his insides were churning. The men, ever alert when it came to self-preservation, knew better than to say or do a thing. Tell found who he was looking for, alone in the far corner. Even in these circumstances, the men had managed to shun Hammerhead. Tell strode over to him.

"I don't need this one," he told the merchant. Then he put his foot on Hammerhead's shoulder.

"Please . . . ," begged the most feared man in his village.

For a moment Tell almost felt sorry for Hammerhead. He'd chosen to be feared over loved or respected. Or, rather, fear had been chosen for him long ago. Who he was wasn't entirely his own doing. Then Tell remembered the unmoored feeling of swinging in that cutthroat trap and the sight of his sister squashed under a man who meant her harm. The moment of sympathy passed.

"You can join those cutthroats you sent after us," Tell said quietly as he pushed Hammerhead over with a thrust of his leg. Hammerhead wriggled and thrashed helplessly, trying to roll himself up. He seemed smaller already. Tell savored the warm feeling of never having to fear Hammerhead again. Then he faced the people merchant. "That's one less."

"Which means you still need the money for three more," the merchant replied stubbornly.

Rumi's face went tight with outrage. She stalked in among the trussed men and grabbed Tell by his sleeve. "He's robbing us. We're leaving."

"But—"

Rumi's eyes flashed at Tell. "Right now," she said loudly. "Look angry," she hissed, giving him a pay-attention pinch. Luckily, looking angry was a specialty of Tell's.

"Your next auction's in eight days," Rumi coldly informed the merchant as they sailed past him. "Good luck selling this lot in the condition they'll be in by then. Their wounds are already hot. They're not going to last a week."

Tell, feeling sick, forced himself to walk away with Rumi, all the while realizing that he would *never* have the stomach for the kind of bargaining she was born to.

The merchant let them get an agonizing twenty paces away before he scuttled after them.

"Wait, wait! Let's not be unreasonable, now. I'm sure we can come to some kind of . . . an accommodation."

Rumi waited, so Tell waited. The merchant reached them, wheezing. He was very unhealthy.

"What else do you have, in addition to your sous? Anything? Just a trinket or two, so that I can fetch something for two men that I've already paid for and fed and housed."

"We have nothing more for you," Rumi said firmly.

The merchant beseeched Tell, "Then choose two more to leave behind, and we have a deal. That means I've thrown in one man for nothing." He shrugged at Rumi in defeat. "Well done. Your father would be proud of you."

"No," said Tell. "I'm not choosing two more." And before Rumi could stop him, he pulled the bag with Rold Roland's rings and tooth out from under his tunic and emptied the contents into his hand.

"This is for all of them," he said as Rumi growled softly at him.

The merchant poked through the polished stone rings until he came to the tooth.

"A tooth? Why would I want that?" he said. Tell turned it over, so that the emerald sparkled. The merchant grunted with a surprise he couldn't hide.

"I see you recognize it," Rumi said.

"And I see your father finally cut him loose; good to know," the merchant replied.

Rumi plucked the tooth back out of the pile. "Now you have information that no one else in this city has. That's your final part of the price," she said as she tucked the blackened tooth away in her tunic.

"And we have a deal for all the men but one," said the relieved merchant. "Good luck with them; they're a nightmare," he said.

"I know," Tell said. "That's why I bought them."

34

"I have a question," Wren said.

"We just talked about that," Lilit retorted. "Watch and listen."

They were back in Lilit's chambers after taking a brief, tense walk in the garden. Her bed, covered in shimmering fabrics, was far too big for one person, or even one family. Other, smaller rooms and cupboards were still to be explored. Wren was beginning to realize that Lilit spent most of her time in here, doing . . . what? Waiting for things to happen outside these walls that she'd set in motion from inside them?

"There's no time for that," Wren argued. "Anyway, I don't mind you knowing what I think; also, my question isn't about what's happening right now. It's about you."

"You're worse than I was! Go ahead."

Wren sat down on the edge of Lilit's bed, testing its softness before asking her question. "Did you really hate your life so much, up the mountain?"

Without the slightest pause, Lilit said, "I was ready to kill myself rather than go back, so yes, I did."

"But you were always so funny. . . . You made us laugh all the time."

"Being funny isn't the same as being happy," Lilit explained, voice suddenly thick with feeling. "Often, it's the opposite."

Wren frowned. She left the bed and peeked into a cupboard full of spectacular clothes.

Lilit came up behind her and shut the cupboard door. "I do want you to understand me—if not now, then one day." She began pacing back and forth, as if talking about her past life gave her the need to move around. "Where should I start? It was miserable and cold all the time; that much you know. Even worse, it was boring. Incredibly so. You're still learning, but once you do, there's nothing but drudgery and obeying thoughtless rules made by short-sighted people, while also trying to make something out of nothing for my family, every single day—a family who barely knew I was there. *That's just the way it is, was, and always would be.*" She spat out the village's favorite saying as if it tasted bitter. "That cursed saying tells you everything you need to know about the village and why nothing there will ever change."

A thought that had echoed many times in Wren's mind as well.

But Lilit wasn't finished. She continued to pace, faster and faster. "Every morning I woke up knowing exactly what was going to happen that day, and the next, and the next. Why do you think the women are so horrible to each other up there? Not because they hate each other. Because that's all there is to do!"

Lilit stopped to make sure her daughter was paying full attention. "Let me be clear. If there'd been a chance to change some of the many things that needed changing, I would've stayed and done it. That would've been enough. I had a lot of ideas . . . better than any of the men, who never had a single thought between them, because it suited them not to. But I didn't have a say in anything. And even though your father . . ." Lilit paused to compose herself.

"Your father listened to me; I'll give him that. He liked my ideas . . . but he did nothing at all about it. At the same time, he was better than most. He never hit me, like the other men. I never hated him." To Wren, it sounded as if Lilit was having an argument with herself. "Nor did I ever love him. Sorry. That's just the truth. You asked."

Wren looked quizzically at her mother. She was quite sure that *wasn't* what she'd asked.

"The other women always said I was the lucky one. Lucky?! That should tell you how miserable life is up there on that freezing mountain. And all for the sake of what?

A shiny stone that cuts you and blinds you and keeps you poor forever, despite its value down here."

Lilit stopped her pacing, breath heaving. Her stare went into the distance, then back to her daughter. She put a hand on Wren's shoulder.

"I've said all these things to myself so many times, and they always made sense to me, but now that I hear them out loud . . ." She ran her hands through her hair, tangling it. "Let's just say that I needed more from life than I could ever hope for up there. You're probably too young to understand that."

Wren felt irritation rise in her. "I'm not too young! *I'm* the one who looked after our family when you left, remember. And now I've left, too. I want more, too."

"Yes . . . *yes!*" Lilit almost seemed grateful. That was surprising. "And you'll have more," Lilit promised. "I'll make sure you do." Then she blinked, brought herself back to the here and now. "Starting with your clothes. You'll need two changes a day. Come." Lilit headed for the door, but Wren didn't follow.

"I have one more question."

"Is this what it's going to be like?" Annoyance pricked Lilit's voice again, her feelings as mercurial as always. "A never-ending stream of questions?"

"I want to know things, just like you do," Wren stated matter-of-factly. "Knowing is a kind of power, right?"

Irritation settling, as Wren knew it would with the

compliment, Lilit said, "I suppose you would be like me; you're my daughter." For the first time, she seemed almost pleased by the notion. "All right. Go ahead."

Wren steeled herself before asking her next question, because she knew it would bring trouble with it. "I understand why you left. But why did you have to destroy us all? You already had a new life down here."

"I haven't destroyed anyone," Lilit said.

Wren's eyes never left her mother's.

"What? Spit it out!" Lilit commanded.

Wren spoke calmly. "Only you could've had the idea to capture the men and force them to make weapons out of black glass."

Lilit's face flushed. "Who told you that? Who have you been talking to?"

"Nobody," Wren said with the power of simple truth. "I saw it for myself, in Rold Roland's warehouse. I saw our men, our neighbors, with nooses around their necks. I saw them all." A sudden insight flashed into Wren's head. "Oh! I bet you told Kennett to use Hammerhead, that he would do anything for power over the others."

Lilit turned from her daughter, but Wren maneuvered in front of her, not allowing it.

"You see, I do watch and listen," Wren told her defiantly. "And think. And I think that only you could've known when they'd be here. And probably how to capture them, too. That's what you offered the Beltons, isn't it? Weapons and the men to make them, in secret. That's why they took you in. You offered power to the weakest ruling family in Halfway."

Lilit's silence continued.

"The women and children—they'll die now. Not just the men." She let those words sink in, then added, "And I know you know that, *Lilit*."

Her mother laughed. "No, they won't; they're tough. They're the toughest people in the world."

Wren wouldn't hear it. "True. But they'll wait for the men to get back until after the first snows, and then they'll be trapped up there and starve to death." Lilit tried to walk away again, but Wren blocked her. She wasn't done.

"What you've done for yourself down *here* means everyone dies up *there*. That's a price you're willing to pay for fine clothes and some servants?"

With that, Wren had found Lilit's snapping point. Lilit lashed out. "Clothes? Servants? I don't care about any of that, you little idiot! I only care about the future. That's what I offered the Beltons—the *future*! All they wanted was not to be the weakest family. I convinced them that Halfway should be run by *one* family, not four. I told them Halfway should be protected by men with weapons like Kennett's men, not manipulated in secret by a handful of conniving, greedy, outdated sorcerers!" Lilit paused for breath, but she wasn't done.

"Yes, using the men was my idea. And the black glass.

And Hammerhead. And it all worked! The Beltons don't know every little detail, nor do they want to, but Kennett does. He knows how powerful my ideas are. More powerful than any sorcerer, because by tomorrow they'll all be gone, and I'll still be here!"

Wren cocked her head. "Why are you so sure you'll still be here? Why would Kennett trust you?"

Lilit tidied her hair without even knowing she was doing it. "Because he loves me. That's something you don't understand."

"But I do understand that you've already betrayed your own people and you're going to betray the Beltons the moment you can. Anyone with half a brain can see that. And you won't stop there. You just can't. Kennett knows who you are. He knows where you're from."

Lilit tried to look serene and sure. "Not anymore."

Wren smiled, a smile that cut Lilit like a blade of black glass. For a moment they almost seemed the same age; the person Wren would become was clear in that tight smile. "You can give yourself a new name," Wren said in a tone that dripped venom like a scorpion's raised sting, "and wrap yourself in all these shiny clothes, and pretend you don't have mountain children, but everything you've done, you could only do because of where you're from. You're still part of us. Your blood is the blood of black glass and always will be. And Kennett knows that, I promise you."

Eyes wild, Lilit stormed for the door. Then stormed

back. She grabbed Wren, ripping the seams at her shoulders.

"You would do well not to talk to me that way. You would do well to make sure I like you. I've already made my peace with never seeing you again. It'll be even easier the second time."

This time when Lilit stormed out, she kept going.

Wren stood in the sumptuous room, letting the echo of the hard words die into silence and letting her heart calm its frantic beating. Then she went to Lilit's bed and yanked the cover off one of her many soft pillows. It made a good bag.

Necklaces, bracelets, rings, ivory combs, ornate jewel cases made of different woods by master craftsmen from faraway lands, all went into the pillow cover. Wren was ready to leave, satisfied by what she had, happy to walk away with so many valuable things belonging to the person who had once called herself her mother, pleased at the thought of how angry it would make her. Then her eyes found a shelf piled with folded pieces of the finest fabric she'd ever seen, in colors she hardly knew existed. She put her full bag down to fetch another pillow cover, but when she turned to pick it up, it wasn't there.

It was in Selt's hand. She hadn't heard him enter. They looked at each other across the bed. Selt sighed sadly.

"I'm leaving," Wren declared. "I can't live here."

"You can't steal from the Beltons either."

"I'm not. I'm stealing from my mother, and it serves her right."

"Everything in this house belongs to the Beltons, including your mother," Selt said flatly.

Wren grinned humorlessly. "That tells me I'm doing the right thing by leaving." Selt shrugged silently. "I'm not taking this for myself. We need to buy food for our village."

"No matter what it's for, if you steal from the Beltons, they'll send me to kill you. I've done it many times. Neither of us wants that. I know I don't."

"But you'll do it?"

Selt nodded gravely.

"Why?" asked Wren.

"Because I belong to the Beltons too." Selt's face was blank, unreadable.

Now it was Wren's turn to look sad. "Only if you think you do," she said. But she left empty-handed.

No one stopped Wren as she walked out into the central garden and found the pomegranate tree. Something had changed. It took her a moment to realize what it was. The beautiful old oak at its center was gone! Just a low stump remained, freshly trampled plants circling it. Wren wondered why she was sad about an old tree, when there were so many other things to be sad about. She picked two pomegranates for Rumble, and, as if sensing it, the old mule began braying from the stables at the opposite end of the garden. Wren hurried toward the sound, then hesitated as Rumble's voice faltered and stopped.

She entered the stables cautiously, expecting trouble.

The stable hand approached her, and she showed him the pomegranates.

"For my mule," she said.

"He's a monster," the stable hand exclaimed. "Worst creature in here."

"He's missing his mountainside," Wren explained.

"I wish he was there even more than he does," the man grumbled, waving her on back.

Wren passed a line of priceless horses without sparing them a glance. "Guess what I've got for you?" she sang out as she reached the half door and looked in on her old mule . . . who had company.

Tell, Rumi, and Cormorin crouched behind Rumble, petting him and feeding him knobs of coarse bread. Or, in Cormorin's case, keeping as far away from Rumble's hooves and teeth as possible. Tell stood, grinning broadly, very happy to see his sister. "I thought hearing Rumble might get you in here."

"I was coming anyway, to take him with me," said Wren.

"You can't," said Tell. "Not yet."

35

As Wren left House Belton for the last time, the foursome caught one another up as quickly as they could. Just as quickly, they wove their way through the streets toward the Mountain gate. Cormorin had a bundle of old tunics he'd pinched from the sorcerer's rag basket.

"What are those for?" Wren asked.

"You'll see" was all the answer she got.

When Wren heard that the men were recovering back at the sorcerer's house, she laughed with relief. But when she heard the price paid for their freedom—that, once again, they didn't have a sous between them—her only response was to remark to Tell, "We don't have food for the winter."

"That's a problem for tomorrow." Tell shrugged. "If today doesn't work, tomorrow won't matter."

And when Tell heard that their own mother was the root cause of the impending chaos in Halfway, he didn't seem nearly as surprised as Wren had expected. All he said was, "We still haven't found medicine for Da's eye, you know." Meaning, he just decided not to think about their mother any more that day. Or maybe ever.

The cruel words Lilit had slashed Wren with, about it being easier to forget her the second time, applied just as much in reverse. Tell and Wren had already mourned their mother once. They knew how to do it and what to expect. You can get used to anything, it seemed, even grief.

Tell had come up with a plan for getting their weapons back that made sense when he'd first told Cormorin about it, but when they reached the Mountain gate and Cormorin actually saw the gatekeepers in the flesh, he faltered.

"I'm not sure it'll work on them . . . ," he now muttered worriedly.

"Of course it will," Rumi said stoutly. "Anyway, there's no choice. Make it work."

"I'm actually not feeling my best," Cormorin confessed. And it was clear that he wasn't. He was shaky and kept looking over his shoulder for things that weren't there.

"None of us is, in case you hadn't noticed." If the idea for this expedition was Tell's, the force came from Rumi. Her driving force? Revenge.

It was business as usual at the gate. The gatekeepers were at their post, taking crude spears and knives from two ragged dung collectors, men who ventured into the wilderness looking for herds of animals that ate grass.

They trailed in the herd's wake and gathered cobbles of dried dung into vast loads, which they carried tied up in squares of tattered cloth on their backs. The dung was used for kitchen fires in the poorer parts of Halfway. It was unexciting work that paid very little, but it was steady because there was always dung and always the need for it. And dung was free.

Once the dung collectors had passed through the gates, the foursome knew there was no excuse to delay any longer. Tell's plan was simple, but like most simple plans, it became complicated right away. Cormorin's part in it was the key. He was going to use the spell from the ditch to freeze the gate- and weapons-keeper, while Tell gathered all of the villagers' bows and knives from the shed. They assumed Wren, Rumi, and Cormorin would be frozen too. Tell would have to work fast.

"You don't understand," Cormorin had said when Tell explained the plan. "I made a mistake last time. Only the sorcerer making the spell is supposed to be able to move. Somehow it was you, instead."

"Just make the same mistake again," Tell had responded reasonably. Now Cormorin gave him a despairing look as they all walked out through the gates. The gatekeepers were instantly alert. "You can't leave without paying tax!" roared the left-hand gatekeeper.

"Tax? What tax?" Wren asked in surprise.

"A leaving tax, of course!"

Tell and Wren had never heard of such a thing. Evidently the People of the Black Glass had found another way out of the city.

"We're not leaving, so we don't have to pay," Rumi explained calmly.

"Then what are you doing out here?" The gatekeepers came closer, looking irritated.

"Ohhh, nothing," Wren said with a great show of innocence. Tell nudged Cormorin, who licked his lips nervously and cleared his throat elaborately.

"Oi!" The right-hand gatekeeper pointed. "What's that on your belt? Is that a knife?" Tell looked down. He had forgotten all about it!

"Now, Corm. Now!" Rumi urged.

Cormorin opened his mouth to cast the spell. Nothing emerged but a squeak.

"What's that you say?" the same gatekeeper asked.

"I think they're up to something, these whelps." The left-hand gatekeeper strode toward them, readying to grab them.

Rumi cursed in frustration and punched Cormorin on the arm, hard. "Now!" she yelled.

Shocked, Cormorin lurched forward and barked out the spell.

Just as the gatekeepers reached them, everything stopped. Massive hands loomed inches from their necks.

Everything stopped, except Tell. Cormorin had repeated

the incorrect spell perfectly. Grinning in triumph, Tell ran for the weapons shed. Then something occurred to him. He looked back at the two gatekeepers towering over his sister and friends. As with the glass in the ditch, his touch on the bows would break the spell. They wouldn't escape the gatekeepers.

He ran back and, with a great heave, tipped them over. It was like trying to tip over giant statues, and it took all Tell's strength, but the gatekeepers ended up on their backs, staring at the sky.

Tell didn't want to think about how angry they were going to be as he thundered back toward the weapons shed, hurrying for the corner where he'd seen the weapons-keeper join his and Wren's bows with the rest of them.

But as he reached the shed, the weapons-keeper, bearing a crescent-shaped sword made of the same material as his new knife, stood in his way. The old man looked as if he were frozen and would just be an inconvenience. Then he spoke.

"You think a pissant little spell from a pissant little apprentice is going to affect *me*? I've known my share of sorcerers, learned a thing or two along the way," he declared, tracking Tell with the point of the sword in a way that made it fully clear he was far more than just an inconvenience.

Tell blinked, then did the only thing he could do. He told the truth.

"Look," he said, holding out his hands to show they were empty and he meant no harm. "Halfway is under attack. We need our weapons; we're going to try to save the city."

The man glanced around. "What attack, boy? I don't see any attack."

"It's from inside," Tell explained. "And it's secret. Three sorcerers are already dead, and one is working for the attackers. We're trying to help the middle sorcerer hold the city."

"How do you know all this?" the weapons-keeper demanded, trying to mask his shock. "If it's even true."

"Our mother is . . . part of it," confessed Tell. "She's working with the Beltons and the Ropers—"

The weapons-keeper spat explosively onto the floor. "Those Belton lice with their Roper curs! All you had to say is you're against them." He spat again. "They've had thieves breaking in here three times in the last year."

"Looking for weapons," Tell guessed. "Well, they've got weapons now, and they're using them to take Halfway."

The weapons-keeper lowered his crescent sword. "Fetch your bows; use them well." Then he slipped the crescent sword into its scabbard, flipped it in the air, and held it handle-first toward Tell. "Take this, too. It'll match that knife of yours."

Eyes wide, Tell took it and remembered the words he needed to say. "Thank you."

"You better hurry. Who knows how long that apprentice's spell will hold those big lugs out there."

Tell ran for the bundle of bows and quivers standing in the corner, bent to scoop them up, then suddenly stopped. "Wait!" he exclaimed. Tell slapped his forehead angrily.

"What now?" asked the weapons-keeper.

"I should've tied their legs together! Tipping them over won't be enough. None of my plans ever work the way they're supposed to!"

The weapons-keeper cackled. "Plans have a way of doing that." He swept past Tell, scooped up all the mountain weaponry while Tell cast anxious glances at the toppled gatekeepers. It could be that his eyes were playing tricks on him, but it looked as if one of them was beginning to move.

He readied his arms for the bows. With a wink, the weapons-keeper said, "I'll tell 'em I got frozen by the spell, too," then swept the bows into Tell's arms.

As the weapons touched Tell's hands, the spell broke, and everything moved at once. Cormorin ran to help with the bows. The gatekeepers grunted and rolled over to push themselves to their feet. As they levered their gigantic butts up into the air, Wren and Rumi had the same thought at the same instant.

With a wild yell, they each swung their hands and smacked the gatekeepers' hamlike butt cheeks with stinging blows. They dashed away, the gatekeepers thundering after them, bellowing furiously, giving Tell and Cormorin time to reach the gate, their arms loaded with mountain weapons.

Behind them, the weapons-keeper had to clutch the doorway to hold himself up, he was laughing so hard.

In a straight line, the gatekeepers would have run far faster than the girls, their one step equaling three of the girls'. In a straight line. Which was not what Wren and Rumi did, of course. They zigged and zagged and danced away from the massive men. This was second nature for Wren. Rumi's determination was something to behold. She copied anything Wren did, and they drew the gatekeepers farther and farther away from the gate, where the men's weakness was quickly revealed.

The gatekeepers were bigger than the biggest Roper, but all they did was stand in one place all day, wielding spears. Trying to keep up with the nimble, darting girls quickly had them panting and sweating, then stumbling with exhaustion.

"Bye." Wren waved, scarcely breathing hard at all as she and Rumi sprinted to join Tell and Cormorin inside the gate, where they were dividing the weapons into four smaller loads, wrapping them in the old tunics, so they wouldn't be seen on the journey back to the center of Halfway.

Despite what was to come, and despite the enormous cost if they failed, the foursome hurtled joyfully back to the sorcerer's house, carrying a bundle each and laughing out loud as they ran.

It was the first time any of them had laughed properly for longer than they could remember. Tell wondered if it would also be the last time, which stilled his own laughter instantly.

36

When they arrived at the sorcerer's house, they found the men of the Black Glass sprawled all over the furniture on the second floor, eating from platters of food, heads down like ravenous hyenas. Bruised, limping hyenas with missing teeth, split lips, and fat ears.

Still, a ragged cheer rose from the group when the bundles were unwrapped and they saw their cherished weapons—weapons that never left their hands other than in Halfway. They fell upon them more eagerly than they had the food, sorting and stringing their bows, checking their arrows, slipping their sheathed knives back onto the worn places on their belts where they usually lived. Being armed made them seem bigger and more dangerous. Tell felt a surging pride as well as he slung his bow across his shoulder. This was how he saw himself, this was who he was.

Mort the older clapped him on the shoulder hard enough

to make him stagger. "I don't feel naked anymore!" he crowed. The rest of the men agreed heartily. Which was the closest to thanks the four were going to get. The men still had not thanked Tell or Rumi for buying their freedom, which Rumi found both appalling and insulting. Despite getting to know Tell and Wren, her opinion of the People of the Black Glass hadn't changed much.

Cormorin disappeared upstairs after issuing them a warning. "Don't touch anything except on this floor. There's poison everywhere, and we haven't had time to make the cures."

That made them all inspect their own fingers worriedly.

"How did you get the weapons?" Curas rasped once Cormorin was gone. "Has to be a story there."

"It was easy," Tell said with a shrug, which earned him a sharp look from Rumi.

"And what's that?" asked Toyot, pointing at the sword on Tell's belt. "Did you steal it?"

"It was a gift." Tell saw Toyot's lustful gaze. "Don't even think about it," he warned. Toyot broke into a crooked smile, showing a bloody gap where a tooth used to be; he definitely was thinking about it.

Behind them the rest of the men were tipping the left-over food into the dirty old tunics and tying them into bundles. No one from the mountain ever wasted food. Then they shouldered the food bundles and started looking around for a way out.

"Wait!" Wren exclaimed. "What are you doing?"

"We're leaving, of course," said Mort the younger. "While we can."

"What?!" Rumi gaped at them, astounded.

Mort the older eyed her out as if deciding whether they needed to explain themselves to her. Rumi stared daggers, as did Wren and Tell. So, as if doing them a great favor, he said, "We talked about it while you were gone. We're going back up the mountain. You can come if you like, but you'll have to keep up. We're not going to slow down for you—there isn't time."

"But—but what about the Ropers?" Wren asked, looking from man to man. "They captured you. They killed the chief. They turned you into slaves."

"We'll get our revenge on them some other time," Toyot said casually. "Next year."

"There won't be a next year!" Tell's voice was steely. "The Ropers and their sorcerer are using the weapons *you* made to take the city. The only force that stands against them is the sorcerer here. They're going to attack tonight, to try to kill her. If they win—"

"Sounds terrible," interrupted Melk. "But none of our business. Our business is getting our families to a place where we can survive the winter."

"You're just a pack of cowards!" The disgust in Rumi's voice was palpable. "We should've left you to be sold. That's what you deserve."

Curas narrowed his eyes at her. "Who's she?"

"*She's* the reason you're still alive," Wren fumed.

"Well, she should know better than to call us cowards," the bantam-size man warned.

"Oh, should I? What single thing have you done to make me know better?" Rumi met his gaze. "As far as I can see, everything they say about you people is true."

"Is she a friend of yours?" Alt, a slovenly ally of Toyot's, who was never far from his side, asked.

"Yes!" Wren and Tell retorted.

"Then we won't slap her. Unless she keeps wagging her lips," said Toyot ominously.

Tell and Wren both stepped up to him. "You won't slap her at all," Tell informed him, his voice dangerously quiet.

"Who are you to say what I do?" Toyot stepped closer, his face reddening.

"Who are *we*?" Tell answered, resting his hand on his new knife. "We're the only ones here who've actually killed a Roper. And we're the only ones here who've faced up to them, not sat around making weapons for them."

Curas stepped between them, held out his arms in both directions, as if holding back two forces. "This is a waste of time. We're leaving." He turned to Tell. "We'll do whatever we want, boy, and you can think whatever you like about it."

Tell opened his mouth to reply, but Rumi spoke up before he could.

"You know what? You weren't worth saving," she said to the men. "Your village deserves to die, and the sooner the better. My family would still be here if you never existed."

If her harsh words affected the men, it didn't show. They ignored her and made for the door . . . to find the sorcerer standing in front of it, and she was clearly in no mood to be nice. Cormorin came out from behind her and circled the room.

"You'll do whatever your master orders you to do," said the sorcerer, her voice precise, golden eyes glowing.

Mort the older smiled as if to a child. "Our master? We have no master. We don't even have a chief."

The sorcerer gestured at Tell. "He bought you with his own money; he owns you."

"Him! He's just a boy. With no mother and soon no father," Toyot scoffed.

"He can't make us do anything, even if he is," Alt added.

"But I can." The sorcerer whispered something, made a hand gesture toward Alt, then pointed at a stuffed chair. "Kill that chair," she commanded.

Alt drew his knife, leaped forward, and proceeded to kill the chair, stabbing, cutting, ripping the stuffing out of it, grunting like a demented animal until the chair was utterly destroyed. "That's enough," said the sorcerer. Alt stopped instantly, panting. "Now stand on your head against the wall," she said in the sweetest of voices.

Tell and Wren watched in amazement as, face blank, Alt walked to the wall, put his head to the floor, kicked his feet up, and leaned upside down against the wall.

"You men can leave tomorrow, if there is one, " the sorcerer said with finality. "Until then, you're not free." She turned to leave, her silken tunic sweeping around her.

Tell heard someone curse, "Sorcerers!" Then, from the corner of his eye, Tell saw one of the men raise his bow, about to loose an arrow into the sorcerer's back.

But before Tell could cry out a warning, Cormorin said a quiet word. The man's bow turned into a golden viper, writhing angrily in his hands. The man screamed, and before he could shake it off, the viper sank its fangs into the meat of his forearm, striking three times so rapidly, it was hard to distinguish between one bite and the next. The man sank to his knees, clutching his forearm, which began to swell immediately. The viper slithered under an armoire, hissing a final warning.

Tell, Wren, and Rumi gaped at Cormorin in awe. He returned their gaze, his eyes glinting, looking more like a sorcerer and less like an apprentice than he ever had. Tell wondered what other surprises he had in store for them.

The sorcerer faced them again, her tattoos writhing as malevolently as the golden vipers. The men clustered together now, nervous and muttering.

"I'm the most powerful sorcerer in Halfway," she told them matter-of-factly. "You are in my house, the center of *my* power. Your lives are mine to do with as I need, and I will sacrifice every single one of you to save this city. You will fight the Ropers tonight, of your own volition, or mine. Is that clear?"

Curas turned to Tell. "What have you done, boy? A sorcerer killed the chief and enslaved us to those Ropers. And now we're in thrall to an even worse one?"

"What has he done, you ask? *He's done his best,*" the sorcerer answered for Tell. "More than any of you." She raised her hand in a way that foretold another spell. "I don't have time to talk. There's too much to—"

Something lurched in Tell's stomach—an idea, a feeling, an instinct. "Wait!" He stepped between the men and the sorcerer.

"I have no time to wait," the sorcerer said impatiently.

"Doing it this way . . ." Tell struggled to get the words right the first time. "It's not right." He turned to the men. "You can leave if you want—"

The men instantly moved toward the door, perfectly willing to leave Alt upside down, another dying of viper venom.

"But before you do, hear me out."

"You said we could leave, so we're leaving," Toyot said as he limped past Tell. But when the sorcerer raised her hand, they all stopped.

"What do you have to say to them?" the sorcerer prompted Tell, clearly curious.

Tell began by speaking to their backs, because they'd stopped but refused to turn around. His voice was halting, unsure, as if his tongue couldn't catch up to his thoughts.

"We're People of the Black Glass . . . and we like to think of ourselves apart from Halfway. We like to think we're above Halfway, looking down on everyone from high up on our mountain. But being here has shown me that we need Halfway far more than Halfway needs us."

Rumi nodded emphatically.

"This is not someone else's fight; it's *our* fight. You know why? *You can't eat black glass.* Unless we have somewhere to trade it, we starve. The Ropers . . . you know as well as I do that if they win, we'll never be able to enter the city again. And then what? We'll be a village of cutthroats. If we're lucky."

Curas was the first to turn and face Tell.

"Curas," Tell said, "you taught me to hunt. I've admired you since I was big enough to walk. I saw you cut your own throat to save yourself in that warehouse. I hope I can be that brave when I need to be."

Now the Mort brothers turned, then Melk and two or three more men. Tell's voice grew in strength with every face he saw.

"Until this week, you're the only people I've ever known. You've taught me what it means to be one of us, good and bad. Wren and me, we've only been able to survive because of what we learned from you. . . ." Tell looked at Rumi and Cormorin.

"And because of who we've met down here in Halfway. Our friends."

More and more men gave Tell their attention. Tell, the boy they had all refused to take in under their own roofs.

"In that warehouse, Wren and I heard you say you'd rather die than be slaves, and you meant it. What happened to those men? Where are the men who taught Wren and me, every single day of our lives, that revenge at any cost was the price of our survival?"

Tell's voice grew louder and louder, stronger and stronger. Wren and Rumi stood a whisper apart, scarcely daring to breathe. It was as if Tell were casting his own kind of spell.

"The Ropers are just people. Why are you afraid of them? If Wren and I can take one down . . . how many can you?"

Tell edged in close, so close that he was almost among them.

"When I saw you trussed up like piglets in the people pens, I cried. If you leave now, I'll cry again . . . because I'll know that this is the day the People of the Black Glass became nothing. Gone, like snow that melts overnight. And you know it too. If we don't fight, it's the end of us, whether or not we survive the winter."

Tell paused, as if searching his own soul for more words. Then he shook his head. He'd said enough. "That's all I have to say. You can leave if you want."

The men stirred and shuffled, torn, embarrassed. Except

for Curas. "The boy's right. I stay and I fight." His voice, raw and rough, matched Tell's conviction.

"Us too," said the Mort brothers. One by one the men nodded in agreement, until only one man was left.

"You're idiots! I'm leaving," Toyot said angrily.

"If you do," said Mort the older, "don't come back up the mountain."

"What will happen to my family if we lose down here?" Toyot shouted.

"The same thing that'll happen if you leave now," said Mort the younger. "They'll be on their own."

"We might as well win, then," Tell said casually, ignoring the poisonous look from Toyot. He looked to Curas. "You're the best hunter here. Everyone knows that. Do you have any ideas?"

Curas nodded. "Maybe. It's all I thought about when I was sitting around that miserable fire with a noose around my neck. I'd hunt those rope-haired bastards the way we people used to hunt big animals before all the big animals disappeared; I'd hunt from hiding, from behind, and from low."

As the men heard that, their eyes lit up. Deep growls began to rumble in their chests. Sounding, Tell thought ironically, like the savages the people of Halfway thought them to be.

Tell released a breath he didn't know he'd been holding, then retreated to join Wren and Rumi.

"Where did all that come from?" Rumi whispered.

"No idea," Tell admitted.

"I thought you'd never stop talking," Wren teased, elbowing him.

"I couldn't," Tell confessed.

Cormorin joined them, grimly pleased. He gave Tell a half bow of respect. "This is the better way. We need all our powers for tonight."

He reached into his tunic, pulling out a small clay jar sealed with wax. He held it out for Tell. "This is for you. Medicine for your father's eye. It's a drawing salve. It may not help, but you never know."

Tell cradled the precious jar in his hands. "Thank you!" he said fervently. Though the light of hope in his eyes was thanks enough.

"Yes, Cormorin!" Wren added, shooting the apprentice a lovely smile. "Thank you very much."

"It's not me you should thank," Cormorin told them. "Oh, which reminds me . . ." For the third time, he uttered the spell that froze everything. Only this time he got it right. Tell was frozen too. It felt as if he were in a silent dream, unable to move, hear, or see anything that was not right in front of him.

And what materialized directly in front of him was the sorcerer, but more as a creature of light than of flesh and blood. Not entirely human. She flicked a finger at Tell, at Wren, at Rumi . . .

. . . and they each unfroze with a gasp. The men were still frozen.

"I hate that spell," Wren muttered.

"It was necessary," said the sorcerer. "No one else can be allowed to hear what I'm about to tell you three." She shot a look at Cormorin. "You four."

They waited uneasily. The sorcerer nodded to herself, as if agreeing with something unspoken. Then:

"My true name . . . is *Sicatrice*."

Cormorin failed to muffle his gasp. Sicatrice smiled gravely at him. "I told you these were strange times." She turned to them all. "Say my name in front of no one else. It can be used to harm me. But *you* can now use it to call to me when you need me. I'll hear you wherever you are and wherever I am if you use my true name."

The foursome shared a stunned look. They understood that things had just changed yet again in their ever-changing lives. They were now part of a powerful sorcerer's realm.

"Thank you," Wren said.

"It's an honor," Rumi added.

"It's an honor if we survive the night," Sicatrice said. "Otherwise, it's just a word."

37

The men had divided into groups and gone into hiding down the streets approaching Sicatrice's house from the direction of the Desert quarter. The Ropers had approached that way the night before, and there was no reason to think they wouldn't again. It was a gamble they had to take. Sicatrice had reappeared for a moment and cast a spell that made them almost invisible when they were in the shadows.

"It wears off," Cormorin warned. He was going to stay in the house to help refresh defensive spells while Sicatrice fought Desert. They knew Desert's attack would be timed to the Ropers'. At least, that's how Curas said he'd do it, and nobody disagreed.

Tell was more than happy to have Curas take the lead. The hunter decided that the three of them would be lookouts and runners, giving advance warning. They were excited to be part of the battle. It felt right.

The three filed silently out of Sicatrice's house from a hidden door on the ocean side. Cormorin told Tell to use only that door coming back. It would be invisible until they touched it.

Once again, the streets around Sicatrice's house were empty, the houses deserted. No lights shone in any window, no faces peered out. Maybe they were always that way, Wren thought to herself.

Cormorin had selected the places they should stand, which was reassuring. As the men disappeared into the shadows blocks away, Tell, Wren, and Rumi paused before splitting up.

"You know what would be clever?" Rumi mused.

"What?" Wren asked.

"Just keep going. Disappear until this is over."

"Nobody I know is that clever," Tell said.

"Just thought I'd bring it up." Rumi gave a wan smile. But they had no doubt of where her heart lay, and she confirmed it immediately. "You're right, Tell. We have to fight them. Even if we lose, we have to fight."

"Watch out." Wren laughed. "You're beginning to sound like one of us."

It was strange. They weren't afraid, though they knew they should have been. But they'd been living with so much uncertainty that it was almost comforting to have everything come down to one action on one night—their lives, the fate of their village, Sicatrice's and Cormorin's lives, the fate of the city, even Rumble's fate. By sunrise, the course of their lives would be clear, or they would be dead, and they were ready for either. Each of them felt the same, or some version of it.

Curas had told them that the waiting would be the worst part of it, and it was. Each of them stood alone on the empty streets—alone but for their thoughts. And their thoughts were dire enough, or sad enough, that the first sighting of the attackers was almost a relief.

Rumi heard them before she saw them, the beat of their footsteps echoing forward. She was supposed to count the Ropers, but when more, and then more, appeared around a corner, she turned and fled.

Tell heard her feet slapping the street just as Rumi flashed out of the dark, running faster than she'd ever run in her life.

"They're coming!" she panted as she charged past him without stopping.

"How many?" he asked, breaking into a sprint to catch up with her.

"Lots!" she wheezed. Coming from the girl who prided herself on counting everything precisely, this was frightening. Did "lots" mean too many even for Rumi to count?

They reached the first group of their men just as Wren hurtled in from her own position. "Lots of them. They're carrying something big."

Tell had a sudden sinking feeling. Kennett had said it

was all or nothing. Maybe there were more Ropers than they'd seen in the warehouse that night? He'd just assumed that was all of them, because there seemed to be so many. He'd never asked. Stupid! A rock for a head!

"Run, boy," said Mort the older, steering him toward a side street. "Tell Curas there are two groups." Tell, fueled by fear, reached him quickly. Curas and his men took off instantly.

When Tell returned to the street where he'd left Wren and Rumi, it was empty. He looked this way and that, heart thudding in his chest, until a hand tugged at his tunic. It was his sister. She and Rumi were almost invisible in the shadow of a stairway. "They want us to stay out of the way," Wren said softly.

"Why?" Tell whispered as he unslung his bow from his shoulder.

"They don't want to have to worry about us," Wren explained.

"They never have before!" Tell scoffed. "Why start now?"

"Because this is a bit different from a mountainside, don't you think?"

"I wasn't scared before, but now I am," Rumi admitted.

As Rumi had earlier, they heard the Ropers before they saw them, feet marching in unison.

Rumi clutched Tell's fingers hard enough to hurt when the Ropers came into view. There were twelve of them, in four rows of three men each. They all held short stabbing spears tipped with black glass in their right hands and, strangely, thick rolls of felt carpet under their left arms. Not only did their feet move as one, but they breathed as one too. In through their noses, out through their mouths, so that each massed exhale sounded like a secret shout. They were not just twelve Ropers; they were one formidable war creature, bound by will and discipline and training, the lust to conquer written on each face, the certainty of victory shining from their arrogant eyes.

And this was only one group. If the other group was the same size, the men were already outnumbered. And facing a foe like none they'd ever seen.

"How can we win?" Rumi whispered despairingly. And although Tell and Wren were silent, they were thinking the same thing.

Once the Ropers had thundered past, the threesome peered from out of the shadows, which was when they got an answer to Rumi's question.

Up ahead, they saw shadows rise out of the ditches and from behind walls: six low, quick shadows that darted in on the marching Ropers from the sides and from behind. A sudden agonizing scream pierced the air and echoed off the surrounding buildings. Then another. And another. And the precise drumbeat of feet was no more, the rhythm of discipline replaced by the chaotic sound of desperate combat. Pants, curses, thuds, screams, moans, and death rattles; the sounds were more vivid than anything they could see on the dark street.

Unable to resist, Tell, Wren, and Rumi crept closer, and Rumi finally saw the people she had feared and loathed all her life—the People of the Black Glass—at their most dangerous. And much to her immense surprise, she felt a surge of pride!

Pride at seeing that the People of the Black Glass were the very opposite of the Ropers when it came to fighting. They were undisciplined and had no notions of honor. They saw no point in face-to-face combat if a strike from behind would do. They never stood their ground. They ran away instantly if things went badly, but turned back just as quickly, ready for anyone stupid enough to think the fight was won.

Curas had said they would fight low. And fight low they did—that's how you catch prey bigger than you are. They took away the Ropers' feet, ankles, knees, hamstrings— cutting, stabbing, shooting arrows from behind whenever possible. When a Roper dropped to the ground, unable to move but still alive, they turned their attention to the next. One of the men followed up to finish off downed Ropers with their own spears.

As five Ropers were left crumpled on the street and the fight boiled toward Sicatrice's house, those remaining maintained a tight, disciplined knot, beset from all sides by the mountain men but holding them off.

Tell, Wren, and Rumi followed carefully—even more

carefully when they saw two of their own men also crumpled on the ground, one speared through. They skirted around the Ropers until Rumi tugged on Wren's tunic to stop her.

"One of them's still alive," she whispered.

Wren turned back and saw that Rumi was right. The Roper glared up at them through a mask of blood from a long slash on his scalp. Still on his back, he clutched a stabbing spear in his right hand, but that was all he could do. Both heel tendons were cut. He couldn't move.

Rumi approached him carefully, a strange look on her face.

"Rumi! Leave him. He's done." Wren kept her bow ready; it wasn't a natural extension of her arm, as Tell's was. But this was point-blank range.

Rumi seemed not to hear. She stood over the Roper, staring down at him with such malice that eventually he raised his spear into a defensive position.

"You killed my family," Rumi said finally. "My father, Kun; my mother, Els; my brothers, Wile and Ben. You killed them all."

The Roper's eyes flared with recognition. "Not all," he said. "Not you."

"That was a mistake," Rumi said, her voice harsher than Wren had ever heard it. "And you'll pay for it. On my family's blood . . . You. Will. All. Pay."

Suddenly, the Roper roared, jerked himself up to sitting, cocking his arm to throw the spear at Rumi.

Rumi didn't flinch.

Wren and the Roper released their weapons at the same moment. An arrow flies faster than a spear, and with a thud, Wren's arrow found a home deep in the Roper's chest.

His spear whistled past Rumi's face in a flash of black glass, leaving a curved slice in her left cheek, which instantly filled with blood. Rumi pressed her hand against it with a yelp. Wren couldn't take her eyes off her arrow. She realized right then that killing to save a friend is much easier than killing because someone told you to.

A whistle from Tell down the street stopped any further reaction. He gestured urgently for them to come.

As they ran, Rumi stopped for a moment to pull the Roper's spear out of the dirt, where it had embedded itself. There was a chip in the blade, but it was still lethal. She ran, holding it at her side; she wasn't going to be defenseless anymore that night.

38

A single glance at Rumi's sliced cheek was the sum total of Tell's reaction to her near miss.

"Something strange is happening," he said, indicating Sicatrice's house.

"What?" Wren asked.

"I'm not sure. Listen." A deep, slow thumping sound echoed down the street. They broke into a run, unable to see the cause of it until they turned the final corner.

When they did, they were confronted with a sight they barely understood. Two groups of Ropers had joined to form a defensive half circle in front of the sorcerer's house. They were keeping the mountain men at bay with spears, using the heavy felt carpets as shields. It wasn't a perfect idea because there's no such thing in a fight like this, but the carpets bristled with arrows and if a Roper went down, the circle formation tightened to protect what was happening inside it—the source of that heavy, thumping sound.

Creeping closer, with only brief glimpses between the fighting men, the trio saw that, of all strange things, the four biggest Ropers had a crudely sharpened tree trunk slung on thick ropes between them. That was what had happened to the old oak from the Beltons' garden, Wren realized with a pang.

The Ropers swung the tree trunk against the wall of the house in long, powerful arcs, slowly punching a hole through the plaster and mud bricks. They'd learned the cost of entering through a sorcerer's door the night before. This time they were making their own entrance.

The mountain men seemed to be out of arrows. But apart from the occasional spear whistling at them through the air, which they dodged easily, they were in no danger. Although neither were they stopping the Ropers from smashing a hole through the wall.

"Why are they doing this?" Tell wondered aloud. "They'll face the same problems whether they go in through a door or a hole in the wall."

"Maybe they believe they won't?" Wren suggested. "They're wrong, though. She's got something horrible waiting for them. I know it."

Suddenly, Rumi grasped them both. "Up there! Where we stood!"

A huge clay pot teetered on the terrace railing four floors

above the Ropers. The spiky plant growing out of it waved and jerked until the pot toppled forward and plummeted toward the street, turning a lazy somersault, spewing dirt, rocks, and plant before smashing into the Ropers below in an explosion of clay shards.

"Cormorin!" Rumi shouted, delighted. "That was my father's pot!"

The Ropers holding the tree trunk were splayed across the ground, not likely to get up. But, quickly, four more dropped back to take up the trunk, the protective formation tightening further.

As they resumed battering the wall, the mountain men began to close in excitedly, sensing the possibility of a decisive victory.

With a sudden inhalation of alarm, Wren said, "I just realized something. I haven't seen Kennett. Not in either group."

Tell echoed her alarm. "Nor have I!"

"What if he's making another attack somewhere else? What if all this here is just . . . a big noise?" Rumi asked.

There was no reply because Wren was already running for the ocean side of Sicatrice's house, to the hidden door. Tell leaped after her, with Rumi doing her best to keep up, but nobody can run like mountain people in a hurry.

Wren peered around the corner at a bare wall and an empty street, Tell joining her. They didn't trust what they saw, which was nothing. Tell moved along the wall, trailing his hand on it—the only way he could think of to be certain he'd touch the hidden door. Wren was behind him with an arrow to her bowstring.

"I don't see anybody," she whispered.

Tell stopped short. "Where's Rumi?" He looked around wildly.

There was no sign of her. They retraced their steps, stepping out into the open at the corner, ready for anything. But there was nothing.

"She was right behind us!" Wren insisted, struggling to keep the fear out of her voice.

"How can she just disappear?" Tell was trying to keep his own panic under control.

A weak moan jerked them back around.

"Rumi . . . ?"

Rumi was on the ocean side of the house, a few steps away from the wall, not far from where Tell and Wren had been moments before. How she'd gotten there was anybody's guess. She was engulfed in unnatural-looking shadows. Sorcerer shadow. Her feet were off the ground, as if she were floating in the air. Her eyes were huge with terror. Her arms were pinned to her sides. She'd lost her spear. She was trying to say something, but it sounded as if her breath was being crushed out of her.

"I'm sorry," she managed to wheeze. Wren ducked in behind Tell.

The cloak of sorcerer shadows smothering Rumi roiled

away, revealing the form of a man holding her like a shield. It was Kennett.

Tell's bow came up automatically, but there was no target that didn't risk Rumi first.

"Open the door, Tell." Kennett's voice was calm, serene even. "We know it's on this wall, and we know you can open it."

"Who's we?" Tell demanded, half expecting to see his mother.

The shadows coalesced and became a human form, but only partially. The Desert quarter sorcerer was wreathed in shadows, which flickered and danced around her. What could be seen of her in brief glimpses was terrifying. Her teeth were filed to points. Her eyes were no longer the eyes of a person—they were as clear as water. If she had once been weak, she was weak no more. But at what price?

"Let this night take its course, mountain boy," Desert said, her voice as sweet as a nightingale's song. "Don't stand in the way."

"You're none of our concern," Kennett said. "Just open the door, and then you can leave with your friend." Kennett twisted his hands, and Rumi gave a wavering gasp of pain. "Or you can watch her die, and your sister next."

Tell was frozen in body and mind, until something sharp nudged him from behind.

"Down," came the softest murmur from Wren.

Tell dropped to his knees just as a bowstring twanged

and an arrow hissed over his head, aimed at what was left of the sorcerer's heart. One inch from its target the arrowhead exploded into dust, as if it had been shot point-blank at a cliff face. Desert smiled through her obscene teeth.

"What do you take me for, mountain girl? Your black glass is useless on me."

"But not for your friend," said Kennett harshly as he pressed a blade of black glass up against Rumi's throat. Their black glass.

It wasn't the cut that broke Tell's will; it was Rumi's bravery. Except for a hiss of indrawn breath, she did nothing but close her eyes.

"Stop!" he yelled. "I'll open the door." The black glass blade paused. Blood trickled down Rumi's neck.

"He'll never let her go," Wren whispered in his ear.

Tell ignored his sister. Walked forward along the wall, feeling for the spell-hidden door.

"Yes! Open it," Desert urged eagerly. "*She* won't be able to stand up to me in person. She's become fat and lazy. This house is practically mine already."

Tell felt a tingle in his fingertips, and stopped.

"Open it," Kennett snarled.

"Let her go," Tell demanded.

"He's not going to let her go," said Wren, her eyes shifting to Rumi. "Tell him, Rumi."

"Tell . . . don't," Rumi whispered.

But Tell opened the door, then stepped back.

Desert was through the door and into Sicatrice's house in a flash. Kennett went after her, still using Rumi as a shield.

"LET HER GO!" Tell screamed.

But Kennett didn't let Rumi go.

"This is the price you pay for crossing me, boy!" Kennett hissed as he backed through the door, dragging Rumi inside with him.

39

Kennett swung his leg to slam the door with his foot. From just outside, in one fluid movement, Tell desperately loosed an arrow, underhand, through the gap. He saw it lodge deep in Kennett's upper thigh, near the place where a big vein pulses.

Kennett howled, hopped backward, still clutching Rumi. Tell bulled the door open and went in after them, shouting over his shoulder to Wren, "Keep it open!"

Wren plugged the doorway with her own body. "Hurry," she shouted.

"You've failed," Kennett gasped, hopping on one leg. "She dies."

"Rumi! The arrow!" Rumi understood instantly. As Kennett brought his blade back up to her throat, Rumi found the arrow with her foot and thrust downward. She felt the black glass edge rasp against Kennett's thigh bone.

The Roper leader howled, paralyzed by intense pain, and in that instant, Tell leaped forward and jerked Rumi from his arms.

He shoved Rumi toward Wren and pulled out his new sword to finish Kennett off.

"Get out of there, Tell!" Wren yelled from the door, clutching Rumi, as a burst of malevolent light roiled through the room. It signaled the beginning of the battle between the two sorcerers. "They're fighting! We have to go!"

Wren and Rumi grabbed the neck of Tell's tunic and yanked him backward, away from Kennett.

"No!" Tell yelled, his blood singing with the desire to finish him off.

A lightning bolt flashed down the spiral stairs, bounced off Desert, and annihilated the side wall of the spiral stairway. Undeterred, Desert flew upward on the remains of the spiral stairway.

And then they were outside. Wren slammed the door shut, and it disappeared. The last sound they heard was Kennett's bellow of rage as he hammered his fist against the inside of the door, trying to pursue them.

Or trying to escape. For his shouts changed tone, rising and rising in a song of pure terror. However it is that powerful sorcerers battle, unprotected humans clearly should not be present when they do.

Once they'd gotten far enough away to feel safe, Tell

sawed strips from his tunic, made a pad for Rumi to hold against the cut on her throat.

"You'll have scars like us now," Wren told her.

In shock, Rumi could only nod.

A fresh night breeze whispered, then hummed, then whistled down the streets as they hurried back to the front of the house, to the other battle. When they rounded the corner, they were confronted with a sight that was hard to comprehend. Apart from the bodies of the dead—quite a few more Ropers than mountain men, they noted with grim satisfaction—there was no one to be seen.

The old oak trunk was sticking halfway out of the wall, as if some unimaginable force had sucked it inward.

"I wonder what's happening inside the house." Wren looked upward to the terrace. For a moment she thought she saw something flying into the house on wings the color of the night. When she looked again, it was gone. Or had never been there.

"Poor Cormorin," Rumi said, voice quivering.

"I hope he found a good place to hide," Wren added.

"He may make the difference," Tell declared. "Nobody pays any attention to him, and he likes it that way, but he's powerful too."

They hovered, not sure of what to do next. Stay? Run?

"You know what?" Wren said, seemingly out of the blue. "I think she lost her mind."

"Who?" Rumi asked. "The sorcerer?"

"No. Lilit. Our mother. How else do you explain her wanting this?" Wren looked bereft.

"Selt already told us," Tell reminded her. "Power creates a hunger for more."

"Shhh!" Rumi hissed. She pointed. "They're coming back!"

"The Ropers?" Wren asked wearily.

A host of shadows was flitting toward them, using the deeper darkness near the walls of the houses.

Tell swore, nocked another arrow, waited. "I'm sick of this."

Wren did the same. Rumi moved behind them. But their precautions were unnecessary. The shadows belonged to men they knew, noticeably fewer than there were at the beginning of the night and the beginning of the ill-fated journey down the mountain.

"There'll be a lot of second wives this winter," Wren said sadly, wondering who had survived.

They were relieved to see Curas and the Mort brothers among them, all showing fresh blood in various places but strutting triumphantly.

"They ran like rabbits, those rope heads!" Mort the younger told them. He pointed at the tree trunk embedded in the wall. "As soon as that tree did that—it just got sucked in!—they took off. Scuttled into a building just down the street."

"Which building?" Tell asked, tensing for further conflict.

"Oh no, boy," Curas growled. "You can make all the fine

speeches you want; we're not going in there after them. There's still plenty of them left."

Rumi's brow furrowed. "Well . . . have we won, or not?" she asked. "Did we help? Did we change anything?"

"Oh, we won," Melk assured her. "More of them died than us, and then they ran away. That means we won."

Tell shook his head slowly. "But it's not over." He pointed up to the sorcerer's terrace, where light pulsed violently out into the night. "They're still fighting in there—the sorcerers. If Desert wins . . ."

"Her teeth are pointed," Wren added.

Curas stood square in front of Tell. "We've done all we can here, boy. We've lost all we can afford to lose. You can't fight a sorcerer's battle. The snows are getting lower every day. We need to move our families now. It's time to go home."

Tell knew in his heart that every word Curas said was true. He looked at Wren. She nodded.

Rumi walked up close to the men she'd loathed all her life. "Come to my father's house—it's my house now. Take whatever you think will help you. It's yours."

The men liked that idea, not that they thanked Rumi for it.

"What about you?" Tell asked her. "What will you do?"

Before Rumi could answer, the men suddenly became alert. "By the mountain's sharp teeth, what is that thing?" Mort the younger exclaimed.

A strange shape, a strange being, moved slowly toward

them, staying deep in the shadows. A creature in the shape of a cross, haloed by a bright darkness that glowed and flickered: the living darkness of sorcery.

Tell, Wren, and Rumi were pushed protectively behind by the men as they prepared to fight again.

The bizarre, spectral creature turned away from the wall, emerging from the shadows.

"Oh," Wren cried with relief. "It's Cormorin!"

Cormorin, carrying Sicatrice in his arms. The three of them rushed to help him, then faltered as they got close.

Cormorin was bleeding from his nose, his eyes, his ears. Sicatrice's eyes were open in an endless stare.

"Is she . . . dead?" Rumi asked, an icy chill shivering through her.

Cormorin shook his head uncertainly.

"And the other one?" Tell asked. "Desert?"

It took Cormorin a long moment to find the word.

"Gone."

"Did you win?"

"Nobody won," the shattered apprentice said so quietly they weren't sure they heard him correctly.

It didn't matter, because Mort the older clapped his hand down on Tell's shoulder and spun him around roughly. "We have to go, NOW!"

The men were all looking upward, not at Sicatrice's house, but in the opposite direction, at a light above them. An orange light. A familiar light. Fire light.

Driven by the night breeze, flames billowed away from the roof of a nearby building, bending, reaching, feeling for the next building.

"Is that the building the Ropers went into?" Tell asked.

"It is! They set it alight! This city's going to burn to the ground! We need to go."

"We'll be hung from the walls just for being here," Curas added.

Yet they couldn't quite pull themselves away, watching in horror as the flames jumped the gap to the building right across the street. Rumi saw Cormorin's stricken face. The night wind was blowing the flames directly at Sicatrice's house. What would happen next was obvious to all.

Cormorin looked hopelessly at his home. "There isn't much left in there anyway."

"We go—*now!*" Curas rasped.

Tell helped Cormorin carry Sicatrice. In the shadows, they traveled across Halfway toward Rumi's house. Behind them, the wind carried a ribbon of flame onto Sicatrice's roof. Moments later, the very center of Halfway began to burn. Without her in it, Sicatrice's house was just another building and could burn just as easily. The Ropers had unleashed another monster upon the city they sought to possess.

Shock piled upon shock. When they reached Rumi's house, they saw that it was under seal, in possession of the family who ruled the Mountain quarter, patrolled outside by a trio of very alert guards and filled inside by functionaries making lists of everything that should, by right, have belonged to Rumi. Except, she was assumed dead.

And so the People of the Black Glass fled the burning city, empty-handed, heavy-hearted, their brains already becoming dull with hopelessness.

Tears ran down Wren's face as she wept for the mule she'd left behind, once again.

Tell felt sick to his stomach; he'd failed in almost every way possible.

And now they all ran for their cruel mountain, because the mountain was all they had left.

40

The Night Before hot springs did wonders for their many wounds. The physical ones, anyway. When the men left well before dawn, Tell and Wren stayed behind with Rumi, Cormorin, and Sicatrice. The three lowlanders were in no condition for the climb back up to the village. They needed another day of rest, and Sicatrice was unchanged.

As far as they could tell, they hadn't been followed. The chaos brought by the fire made sure of that.

"We'll take a couple of days to pack up," Curas had explained to Tell on the way out. "But we'll be coming right back down again. Take your time. You can even stay right here and wait for us. You earned it."

"What about our da?" Tell had to ask.

Curas shrugged. "If his eye's better, he'll be with us." There was no need for Curas to say the rest. Even though it had been less than thirty days, if his eye was not better, their father would be abandoned on the mountain, along with anyone else unable to make the journey down.

"We have medicine for his eye," Tell told him stubbornly. "We'll be right behind you."

"Carrying a dead sorcerer and two others who've never been cold in their lives?"

Tell shook his head at Curas. "She's not dead."

"She may as well be," Curas said. And then the hunter did something no man of his village had ever done to him other than his father. He reached out and gave Tell's shoulder a gentle squeeze.

"You're almost a man," he said. "I would like to see you become one. But you surely won't if you take on too much; things are too dire right now. Think about that."

With the men gone, Tell, Wren, and Rumi lost no time getting into the hot, sulfurous water. Rumi had heard talk about the hot springs every year, when the People camped in her father's yard to trade their glass. Not for one moment had she ever imagined using them. But here she was.

It was not fully light, which made undressing easier. And once you've faced death and the death of people you love, being naked together in a hidden hot spring doesn't seem to matter much.

Cormorin, however, hesitated noticeably before taking off his tunic, and when he did, they understood why. From knees to shoulders, his body was crisscrossed and layered with scars. The scars of many, many childhood whippings, far worse than anything Wren had seen on Rumble's back. Nobody said a word, but nobody looked away, either. Cormorin's scars were a part of who he was, and that was that.

After the initial groans and sighs of pleasure, Wren's eyes widened with excitement. "We need to get her in here," she said emphatically. "This water heals all wounds."

Cormorin gave a bleak shake of his head, his red hair plastered to his head. "Not hers." But Wren insisted, so they fetched the sorcerer from the bed of furs they'd made for her and carried her to the steaming water.

There was no thought of undressing her. They simply lowered her in gently in her tunic. It was the oddest thing: she had a pulse, her eyes were open, her body was not stiff. . . . She just wasn't there and had still shown no sign of coming back from wherever she was.

But when they lowered her to the point that the steaming water reached her throat, Sicatrice's eyes suddenly closed.

"Is that a good thing?" Rumi asked.

"I don't know." The sadness in Cormorin's eyes was gutting. "I don't know anything anymore."

"What did they do to each other last night, in her house?" Wren asked, unable to hold herself back any longer. Cormorin didn't seem to hear. She began to ask more loudly, but Tell prodded her with his toe and shook his head. Wren stayed her questions, with great difficulty.

But that didn't stop her from calling to Sicatrice throughout the morning, using her name out loud. Nothing changed. Nothing happened. Finally Wren sent a shrug Cormorin's way and gave up.

They spent much of the day soaking and resting, trying not to think of the past or the future. None of them were looking forward to the climb back up the mountain, nor to what they would encounter when they got there. Tell warned them that they'd have to climb as fast as they could, to get the salve working on Seka's eye as soon as possible.

Late in the day, Tell's grumbling belly drove him up a tinkling stream of cold water that kept the hot springs from being too hot to soak in. He crested a rocky rise and found a small, sheltered valley cupped like a bird's nest between the harsher ridges. There he quickly shot and dressed two fat rabbits.

They gnawed the fire-roasted meat to the marrow, while Tell scraped and stretched out the rabbit furs, telling Rumi that she would be needing a coat up the mountain. Rumi managed to smile tightly in a way that made Wren laugh out loud. Kun Anton's daughter, the apple of his eye, could no longer be considered spoiled.

As night fell, they gathered the remaining furs from the secret cave and made them into beds. Sadly, there were more than enough for their needs. Without having to discuss it,

Tell and Wren didn't touch Hammerhead's, even though good furs were a precious commodity. When Tell had told Wren earlier about leaving him at the people market, she had nodded once and said: "Good." She stopped thinking about Hammerhead right then, and forever.

They huddled around the little fire, lying as close to each other as they could. They hadn't expected to sleep much; they expected to be harassed and haunted by all the things they'd seen, heard, and done. But exhaustion and a day in a healing hot spring did their work, and they all slept soundly.

So soundly that they didn't hear the hooves on the path below until it was too late. Many hooves. A big group of pursuers! Tell and Wren woke together, wide-eyed and panting, jerked upright by the sound. They woke the others with fingers over their lips. They left Sicatrice lying with her eyes closed, because it made no difference either way.

The sound of the hooves was directly below them. They had allowed themselves to be trapped, and the thought made Tell's stomach churn with anger at himself; of course the Ropers would come after them; of course they would seek revenge. All Tell and the others could do was keep quiet, put arrows to strings, and trust that the hidden hot springs would stay hidden. When Wren looked to Cormorin for his kind of help, he shrugged. He couldn't.

All went quiet. With a sinking feeling, Tell guessed that they stopped right at the concealed path. He gestured to Cormorin and Rumi to get ready to pick up Sicatrice;

they'd have to try to carry her to the secret cave.

Still as stone, they listened anxiously until they heard the sound of a single set of hooves turning off the main path and climbing slowly toward them. A single rider. A scout, unseen behind the jumble of huge boulders that concealed the hot springs.

Tell and Wren drew their bows, ready to loose their arrows. Cormorin and Rumi picked up Sicatrice, about to start their futile scramble upward.

Closer and closer came the hoofbeats, slowing noticeably at the tricky parts of the path but never stopping. Tell rose to his feet, choosing the best shooting stance over concealment that wouldn't last but a moment, anyway.

The approaching horse passed the last big boulder . . .

. . . and revealed itself to be not a horse, but a mule. A mule called Rumble, carrying nothing but a cloth sack on his back. Compounding their shock, the person walking at Rumble's shoulder was someone they never expected to see again.

Selt.

Wren wasted no time in firing off her first question of the day. "Have you come to kill us?" Her arrow was aimed unwaveringly at Selt's chest.

"No," said Selt with half a smile. "Just the opposite."

Only then did Wren lower her bow and rush to embrace her mule. Selt walked to the edge of the hot springs and looked across at Tell, Rumi, and Cormorin through swirling ribbons of steam.

"I have a message for you. Two messages, really."

"From who?"

Selt gestured toward Rumble. "I think you know the answer to that."

"What's the message?" Tell asked in a flat tone.

"You'll be killed on sight if you return to Halfway. That's for all of you, including her." Meaning Sicatrice. "This ruling is absolute and eternal. Halfway is forbidden to you for the rest of your lives."

"Look!" Wren interrupted, holding up the cloth sack that Rumble carried. "Honey cakes!"

"And the other message?" asked Tell, refusing to be distracted by his rumbling belly.

Like the honey cakes, the second message was confusingly different from the first: fifteen sturdy mules waited patiently on the path below, heavily laden with carefully wrapped packs of food and warm clothing. More than enough to survive the winter. Enough to sustain the village in comfort.

"How can she tell us she'll have us killed on sight and send all this at the same time?" Tell asked when he saw the mule train. "Plus honey cakes."

Selt simply shrugged, as if to say, *That's Lilit for you.*

"What happened to Halfway?" Rumi asked.

"Ah, that. Yes. Well . . . the fire you so callously started has burned all the way to the edge of the city—"

"We didn't start it! They did!"

"That's not what Kennett says," Selt explained. "And he's there; you're not."

"He's alive?!" Tell exclaimed.

"Somewhat," Selt said in a strange tone. "So far."

"And Lilit and the Beltons . . . ?"

"Are being celebrated by the other three families for stopping a vile attempt to take over Halfway."

Tell, Wren, and Rumi frowned in confusion. Cormorin gave a bleak laugh. He understood.

"This vile attempt?" asked Cormorin. "Would it be a collaboration between my sorcerer and members of a mountain village known for their savagery?"

"And for their black glass, which they used to make weapons in a secret hideout, and kill all the other sorcerers," added Selt helpfully.

Wren exploded. "That's . . . that's just . . . that's . . ."

"Very convenient," concluded Selt.

"But you know it's not true!" Wren was outraged.

"I do," agreed Selt.

"So does Lilit!"

"She does."

"And Kennett!"

"Yes."

"And the Beltons!"

Selt nodded. "And the Beltons. But nobody else. Nobody who isn't already dead or banished."

Tell laughed loudly.

"What's so funny?" Wren asked furiously.

"Now I know why she sent these mules. And the honey cakes. It's to make her feel better about all the lies she's telling about us. The entire story is her idea. Nobody else is that clever."

They all considered that.

"Actually," Selt said to no one in particular, "I can think of two people who might be."

They made Sicatrice as comfortable as they could on Rumble's back. Cormorin wasn't looking forward to walking so close to a mule who seemed likely to kick him off a cliff at any moment, but he would stay by his sorcerer's side all the way up the mountain.

"You can ride on a mule when you get tired," Tell told Rumi.

"When I get tired, I'll keep walking anyway," replied Rumi with a glare. Tell hid his grin.

Wren approached Selt. "Are you coming up the mountain?"

"I would've, if that horrible old mule hadn't found you."

"Which is why I love him," Wren said, stroking the horrible old mule.

"Then I suppose I should too," admitted Selt. "However, I can't tell you how pleased I am not to be coming with you. All this . . . ." Selt gestured at the landscape and shuddered. "There's too much of it."

Wren's smile came to life slowly, as it began to sink in that they'd be heading back up with eye medicine, food aplenty, and two new friends. Three, if Sicatrice ever returned from wherever she was. Their father was in for a surprise. She couldn't wait to see his face when she handed him a honey cake and introduced them all. On second thought, though, it was highly unlikely that the honey cakes would survive the journey. She tucked one away for him, vowing to not touch even a crumb of it.

And as Selt turned away and started downward, most relieved, and as Rumble looked balefully over his shoulder at the rest of the mule train, then started upward, Rumi caught up to Tell at the front of the line.

"You know what all this is, don't you?" she asked him, gesturing behind them.

"Yes. It's a mule train full of food."

"No," Rumi said. "It's power."

As Tell breathed in the clean air, stretched his legs, and walked upward with the jar of eye medicine tucked safely in his tunic, he began to think about that. He admitted to himself that it excited him. It also frightened him.

Far above them, the first snow of winter began to fall: little fluffy flakes as small and delicate as the breast feathers of songbirds. For the first time since they were old enough to understand their world, Tell and Wren realized that they didn't need to fear its arrival.

TO BE CONTINUED

TO BE
CONTINUED